Praise for *Her Mother's Daughter*

'It'. n a long time since I found a book so utterly engaging
and eloping. Mental illness and the long-term effects of emotion d sexual abuse are drawn with insight and subtlety.
Th 1g is vivid and raw, the characters real, and the voices
of n and daughter feel pitch-perfect. I raced through it, so
imm that it kept me up half the night.' – Charity Norman,
auth *er the Fall*

'A ve ng, authentic portrait of an Irish family with deep
secret aire McGowan, author of the Paula Maguire series

'A com lling read that is raw and poignant' – *Woman*

Alice Fitzgerald is an author and journalist whose work has featured in magazines and on websites, including *Hello!*, *Cosmopolitan*, Refinery29 and online literary journals. *Her Mother's Daughter* is her debut novel. Born in London to Irish parents, she now lives in Madrid.

@AliceFitzWrites

ALICE FITZGERALD

Her Mother's
Daughter

ALLEN&UNWIN

First published in Great Britain in 2018 by Allen & Unwin
This paperback edition published 2018

Allen & Unwin
c/o Atlantic Books
Ormond House
26–27 Boswell Street
London WC1N 3JZ
Phone: 020 7269 1610
Fax: 020 7430 0916
Email: UK@allenandunwin.com
Web: www.allenandunwin.com/uk

A CIP catalogue record for this book is available
from the British Library.

Paperback ISBN 978 1 76063 065 2
Ebook ISBN 978 1 76063 824 5
Printed and bound by CPI Group (UK) Ltd, Croydon, CR0 4YY
10 9 8 7 6 5 4 3 2 1

For my family; I love you

prologue

JOSEPHINE

18TH OCTOBER 1997

With each step I feel lighter, like the years of wading through quicksand are being washed away. It's as though I'm treading water and at last the surface is below my chest. I can breathe again.

It starts raining, and me with no umbrella. For some reason this makes me smile. Then I remember why. I don't run to the station or even increase my pace. Instead, I let the raindrops fall onto my face, trickle down my cheeks and seep into my collar.

Oh, Michael, remember when we danced in the rain on our way to Buckingham Palace?

It's funny, remembering who you were, knowing who you have become. You can never quite imagine how things will pan out, no matter how hard you try. Siobhan and me playing the game when we were little: Who do you want to be when you grow up? Where will you be when you're twenty-five? Thinking twenty-five was old. Thinking that home was the whole world.

The trees shiver in the rain and I realize just how many there are; one every few metres on both sides of the road. They must be a hundred years old or more. I couldn't tell you how many times I've gone up and down this road over the years, and I don't think I ever noticed them.

A gust of wind blows and a shower of leaves breaks off and swings its way to the ground. They're wet and soft when I tread on them, not crisp like the ones Thomas loves. He'll be out tomorrow in search of the crunchy ones, running and jumping on them with both feet. And Clare will be after him, playing Hopscotch on the flagstones, just like all the other days.

CLARE

7th JULY 1997

This year we're going to visit Mummy's family for the first time EVER. When I ask why we've never been before but we see Daddy's family every year, she tells me to be quiet, like a good girl. But I've heard her call them a shower of cunts, and that must be something bad because the look on her face when she said it was a dark one. She was all white and her lips were thin. I wonder what cunts are. I imagine them falling out of the sky like rain.

I scratch my head and rub my eyes. Then I climb down the ladder, which takes me fourteen seconds. I go over to my calendar, hanging on the wall by the window and the chest of drawers with My Little Pony stickers on it, and put a big fat X across Saturday, which means now there are only eleven days left till our holiday.

Mummy comes in, bright and breezy like lemon squeezy. That's a song we sing when we're all happy.

'Morning, darlings.' She smiles, comes and holds my face in her hands and kisses me on the forehead. Then she goes over to our bunk beds and does the same to Thomas.

'Morning, Mummy!' I skip over to the curtains and pull them back, then tie the ropes with dangly bits around the ends, so it looks like a theatre, the way she likes.

'Shall we go and have some breakfast?' Mummy asks. She comes to look out the window and rubs my hair, twirling my ponytail around in her hand to make it curly like a pig's tail.

It's a Nutella-on-toast day. I can tell because Mummy is speaking in her nice, soft voice, which means everything is okay and she loves us. When things are not okay, her voice is low and rumbly like thunder and her eyes are dark like clouds and she doesn't ask if we'll have breakfast, she says, Wash your faces and get downstairs.

We put on our dressing gowns with Mickey Mouse ears on the hoods and tie the belts tight around our waists, so they keep the cold out, and we put our slippers on. Mummy has her nice green silky dressing gown on today. It's got a brown stain on the front from the other night, when she was drinking her strong apple juice and she spilled it. I know this because she tiptoed into our room and woke me up to ask me if I'd like some hot chocolate. When I said yes, she helped me down the ladder. Downstairs, I tried not to listen while I drank my hot chocolate, because she was saying things that weren't nice. When she finally let me go to bed, I got into Thomas's bunk and snuggled up close, to keep the bad dreams away.

I run down the stairs two at a time, closely followed by Thomas, then Mummy.

Daddy works on Saturdays, so it's just the three of us. That's fine now, but sometimes I wish he was here to tickle us and make us laugh, or put his arms around Mummy and make her smile.

I sit down at the kitchen table and Thomas climbs onto the chair next to me. He has all these little golden hairs that Mummy calls baby hairs, and they're sticking out everywhere and make me laugh.

'What's for breakfast?' I ask, even though I'm pretty sure.

Mummy is filling the kettle for her coffee. 'How about Nutella on toast?'

'Yeah!' me and Thomas shout. If we're really lucky we'll get to put it on ourselves and I can scoop loads on, so it's dripping off the edges.

'Shall I put the bread on?' I ask.

Mummy pushes the button on the kettle and gathers her hair into a ponytail and ties it up so it's out of her face, the way she likes when she's around the house.

She likes us to help and for me to be a good girl and Thomas to be a good little boy. Only you have to be careful because once I washed the dishes and she dipped her finger in the water and said it was cold and hit me around the back of the legs with a tea towel. I haven't washed the dishes since.

I take the bread out of the breadbin, then slot four slices into the toaster. I get the Nutella out of the cupboard and two knives out of the drawer by the sink, and put them on the table.

'Don't just sit there, do something,' I tell Thomas. 'Lazy good-for-nothing.'

He sticks his bottom lip out.

'Clare, don't you speak to your brother like that,' Mummy snaps.

'Sorry, Mummy,' I say. My bottom lip goes loose and I try to hold it still. 'I was only telling him to help.'

'Well, that's no way to do it.'

Thomas goes over to Mummy and puts his arms around her leg, while she stands in the middle of the kitchen twirling his hair round her fingers. She says he has the eyes and hair of a little cherub.

I sit at the table, looking at them and feeling a bit jealous. I don't say to Mummy that it's how she tells us to help.

The bread pops and I jump.

Mummy taps Thomas on the back. 'Get the plates out, like a good boy. Now, we're going to have a fun day out. There'll be no tantrums from either of ye.'

I smile and shake my head. 'No, Mummy.'

Thomas stands up straight and tall, like one of his plastic soldier men. 'No, Mummy.'

'Can I get a nice dress?' I ask. Today we're going shopping because Mummy needs clothes to look beautiful, for going home to see her family. She wants to look her beautifullest and skinniest. She always looks beautiful, but she wants to look even more so than normal for her family. She's been on a diet for ever and ever, and I've heard her say to Aunty Maura (Aunty Maura isn't really our aunty, but she is Mummy's best friend) that she doesn't want them talking about her behind her back. I wonder why they would do that, because they're going to be so excited to see her that they'll only want to talk to her face.

'If you behave,' she says.

'What about me?' Thomas pipes up.

'You can get a dress, too,' jokes Mummy, which makes him put a grumpy face on. 'Only joking,' she says, tickling his sides. 'We'll get you your own outfit.'

Thomas smiles, all happy with himself, as he carries over the plates with toast on. When he gets to the table he sticks his tongue out at me and I look to see if Mummy's watching. She's busy pouring the boiling water into her coffee mug, so I stick mine out at him.

'Cunt,' I whisper. As soon as I've said it, I realize it was too dangerous. I whip my head round, squinting my eyes just in case, but Mummy's getting milk out of the fridge.

After breakfast, it's bath time. Me and Thomas have a bath together every Saturday morning because we're small, so we can't waste all that water twice, even though Thomas wees in it every time.

Mummy pours in the bubble bath. I decide to take advantage of her good mood. 'Can't I have one by myself, just today?' I say in my sweetie-pie voice.

'If you're not careful, I'll wee in it, too,' she says.

I fold my arms across my chest in a huff-puff. Then my head itches, so I scratch it.

'You ought to see how we washed when I was a little girl,' she says in her grumbling thunder voice. 'Then you wouldn't complain.' She swirls her hand around in the water and brings up a handful of foam. 'Six of us bathed in the same water, and when it was your time to go last, there was more piss than water.'

The tears sting my eyes on their way out and my chest heaves.

'Oh, stop your whingeing,' she says through curled lips.

'Mummy, I need to go to the toilet,' says Thomas. He has taken off his dressing gown and his pyjamas with aeroplanes on and is naked beside me, cupping his winkie with both hands and jumping up and down.

'In the bath.' Mummy holds her hand out for Thomas.

Thomas looks at me, then at her.

'In. Now!' She puts her hands under his armpits and lifts him over the edge.

Thomas sits in the bath and looks sheepish, like when he does a poops and doesn't own up to it.

'Come on,' Mummy says to me. 'In you get.' Her face is white and she looks dead serious.

I untie my dressing gown and take off my pyjamas with gold stars on, holding my tears in, so Mummy doesn't give me a belt across the back of the legs as I climb in.

Usually the water is so hot that I don't sit down at first. I dangle in the air, holding on to the edge with my hands and feet and nudging myself in until my bum feels the heat. But now I just get in. It's no time for donkey games and silly buggers.

I sit in the hot suds, my fingers turning into pink prunes while Mummy washes Thomas's hair. I hate prune-fingers. They're like old-lady fingers. Not that I know what old-lady fingers look like; I've never seen any up close. Daddy's mummy died before I was born, and I'm only going to meet Mummy's mummy for the first time ever this summer. I will make sure I look at her fingers when she's playing with my hair and rubbing my face. I hope I don't forget.

When Mummy has had her bath and dried her hair into big red waves and put make-up on, so she's shiny and new, all that's left is to paint her nails. She chooses a red one from the fridge, and sits down in the armchair with a fresh coffee beside her. She shakes the little bottle of paint.

'Can we watch, Mummy?'

She nods as she rolls the bottle between her hands.

'What does that do?' She likes it when I ask questions like this, and I want to get out of her bad books.

'Warms it up, so it's easier to paint.' She unscrews the top and paints her thumbnail in three strokes, one in the middle and another on either side. It smells a bit like when Daddy painted the walls in the sitting room and Mummy said the fumes could knock out a horse.

'Will you paint my nails?'

She looks at me, then takes one of my hands in hers to inspect my nails. 'Go on, then.' She smiles.

The paint is cold as Mummy dabs the brush on each one of my nails. When she has finished, I hold them out to look at; they're all shiny and new, like Mummy's.

'And me!' Typical. Thomas always copies me.

Mummy laughs. 'Boys don't paint their nails, silly!'

'Why not?' Thomas asks, frowning and pouting his lips the way he does when he's getting angry.

'Because painting nails is only for girls,' I tell him in my I'm-older-than-you-I-know-more voice.

'But why?'

'Because we like to make ourselves beautiful.' I wave my hands around to dry my nails while Mummy finishes painting hers. Then, when she has finished, she blows on them. I blow on mine, too.

Thomas is bored, so he turns on the TV and sneaks out to the kitchen to eat a biscuit from the jar without asking. I know because he has a crumb on his lip when he comes back, and I heard the sound of the jar being opened and closed. He must have climbed up on a chair to get to the jar; he's lucky he didn't fall and chip his tooth. He's already chipped one, from when he was climbing on the tree in the garden, but it's just the corner, so you couldn't tell it was chipped if you weren't there to see him cry.

'I'm going to the loo,' I say, bouncing off the sofa. In the kitchen, I lift the lid of the biscuit jar off in one clean movement, take two biscuits and, ever so slowly, put it back on. It makes the teeny-weeniest sound. I eat the biscuits in the toilet while I wee.

For the seventeenth time, Mummy turns to one side and looks over her shoulder at her bum. I've been counting. Me and Thomas are in the changing room, watching her in the mirror.

'You look gorgeous,' I say, because that's what Daddy says when she comes downstairs all dolled up, and it makes her eyes shine.

'Thank you, darling.' She turns the other way, looks over the other shoulder, smooths the flowery material down over her hips. Everyone at school always says she is more beautiful than their mummies. That makes me smile inside.

'Can we go now?' says Thomas. He is like Daddy. He hates shopping.

'Soon.' Mummy takes the dress off and gives it to me to put on the hanger while she tries on another one.

I watch her fingers pop the buttons into the gaps. 'What are Granny's hands like?' I ask.

'What?' She jumps, like I've crept up on her and shouted Boo!

'What are Granny's hands like?'

She shakes her head. 'Just a woman's hands, Clare. What a strange question.'

'I just wondered if they're like yours and mine and Thomas's.' I get Thomas's hand and put it flat against mine.

His is smaller, so the tops of my fingers have nothing against them. We clap them together.

'I shouldn't think so,' she says. She ties the belt around her waist and looks at herself in the mirror.

This one's pink and flowing and has a big white collar.

'It can't be too much, or too little,' she says.

I watch her in the mirror, because I don't know what too much or too little is.

'Why aren't Granny's hands like ours?' I ask.

She bites her fingernail and some red comes off on her lips. 'Oh, damn it!'

'It's okay,' I tell her in my soothing voice.

She looks at me and then shakes her head and laughs.

'What's funny?' I ask.

'Nothing,' she says.

She's laughing on the outside, but she's sad on the inside.

When she's decided on hers, Mummy chooses a dress for me. It's all frilly and I think of saying I don't like it, but she might pinch me hard under the arm and I wouldn't be able to hold back the tears and everyone would turn around and look at me and I'd have a big purple mark for days.

Thomas gets a navy-blue T-shirt with white stripes and a pair of blue trousers.

I wish I could get a T-shirt and trousers instead of a frilly dress. But, Mummy says, there is a price to pay for beauty.

Because we've been good we can go to the coffee shop. We're so lucky because we're going to have pizza tonight AS WELL. That's two treats in one day. Every weekend we have a Family Night Out, when we go to one of Mummy and Daddy's favourite restaurants and they have wine, and me and Thomas can have whatever we want until we can't eat any more.

I get lemonade and Thomas gets orange juice. Mummy gets a hot chocolate with skimmed milk, which is hot chocolate with watery milk so it won't make her fat. Me and Thomas are allowed to share a chocolate-chip muffin between us, even though Mummy says we shouldn't.

I suck my lemonade through the straw and swing my legs under the table. It's sweet and cold and I keep sucking until I have to stop, even though I don't want to, just so I can come up for air. I take a deep breath and go back for more. Thomas does the same and we kick each other under the table and smile through our straws.

Mummy breaks a big piece off the top of the muffin with all the chocolate chips in it. There's so much that she can't close her mouth and I can see the chocolate-sponge smudge all over her teeth. I grip my lips tight because she said it was for us, and then took the best part, like she always does. I secretly hope she gets fat. She deserves to.

'I'm doing you a favour, Clare,' she says, looking at me. 'You need to start eating a bit less.'

I stop swinging my legs.

She taps her hips and shakes her head. 'A moment on the lips, a lifetime on the hips.' She takes a sip of her hot chocolate. 'And stop scratching your head.'

'Sorry.' I tuck my hands under my legs.

I break the rest of the muffin in two and give the big piece to Thomas, because he's a growing boy and it doesn't matter if he has a big piece. I'm a girl, so I have to look after my hips. I take the small bit for myself.

I put it in my mouth. It doesn't taste that good, now that

I know a moment on the lips is a lifetime on the hips. I chew thirty-four times because I remember Mummy telling me that's a good trick, and by the time I swallow it's turned to mush on my tongue.

When we're ready to go, I stand up and look down at my hips and my legs. I'm sure they've got bigger.

JOSEPHINE

18TH JUNE 1980

The tea towel is coarse against my skin. I am drying my hands with it, looking at all the small black balls of burn, when Sean comes in, runs over to me and wraps his arms around my waist.

'Don't go, Josephine,' he says into my chest.

I hold him tight and get the stench of his hair. 'Your hair stinks,' I tell him, and we laugh, even though it hurts my throat.

I break away. I want to get out as quick as I can, go running in my nightdress through the door and not come back.

Sean looks up at me with big brown eyes and I hate myself for leaving him.

'You'll be good, now, won't you?' I straighten his tie.

He nods.

'You'll work hard, and you'll go to college. And as soon as I send you money you'll come to visit?' I'm desperate for him to come; to know that he will. It was me who raised him, after all. I remember the day he was born and a shiver runs all the way down my spine.

'I will, Josephine.' He throws his arms around me and squeezes tight.

We stay like that for a few seconds until I break away for the last time. I wipe my eyes. 'Off with you now, or you'll be late for school,' I tell him.

'When will you be back?' he asks.

I shrug. 'I don't know, but remember you can always count on your big sister, wherever I am.'

'I will,' he says. He shrugs, too, and I remember when he was small and we were together day in, day out, and he'd copy everything I did. Those were happy times.

'You little blighter, you.' I put my hand to my mouth and blow him a kiss.

He slaps his cheek and shrieks, 'Got it!' and, with that, he runs off to school.

The curtains are still drawn in my room, but there is enough light to get dressed. The bed is bare; I already stripped it and washed the sheets. The wardrobe stands empty, with its dark knots curling through the rotting wood. I won't miss this room, where I have slept all my life. With the towel still around me and my back to the door, I get dressed as quickly as I can in case someone comes in. I pull my knickers up and place the triangles of my bra on my breasts and fasten it on my back. I take my good yellow dress with flowers and pull it quickly over my damp skin.

There's not a sound in the house. They'll all be about their daily chores. I wonder if anyone will come back to see me off. I scrub my hair with the towel and remember last night, and the songs Daddy and Uncle Patrick were singing. I was sure to stay well away from the pair of them, like I always do when there's drink flying. There was whiskey and gin and cigars. A real party. Granny and Bernadette came up to the house and a few girls from my secretarial class, which Daddy and Patrick loved. The boys, too. By the end, Daddy was singing rebel songs and the men were all crying with the melancholy that comes with the songs, and the drink. I stayed with the girls, and we had a drink and a bit of craic. Mammy pulled me close to her and whispered in my ear: 'Off to open your legs for England, are you?' I nearly died. I looked at her and she was smiling away, so I wasn't sure if I'd misheard. 'What?' I said back, but someone had already called her away.

It's daylight when I step through the hole in the hedge to go over to Bernadette's, careful not to catch my dress on the branches. The dewy grass wets my ankles and the light-brown leather of my good shoes quickly turns dark around the toes. In the distance, I can see the long stems dance like thousands of little fairies. I would have loved to be a dancer, or an actress. Maybe in another life. Or maybe in London I'll be spotted on the street and turned into a film star. I knock on Bernadette's back door. Her mother opens it.

'Howareya, Josephine?' she says.

'Grand now, Mrs Tolbs,' I say. 'I've come to say goodbye to Bernadette.'

'Bernadette's not in, love,' she says, 'she's gone to the shop.'

'To Chase's?' I ask, because then I can go and meet her on the way back.

'No, she's gone into town.'

I know then she's lying. Heat pricks at my eyes like a burning poker and I stand and look at her, not knowing what to do. Bernadette is like a sister to me. We're even closer than me and my own sister.

I turn to go down the path and there's a creak on the stairs.

'Mam,' calls Bernadette from the hall.

Mrs Tolbs, as I call her, nudges her head to the side, as if to say, 'Go on up with you', and I run through to the hallway and look up at Bernadette, who is sitting on a step and holding onto the bars of the banister. She looks like she's seven again.

'Weren't you going to say goodbye?' My voice sounds forlorn, like I've already lost her.

She shakes her head, then comes down the stairs and hugs me.

'Come with me,' I whisper, but I know she won't.

'Josephine, I don't know what I'm going to do without you.' She holds my hands tight in hers.

'You'll be grand, you'll see,' I tell her.

For a moment I think maybe her father will die and she'll be able to join me after all, but then I realize that once he dies, she will be needed at home more than ever. God forgive me for wishing her father dead. Her father who is a lovely man and who has done everything for her, and who drove us to college every morning.

How funny that, after all these years of wishing I was her, with her nice home and her nice parents and her weekends and evenings all to herself, with no one to cook for and no one to look after and no washing up to do, now I am the one getting away and she is jealous of me.

'You'll look after my sister, won't you?'

'Of course I will,' she says, laughing.

'I mean it, Bernadette.' I tug at her hands with mine, clammy now. 'You'll keep an eye on Siobhan for me, won't you?'

'I will, don't worry,' says Bernadette, and she pats my hands.

*

'Sorry for fibbing, love,' Mrs Tolbs says when I'm leaving, 'but Bernadette was so upset.'

'That's all right,' I tell her. I can see she's relieved it's me going and not Bernadette. I'm relieved, too. 'I'll always be grateful for everything, Mrs Tolbs,' I say, giving Bernadette's hand a squeeze. It was Mrs Tolbs who talked to Mammy and Daddy about me going to morning college to get my secretarial cert. She said they were driving Bernadette, so it would be the same to them to drive me too, and that they'd make lunch for me as well. Mammy slapped me around the face that night and said how dare I take our business outside of the house, but I didn't do anything. It was all Bernadette.

I turn left at the fork to Granny's. She hears me coming and lifts the nets and waves. By the time she is holding me at the back door, the howls that come from me sound tortured.

When I've calmed down, she smiles. Her pink crinkled eyes go small, like always. 'My little Josephine,' she says.

I start again. The snot runs from my nose and she is blurry through the tears. 'Shhh,' she soothes.

She is the one who has paid for my ticket, given me the money, convinced Mammy and Daddy to let me go.

'I've made you sandwiches, and I've got you a Saint Christopher to watch over you,' she says.

I turn around and she puts it round my neck. It's a small gold pendant on a fine gold chain.

'I won't take it off,' I say, rubbing it between my finger and my thumb. 'I'll keep it with me for ever.'

It's hard to remember today is a good day when it hurts this much. I only allow myself to look back at Granny when I've reached the end of the path, and she is so small in the window that I can only catch the movement of her wave.

I cup my hands around my mouth and take a deep breath in and then I shout as loud as I can, 'I love you, Granny!' I stand just a moment longer to wave her goodbye, and head off home.

In the back yard there is no noise, but for the faint, rhythmic swishing of Mammy dipping washing into the basin and pulling it out.

'Mammy,' I call. The echo of my voice bounces off the cold, grey cement and the white pebble-dash walls of the house. I walk around the back and she comes into view.

'Jesus,' she says, putting her hand to her chest. 'You nearly gave me a heart attack. Fine parting gift that would've been.'

'Sorry.' I smile sheepishly.

'Are you going?'

'Yes, I think so.'

'Well, Brendan's waiting for you. You'd better hurry on – he hasn't got all day. Some of us have jobs to keep.'

'I'll say goodbye now then, will I?'

A car speeds by on the road. I nod my head instinctively. Hello, how are you? I say in my head, even though I can't see them. Will it be like this in London, I wonder, everyone knowing everyone and saying hello as you go by?

'May as well,' says Mammy. She lets go of the trousers, and they are swallowed up by the soapy water.

I imagine they are a baby drowning. I think of saying things to her, things I have imagined saying for a long time, things I have never dared say to anyone. For a moment I even consider asking what she said last night. I go to kiss her, but she puts her hands up.

'I won't get you wet,' she says. Her front is soaking, as if her breasts are leaking milk, like in the days after she had given birth to Sean. 'Your daddy has left you some pounds in the kitchen.'

'Is he here?' The blood whooshes around my body.

'No, he had to work early.'

I keep my face like a mask, hard and plastic.

'Well, that's it, isn't it?' she says. 'You rear your children and then they up and leave.'

I flush with guilt, and with all the words left unsaid, and tell her I will send money soon.

She nods, plunging her hands into the basin of water and dunking the trousers.

'Will you miss me?' The words are out before I can catch them. Then, after a moment of silence, 'Ignore me,' and I laugh like an eejit.

She wrings the trousers and hangs them on the line, her curly grey hairs twinkling in the early-morning light. For anyone looking on, it would all seem so idyllic.

The excitement sets in on the boat. This is real; it's really happening, I think, rubbing my pendant between my finger and my thumb. I find a seat over by the window and ask a lady to look after my suitcase while I go out onto the deck. The wind is cold and wet and salty and I hold tight onto the rail, which isn't as high as I thought it would be. I could just throw myself right off, if I wanted to. I look down, where the sea is murky, slapping against the belly of the boat and coming up in froth and bubbles. Far away, the ripples are blue-green and shiny white under the grey cloudy sky. I try to see where the sea meets the sky, but it's no use. There's just a haze of blue-green-grey-black-green-blue.

I breathe the salty sea air in deep, the screams of the seagulls and the shrieks of the children. I watch the people lined up on the deck wave to the port, as the ferry heaves itself into the sea. A loud horn vibrates through the air, through the deck's floor and through my body, sending the gulls to fly in wild circles.

My tears taste of seaweed. They are not tears of sadness, but tears of joy. Of hope. Of everything waiting for me on the other side. I hold onto the rail to keep steady. When I dare, I release one hand and wave to the crowds. I get carried away and start blowing kisses – sure no one knows that none of my own people are among them. I blow a string of kisses, giddy now, as I say goodbye to Ireland.

When I can't hold it any longer I go looking for the toilet. The boat sways violently and people are lying like starfish all over the floor, so I tiptoe around their splayed limbs. Near the toilet, I pretend to itch my nose against the stench.

In the cubicle I am careful not to touch the seat or wet my good yellow dress, but the boat shudders and, as I grab the sides of the cubicle, the dress slips from my hands.

Someone groans next door and there's the gush of liquid. 'Jesus,' she says through a blocked nose, and I imagine her wiping her mouth with the back of her hand.

I clutch my dress back up and get out as quick as I can. 'Are you okay in there?' I ask.

'Yes, thanks,' she says.

'Have you been in there long?' I ask. I'm dying for a

distraction. In the mirror, I can see that I'm red and puffy-faced after the sharp wind. My brown eyes are still watery and my lips are dry.

'First time?' she says.

It takes me a few seconds and then it dawns on me that she means to England. 'Yes – yourself?'

'Me, too. Where you headed?'

'London.'

'No way!' she says. 'Me, too!'

'Get away with you! Whereabouts?'

'Shepherd's Bush.'

'Same as myself! It's a small world, isn't it? What's your name?'

'Maura. Yours?'

'Josephine.' I check my dress; it's clean. I wait a minute for her to come out, but she tells me she's not going anywhere until we pull into the port, so I wish her good luck and tell her I'll look out for her in Shepherd's Bush.

Back in my seat, I regret not fixing a spot to meet so we could find the coach together from Liverpool to London, or telling her the name of the house I'm going to. We could have been friends.

After the coach journey and two buses, I arrive at the address Mrs Tolbs wrote down for me on a piece of paper, where a friend of hers stayed and where she's reserved me a room. It's past midnight on a Thursday. The streets are dark and empty, apart from rows of foreign-looking houses, and again I find myself wishing I wasn't alone and that me and Maura might have come together. I stand at the door and check the number again. I bless myself and ring the doorbell and start counting.

When I reach thirty and no one has come, I shake my head. The voice in my head starts: You fool, you fecking fool. Good for nothing. You really never were good for anything. Your mother was right. She was right all along. It was Granny who was mistaken – believing in you, thinking you were worth something. More fool her. You're done for now. Wait till you go back with your tail between your legs. How they'll laugh!

My breath comes short and sharp and I'm struggling to keep the tears back, when there's a creak of floorboards inside. A moment later the front door opens and a man looks at me, his eyes half-closed and a frown on his face.

I swallow the tears back into my chest. 'Hello. Sorry to bother you so late. I understand you have a room reserved for me? My name is Josephine.'

He nods and beckons me in. 'You have passport?'

I nod.

'Money?'

I nod.

He looks me up and down. 'I show you room, we sort paper in morning.' His accent is not English, his skin is brown and he has a wispy beard. His face is kinder than my father's.

Inside is lit with dull yellow bulbs. A small reception desk sits by the stairs, and we stop there for the man to pick up a key. I follow him up and along the landing to the end, where he stops, unlocks a door and turns to me. 'Rules are,' he says, 'no boys, no parties, always pay up front.' He points out the bathroom, three doors away, and turns on the light in the room.

I nod, then look past him. The walls are yellow from smoke, almost brown around the cornices, but for a square in the middle of the far wall where, I suppose, a picture used to hang. There's a single bed in one corner, a small cabinet beside it and a chair by the window. A narrow, light-coloured wardrobe stands along another wall beside a small square mirror. Round, blackened circles dot the carpet in front of the window. There are other bare patches, too, in the middle of the floor. Moths. I will have to make sure I keep my suitcase closed or they will have my best clothes.

'Great, lovely.' I release a long breath I have been holding in; I mean it.

We bid each other goodnight and he leaves.

I carry my suitcase inside and close and lock the door behind me. Once I've turned the key, I try the handle and the door shakes in its frame. I smile. I've never been able to lock myself in before.

The mattress is softer than mine at home and I sink right down into it. I rub my hand over the bed, and then I go over to the window to let in some air. I pull the grey net curtain to one side and cup my hands around my eyes, but all I can see is black. I unlatch the window and pull the lower pane upwards. It sticks and I have to make sure I pull it up evenly with each hand. The cold night air whooshes in. It smells different here; the sweet grass smell from back home is gone. The air feels dry on my face. Back on the bed, I sit and cross my legs and get the box of cigarettes that one of the girls gave me last night. There's a lighter inside. I light the cigarette and breathe in, coughing as the end turns orange. I exhale, watching the smoke shoot from my nostrils and circle in grey wisps in front of my face. I do this until the full moon of the filter is yellow and there is a curling worm of ash, and then realize I have no ashtray. I run to the window and reach outside, stubbing it on the brickwork next to the windowsill, light-headed and giddy.

I close the window and look through the small holes of the net. A fly's vision is something like that – one of the lads told me once. I remember how they would catch a fly and pull its wings off one at a time and leave it on the ground to die. The cigarette leaves me with the jitters and I rub the tips of my nails against each other, looking for jagged edges. I rub my chin and scratch a spot until it stings. A moth flies up in front of me and I try to clap my hands around it, but it gets away.

I have a horrible taste in my mouth and am awfully thirsty. I imagine washing the nets around the back of the house and the water turning a dark yellow-grey.

So here I am. I smile. I need only think about myself from now on. Only wash my own dresses, my own underwear and the few garments I own. I take out another cigarette. What the heck – it's time to live life. I don't even smoke, I laugh to myself. But what else have I got to do? I breathe in deep, and after a few drags I'm tipsy with the nicotine and I can't stop smiling. I could scream but I dare not make a sound. Scream with sheer delight, that is.

I undress, careful on my unsteady legs, and leave my dress over the back of the chair. I put on my nightdress and get into bed. The fluorescent tube overhead has dead flies in it, but the light switch is by the door and tiredness is heavy on me. I close my eyes and drift off to sleep.

Later, I wake to the dead flies and the buzz of the light. I go and switch it off, treading carefully back to bed in the darkness.

I lie curled up like a baby and think of home. I think of me and Bernadette in the churchyard with a bottle of rum taken from the cabinet, and I think of Daddy's whiskey-breath singing sad songs, and I think of Siobhan, who didn't come to see me off. They run through my head, distant memories, far away now.

CLARE

7TH JULY 1997

Daddy's white Sierra is parked outside. I know it's his by the number on the yellow plate and the missing mirror that Mummy pulled off one night, when her eyes were shining wet and her face belonged to someone else.

I unclick my belt, then Thomas's, and we jump out of the car and run to the front door.

I ring the doorbell. Ding-dong.

Daddy opens and I run to him and he picks me up and kisses me. Daddy, Daddy, Daddy! His blond stubble tickles and his blue eyes are smiling. He puts me down and picks up Thomas. He's been working all week until late, so we've only seen him for dinner and until we go to bed, which is hardly anything. His hair is curly now because he's been working, but when he is showered and smart and handsome, his hair is combed back and neat like Mummy likes it. He smells of the black liquid stuff that goes hard and makes up the roads, because that's what he does for his job. When he lifts us up and kisses us at times like this, Mummy tells him off. She says the smell of him would knock out a horse and does he want to poison us all?

Mummy walks up the path to the front door where we are, with the bags in her hands, and I feel bad because she doesn't like it when we leave her like that and run off to Daddy. She says anyone would think she was our nanny. She turns her lips into a smile.

Daddy smiles back, touches her cheek and then kisses it. Thomas kisses the other.

'Get your dresses?' Daddy asks in the voice he reads us bedtime stories in. He rubs her arm.

She nods and sighs. Then, after a second, she says, 'You stink,' but she smiles, so it means he stinks but she doesn't mind today. That's because she's too sad even to get angry.

Mummy has not been one little bit happy since she got a call from her sister.

It was me who picked up the phone. Aunty Whatshername asked me what my name was and I said Clare. Then she asked how old was I now? I told her I was ten. And Thomas? she said. How old is the little one? She said it like she knew him, even though we've never met and I'd never even spoken to her before. Six and a half, I said. Mummy started waving her hands madly in the air, like she was trying to bat a fly away. While I was trying to work out what she was trying to tell me, Aunty Whatshername asked if Mummy was there? I looked at her, waving her hands around wildly. 'She can't come to the phone now,' I said. 'She's painting her nails.'

Mummy's face went white, and her eyes opened wide. She marched over to me and took the phone. 'Go up to your room, children,' she told us. Then she put a smile on and, into the phone, she said, 'Hello, who's that?' But she said it in a light airy-fairy voice like she wanted to speak to Aunty Whatshername, when I knew she didn't.

'What's wrong, love?' Daddy asks.

'Nothing,' says Mummy. 'I'm just under pressure to get ready for home, that's all. Clothes for me, the kids, you. Presents. Everything.'

But I know better, because of what she tells me at night-time when she gets me up for hot chocolate and Daddy is out for the count.

When Daddy is showered and smelling nice and Mummy is getting all dolled up, it's time to call a cab. Me and Thomas stand at the door so we can hear the beep to tell us it's there. I hear it first. I open the door and wave to the driver to say we're coming, and then I shout out loud so my voice travels upstairs: 'The cab is here!'

Daddy comes along the hallway and picks up his keys from a little glass dish on the wooden cabinet and we wait while Mummy comes down the stairs. She has dressed up and her hair is in waves around her face, like she's a film star. She's wearing one of her new dresses, the flowing pink one. Daddy whistles at her, like he does every Saturday night. Thomas tries to copy, but he can't whistle, so he blows spit bubbles and it makes us all laugh, even Mummy.

Tonight we're going for an Italian. Me and Thomas get Coke because it's our favourite, but it's the one from the tap, so it's watery, like Mummy's milky coffee. You can go up to the counter and fill it up to the top as many times as you want, so we don't care that it's watery.

'Coke, please,' I say when the waitress looks at me.

'Coke, too, please!' says Thomas when the waitress looks at him.

'Aren't they adorable?' the waitress says to Mummy.

Mummy smiles. 'Yes, they are.'

The waitress brings our Coke and serves Mummy and Daddy wine from the bottle. When she's gone, Mummy tuts. 'Coke will rot your teeth,' she says, looking from me to Thomas.

'It's everyone's Saturday-night treat,' says Daddy. 'Sit back and relax, love.' He winks at her, the way he does when she is about to get angry, and she smiles even though she doesn't want to, and then laughs and takes a big sip of wine.

He takes a sip of wine, too, and then I take a sip of Coke because I know he has made everything better.

We get garlic bread with cheese, a deep-pan pizza with pepperoni and the salad bowl that goes in the deal. Mummy is in charge of going to the salad counter because once, when Daddy went, he didn't fill the bowl high enough and Mummy got annoyed; and Thomas and me would drop it.

She fills it really carefully, layer by layer by layer. I go with her to watch. She picks up the cucumber slices with the big tweezers and makes a base, then the same with the tomato wheels, then a big spoon of grated carrots, and then she pushes it all down. We go round to the other side of the salad bar, making our way between all the people, and she gets potato salad and coleslaw and black olives that look like beetles, and lots of slices of the thing that makes you lose weight.

'It's huge!' says Thomas when we go back to the table.

'Don't draw attention to yourself, Thomas,' Mummy says.

Thomas pouts and kicks me under the table.

I stick out my tongue at him.

'Here we go.' Mummy rolls her eyes.

'It's all right, love,' Daddy says. 'Simmer down, you two,' he coughs. Then he lifts his hand in the air like he's just remembered something. 'How many days, now, Clare?' He points at me, waiting.

It's my moment to tell him the number because I count it every morning when I cross off the calendar. 'Eleven!'

'Hang on a minute,' he says, waving his finger in the air. 'Yesterday was thirteen, so how could today be eleven?'

'Liar, liar, pants on fire!' I say in the sing-song way we do at school when someone is lying.

Daddy comes at me with his finger and pushes it under my arm and I wriggle because it's tickling so much.

'It *is* eleven days, silly billy,' says Thomas.

'It is indeed, Thomaseen,' Daddy says. 'Thomaseen' is Thomas, but little Thomas, and Mummy and Daddy use it sometimes when he's cute or funny, but not when he's naughty. 'You two will meet your grandparents, won't you?'

Me and Thomas nod at the same time. Mummy calls us parrots when we do that.

'Are ye excited?' Daddy asks.

'Really, really, really excited!' says Thomas, and he starts bouncing on his chair.

'Tell us about your day, Michael.' That's Mummy, changing the subject.

'Come on, Josephine,' Daddy says.

'Don't.' Mummy puts her hand flat out in front of her, like she's pushing Daddy away, even though he's sitting at the table. 'Let's talk about something else.'

Daddy clears his throat and drinks his wine. When he's swallowed it down he tells us about his day, and how he made some roads outside London nice and smooth because they had potholes in them. Then he tells us what sinkholes are. They are like potholes but a million times bigger, when the earth swallows itself up and leaves a big hole. While he's talking, I look from Thomas to Mummy to Daddy, and back again. I watch Thomas listen, and feel the happy kick of his legs under the table against my feet. I watch Mummy watch Daddy, holding her glass of wine in her hand, her red nails shining. She takes a sip, puts down the glass and scratches her nails on each other.

She sees me looking at her. 'Clare, stop scratching your head. Put your hands on your lap.'

I do as I'm told, but then I feel another itch at the back of my head so I scratch it, then another at the front so I scratch it quickly, and then I take my Coke in both hands and drink it.

Garlic bread with cheese on top is one of my favourite things ever.

'I won't have any,' Mummy says. She takes a big gulp of wine while we pick up our pieces. Daddy takes a large one and I take the smallest one because I'm trying to be careful with my hips. Thomas chooses the biggest one left on the plate.

I start by nibbling the cheese hanging off the edge, but Thomas takes a big bite from the middle.

'Thomas, give us a bite to try, will you?' says Mummy.

He lifts his piece of garlic bread with cheese up, and Mummy bends down and bites into it with a big open mouth so she doesn't smudge her lipstick.

I'm eating the last bit of cheese that was like a dribble, when Mummy asks me for a bite of mine, to see if it tastes the same. I give her my piece because she can't reach across the table. She takes it and bites right into it. When she gives it back, it looks like a moon that's disappearing at night, being eaten by the black clouds. It has a semicircle of red drawn on it, like it's bleeding.

'Yes,' she nods. 'It tastes the same.'

'Have that last piece,' Daddy says to her.

'Not at all,' she says, 'you have it.'

'Are you sure?' Daddy says.

'I'll just have a bite, and then you have it.' She bites into it, passes it to Daddy and he pops the rest in his mouth.

I drink my Coke, but my face is hot because Mummy ate practically my whole piece of garlic bread, and then ended up eating more than anyone.

The pizza arrives and the Pizza Girl rolls her wheel through it once, twice, three times, four times, and serves out the pizza piece by piece, so the cheese hangs off in strings until she cuts it with the wheel. When she goes away, Mummy serves us some salad on each of our plates, so we all have one slice next to a little pile of salad. I give my black olive-beetles to Daddy because he likes them, and because I don't want to eat a beetle without even noticing.

'Can I have more of that, please?' I ask, pointing at the stuff that Mummy says makes you lose weight.

'Good girl,' says Mummy. 'That's celery,' she says, as she serves me an extra spoonful.

I smile, and think it's a good thing she ate some of my garlic bread. Now the celery will cancel out the pizza, too, so I will have eaten hardly anything, and nothing will go to my hips.

The pizza is cheesy and has loads of wheels of pepperoni, which I love. After one slice I'm still hungry, so I have another one. Mummy has three and a half slices, which she says is very naughty indeed, and I'm jealous because I want another one.

When we've finished our pizza and Mummy and Daddy are drinking their last glass of wine, me and Thomas go up to get more Coke and the ice-cream that squirts out of the machine. You get to be an ice-cream man for a minute when you push the button and the ice-cream squirts out, and you have to move your plate round and round so that it comes out in circles. I try to make mine look like a meringue but it doesn't really work. When it's Thomas's turn he won't let me help him, so his just looks like a worm on a plate.

The ice-cream is so good that I forget about my hips and gobble it all up before Mummy can ask for some.

Then the waitress calls a cab and we all go home.

Mummy takes out the records from the expensive cabinet we're not allowed to touch, with the wine glasses that you can see behind the glass. Me and Thomas sit and watch. Daddy comes in and moves the sofa backwards while we squeal and roll around, because we're still sitting on it.

Mummy looks up and laughs. 'What shall we put on?' she asks.

Daddy tells her the name of a record and takes his and Mummy's coats off and puts them over the back of the sofa, then he takes mine and Thomas's off and goes to the front door to hang them all up.

When Mummy has the record, she goes over to the player and puts it on the wheel with the pin on one side. She slides the pin until there's a crackle, and then the music starts up and she goes over to Daddy. He pulls her to him and puts his arm around her, and they dance.

Thomas and me get up and hold hands. We swing them from side to side with the beat of the music. We all put our hands up in the air and wave them in time to the words. Then, when the next bit starts, Mummy sings to us that we're her angels and she loves our smile and our everything. And we all hold hands and put them up in the air again. We sing at the tops of our voices. Mummy is smiling and her eyes are shining, and in moments like this I am so happy. I run over to her and throw my arms around her. She takes my hands from round her waist and lifts them in the air so we're holding hands, waving them in the air to her, then to me, then to her. She spins me round and round, and then she lets me go. I sway, and the room goes blurry, until my hands find hers again.

When it finishes, we're all out of breath and stand still for a minute while Daddy chooses the next one. He flicks through the records and Mummy goes to the side of the cabinet and pours them a drink. It's the same drink that she says is apple juice, when she's sitting at the kitchen table drinking it by herself, but I can tell it's not really juice, because it's too dark and smells horrible and strong. 'Kids, would you like a chocolate biscuit?'

'Yeah!' we chorus. I jump up and run to the kitchen and Thomas runs after me.

Daddy turns round. 'Maybe we should put them to bed.'

'Do you two want to go to bed?' she asks us, smiling, as we come back with our biscuits.

'Noooo,' we shout, jumping up and down, holding hands.

'Ah, go on, Michael, let's have a drink and some fun.' She hands him a glass and sways to the music that starts up.

I watch Daddy, from the arm of the sofa, while I eat my biscuit. I feel a teeny bit guilty because it'll go straight to my hips, but it's my Saturday Night Treat, so I decide it's okay. Just this once.

Daddy rifles through more records, picking them up and reading their labels one at a time, studying the big ring of colour in the middle. He puts some in a pile on the carpet and the rest back in the cabinet. 'These are the ones we're going to listen to,' he says to me.

Mummy holds her drink in one hand and a cigarette in the other and, as she turns from one side to the other, her flowy pink dress swishes from side to side.

'Twirl around, Mummy,' I say. I love watching her twirl in her dresses. Love watching them sail through the air, like she is a picture on the front cover of a magazine. Her lips are still shining bright red. I want my lips to be as red as hers. Mine are thin and pale like penny sweets. They're dull and don't shine at all. I watch her, and her dress swirling around her, and I can't wait to be like her when I grow up. To colour in my eyelids, draw black frames around my eyes, have bright-red lips.

'Let's dance,' she says, taking one of my hands, then one of Thomas's, and leading us in a circle in the open space between the fireplace and the sofa. She takes her shoes off and leaves them to the side. She lets go of our hands every now and again to get her drink, until the glass is empty. Her face is flushed and her eyes are big and shiny, the way they get when she has been drinking. She sings in time to the words and I'm sure the sound of her voice is travelling through the whole house. I join in when I know the words, and so does Thomas. We watch them dance together, Daddy spinning Mummy around under his arm, her dress rising, falling, rising, falling. They laugh and we laugh, and I copy Daddy and spin Thomas around, too. It's late and we're lucky to still be up; to be allowed to stay and watch Mummy dance like a film star.

The song finishes. The small pin hangs in the air. I lift it up and push it to the side like Daddy has shown me, and lift the record off the wheel. I take a new one from the top of the pile on the carpet and place it so that the nib goes through the hole in the middle. Then I lift the needle and bring it all the way to the edge of the record. A crackling noise like when the radio is wrong fills the room, and just when I think I've done something wrong, the music booms out. Mummy goes to the cabinet and fills up their glasses and we dance.

When the song finishes, I go back over to the player to put the next one on.

I'm sliding the needle to the edge when I hear them whispering. I turn and see Mummy's lips are white and thin and her eyes are cold. She's not smiling any more, or twirling. Daddy looks tired.

'They're back again,' Mummy hisses.

'What do you mean?' Daddy says.

I bend down, open the cabinet doors and put all the records in, careful not to scratch them.

'You know what I mean. Riddled – riddled, she is. Her head's crawling with them. How are we going to take her to meet my mother and father like this?'

I turn round and Mummy is pointing at me. Her eyes are big and round, and her arm is straight in the air, her lovely bright-red nail pointing straight at me. Then she puts her hands in her hair and scratches at her head.

It reminds me my own head is itchy. I scratch it.

'Calm down,' Daddy says.

'I will not calm down,' she screams.

I walk across the room, behind the sofa, and duck under the dining table. All I can think about is that my hair is crawling – riddled. I think of things that crawl. Maggots. I shut my eyes tight and scream with all my might to drown out her voice. I scream and scream, and don't stop even when my throat hurts. I imagine the fat maggots I've seen on the end of a fishing rod crawling in my hair.

I keep my eyes squeezed tight shut and my arms wrapped around my knees. I don't look up when Daddy comes to talk to me, and I don't come out, even though he asks me to. I wriggle like I'm a snake when he tries to grip my hand, so he won't catch me. My chest is popping in and out, in and out. He passes me my pump, which I take without touching him. I put it in my mouth and breathe in while I count to three, then repeat.

What are they going to think of me now, my granny and granddad who I've never met before? They will dip me in the river to catch fish with all the maggots in my hair.

JOSEPHINE

19TH JUNE 1980

The room is flooded with light and I can see straight out to a pink blossom tree. I jump up and run over to look out at it, and there are rooftops and more trees, and the road I can't see but know is below. I open the window and in wafts the smell of flowers and fumes and the beeps of horns. I leap onto the bed and bounce on it like a child until I'm out of breath. I made it! I say it out loud. I kneel down beside the bed and bless myself and say a quick prayer. Then I bless myself again, put my dress on and get my things for a shower, making sure to lock the door behind me.

The water is hot over my face and I stand there for a few minutes, feeling it run over me, not scared of someone coming in, not hurting because it's so cold. The power of the spray is strong, not like the piddly stream that came from the plastic tube attached to the bath taps at home. I scrub my skin and my hair and even shave my legs, humming as I go.

I get dressed and towel-dry my hair. I decide I'll buy a hair-dryer as soon as I can. I'll blow-dry my hair, with smooth legs, while I smoke a cigarette. Like a real city girl.

CLARE

8TH JULY 1997

I wiggle my toes. Something is wrong because they're cold and the soft warmth of my duvet isn't there. I blink, one, two, three times, and shiver when I see the shiny silver leg of the table. My eyes are sticky. I scrunch my face up and my cheeks are tight from the tears. I remember Daddy trying to get in under the table, and me screaming as loud as I could so that he and Thomas would get away. Mummy didn't come near me. Cold air is coming from the bottom of the French doors and when I sniff, my nose is full of snot. I look up at the faint light coming from the three bulbs in the ceiling. They left them on dim for me, so I could find my way to bed. They must have thrown a blanket over me after I fell asleep because it's draped over me now, but it's thin and not heavy and soft like my duvet.

I crawl out from under the table, and when I'm clear of it I stand up. That's when I see Daddy's feet poking out from the side of the sofa. I know they're his because they're big and Mummy's are small. He's still dressed, and his shoes are at the side of the marble floor that's there in case chunks of coal fall out of the fire. He has a blanket over him, too. I bet his back will hurt today. I scratch my head and then I remember and want to cry, but I don't want to wake Daddy up, so I tiptoe to the door. It's already open a bit, so I don't have to turn the knob. I just pull it towards me and step through the small gap and then pull it closed again.

The kitchen light is off, but I can see anyway from the light by the front door that they leave on every night. I go up the stairs on all fours, and step over the one that creaks.

I push our door open and go in. I take my clothes off and leave them on the floor, even though I shouldn't. The curtains are pulled closed but some light is starting to peep through, so I can see my pyjamas hanging on the post at the end of our beds. I put them on and creep up the ladder, left, right, left, right, and I crawl along the wall and lift up the duvet until I'm snuggled underneath.

When I wake it's the light of day, and the sadness in my chest isn't as big as it was. I turn to face the wall and pull the duvet high over my head so that, when Mummy comes in, she thinks I'm asleep and leaves me alone. But she doesn't come. That means she's going to stay in bed. I'm glad. I don't want to see her rotten face, I think, and then I giggle at my naughtiness. Her rotten, crawling face. I lie still, looking at the wall. Then the door opens and Daddy comes in.

'Good morning, sleepyheads,' he says, but I stay facing the wall and close my eyes quick, so he doesn't know I'm awake.

'Morning, Daddy,' Thomas says.

He comes over and leans in to Thomas's bit of the bed and tells him he's nipping out and he'll be back in half an hour.

'Okay,' Thomas says.

'Mummy's asleep,' he says, 'don't disturb her now, will you?'

'No, we won't,' Thomas says.

No way will we, I say in my head.

When he's gone down the stairs and unlocked the front door and closed it behind him, I get out of bed and climb down the ladder and go over to my calendar and get the pen and do a big fat cross on Sunday. I push it hard into the page and the X comes out much fatter than the others. Ten days to go. I can't wait. We'll be in Uncle John's house with all our cousins and loads of adults and I won't have to talk to her hardly at all. Then when it's time to go to her house, I'll stay with Thomas and won't speak to anyone. I've already heard her say the only reason we're going is because someone is dying. I heard her on the phone in the sitting room until she spotted me and told me to go and play with Thomas upstairs. 'She's sick and dying.' That's what she said. But she doesn't know that I heard her, and I know her mum is dying. She can't remember telling me the other night, either, when we were in the kitchen and she was crying.

I remember the worms in my hair, but figure if Granny is dying, she and Granddad will be too sad to worry about dipping me in the river. That's a relief.

Mummy has been drinking more and more apple juice lately. It must be because of Granny dying. I would be sad, too, if one of my parents or Thomas was dying. Even though Mummy is horrible sometimes, and screamed that I had worms crawling in my hair. I would cry for years if she died, so I understand. Daddy says that our trip is just what she needs. After all, she hasn't seen her family since before she got married to Daddy, which was ages ago because I'm almost a grown-up, and they married even before I was born.

'Boo!' Thomas growls in his deep voice.

I turn round.

He is sitting up in his bed with his wispy honey-blond hair sticking up all over the place and his big, round blue eyes that are puffy around the edges from sleep. 'Don't be sad,' he says, sticking his bottom lip out to make a sad face.

I remember last night. Someone being nice to me makes me want to cry all over again and the wave of sadness comes up into my chest and it starts to shake, and my shoulders shake too. I sit on the floor and cross my legs and cover my hands with my face and cry.

Thomas gets out of bed and hugs me, even though his arms are short and he can only hug me around my waist. But it doesn't matter, I hug him back anyway, and kiss him on the top of the head to show him I love him.

'I have maggots in my hair,' I say to him when I catch my breath.

'If we get them out, we can go fishing with them and catch lots of fish!' He tickles me under my arms and I can't stop myself from giggling, even though he's not doing it very hard. He shakes my hair about and says, 'All gone. Now let's go fishing.'

'Where?'

'In the garden.'

'Okay.'

We get dressed, without having a bath or brushing our teeth or our hair. I remember Mummy sleeping in her room and warn Thomas when we're in the hallway by putting my finger to my lips to say shush. We creep along the hallway and down the stairs, Thomas following behind me, holding onto the rail and stepping down with his right foot first, so he takes longer than me. I lead the way to the kitchen, through the utility room and stop at the back door. I get the key from the drawer beside the door and open it.

The garden smells of early morning, before anyone gets up and when the air is quiet and still, but for the sound of the birds singing. It smells of grass and snails and earth. Even though it hasn't rained, the grass is all wet from the water that comes during the night. The air is cold and all the hairs on my arms stick out like the hairs on spiders, short and pointy. We run outside onto the patio. The patio is next to the French doors, and that's where we have a wooden table that sometimes we eat on, when it's warm and when Daddy takes his top off and burns all the chicken on the barbecue. Then there's the big patch of grass where me and Thomas play, and sometimes Daddy puts the sprinkler out to water the grass and we run through it, over and over again, getting soaked and squealing. We love it. The swingball is in the middle. Daddy has been teaching me. It's fast and scary, and you can't take your eye off the ball for a second because it will belt you. At the end of the garden are the flowerbeds where Mummy grows her flowers. Mummy is a bit of a green-fingers. We're not allowed near them, but sometimes when she's inside we pick flowers and I put them in my hair, and Thomas puts them behind his ears or poking out of his top pocket.

Thomas runs over to where the swingball and badminton rackets are and gives me one of each and keeps two for himself. Then we start playing. You can only stand on the racket. If you step off it, the sharks get you. You place it down, jump on it and then put another one down ahead of where you are, and you have to jump onto it without standing on the grass. When you're safely on the racket, you fish.

In our garden we have eight balls, big ones and little ones, bouncy ones, tennis ones, footballs, and we have shuttlecocks and daisies and weeds and snails. We have to make our way around the garden as fast as we can with our two rackets, putting one down, jumping on it, picking up the other one, putting it down... and fish as much as we can.

When I have three bouncy balls, a tennis ball, five daisies and two snails, all I can think about is beating Thomas, because he's closer to the tennis ball by the fence and if he gets it first he might win. It's hard to tell, because we hide small things like daisies and snails in our pockets, so it's easy to be tricked. Just when I'm getting warm and going as fast as I can to get to the tennis ball, I hear the jingle-jangle of Daddy's keys.

Thomas runs over to him, but I stay on my racket. He hugs him and Daddy goes down onto his knees and looks at me, waiting for me to go over as well.

'I have a present for you,' he says.

'What?' I can't help myself. Mummy always says that curiosity killed the cat.

'Your favourite.'

I open my eyes wide. I bet it's a trick. 'Strawberry milkshake?'

'You got it.' He winks.

I run to him and hug him tight, and he hugs me back and the bristles on his cheeks tickle my face. This is a big treat, only for special things like when we go to Mass or when I've got a good mark in a test. I know he's cheering me up, because we've never had one in the morning before. I run into the kitchen and, sure enough, there's a paper bag on the counter. I grab it and run outside.

Daddy is already sitting at the garden table with Thomas on his lap. I hand out one of everything to each of us, which is one milkshake and one muffin for me and Thomas – strawberry for me, and vanilla for him – and a coffee and a muffin for Daddy. Another coffee and muffin are left in the bag. I close it and leave it on the table.

I put the straw in and start sucking, but it always takes a minute to come out, so I keep sucking, and then all of a sudden the strawberry milkshake fills my mouth. Yum, yum, yum. I suck more and more and keep going until – bang! A sharp pain hits me in the head. I put my hands over my ears, even though the pain is coming from inside, and then Thomas is doing the same. Daddy starts laughing and I'm holding my head in my hands, and so is Thomas. He gets down off Daddy's lap and starts rolling around on the grass, and we're all laughing because it's so funny.

When we've finished, Daddy says it's bath time. We already had our baths yesterday and our hair washed and dried, but we're going to have another one with Daddy. He runs the water and pours in the bubble bath and we get undressed. I dip my fingers in first and then my toes, and then slowly, slowly I lower myself in until I'm all underwater, apart from my face.

'Move over, little monkey,' says Daddy, so I sit up and he lifts Thomas over the edge until his feet are in, and he kicks and splashes me in the face.

When Thomas is in, Daddy takes a bottle of shampoo out of a plastic bag and rubs some into my hair. It smells so bad I think for a minute my milkshake's going to come back up. I've smelt it before, once or twice. It's going to kill the worms.

I try not to think about it, about worms dying in my hair and falling into the bath before my eyes.

When Daddy's finished with me, he rubs the shampoo into Thomas's hair and we hold our noses and try not to breathe. Daddy makes us leave it in for ages. He combs Thomas's hair through with a really thin comb that takes for ever. When he's finished, he combs mine for much longer because I've got more hair, as I'm a girl and mine is long. After a while, he rinses our hair.

We get out of the bath and Daddy wraps our towels around us and combs our hair again. Then he dries and plaits mine, but he's not very good at plaits, so I take them out and do them again.

'Great,' says Daddy. 'Now go up and get dressed for Mass. Clare, choose something nice for you and your brother,' he says, looking at me.

I can't believe it. I never get to choose what clothes I can wear. I decide that maybe today isn't so bad, after all.

'Okay!' I chirp like a bird. That's what Daddy says I sound like sometimes when I'm happy and my voice goes all sweet, like a tweet-tweet.

Even Thomas is excited and he doesn't care about things like clothes. I pick out his favourite yellow T-shirt with red-and-blue stripes and a pair of his denim shorts that are old, with threads hanging out around the pockets, so he's not allowed to wear them. And I choose his favourite brown boots to finish his outfit. When he's dressed, he looks in the mirror and gives me a big hug. 'Thank you, Clare!' he says.

'You're welcome,' I say. Whenever anyone does anything nice, you say thank you; and when anyone says thank you, you always say that they are welcome.

I pick out a short pink polka-dot skirt that Mummy never lets me wear, and socks that aren't frilly, because she always makes me wear frilly socks, and a stripy red-and-green polo that she says is old and only ever lets me wear at home. When we're dressed, we go downstairs and decide to play cards.

I'm letting Thomas beat me at the memory game, when we put all the cards face-down and have to look for matches, when Mummy comes into the sitting room. She is in her dressing gown and has a cup of tea that she is holding with both hands. She has no make-up on and she looks as grey as the clouds in the sky yesterday.

'Morning,' she says, smiling just a little.

'Morning, Mummy,' says Thomas.

I push my lips tight shut together and don't say anything.

She sits down on the sofa and rubs a curl of hair away from her face. Her nails are just as bright and glistening red as they were yesterday, but there's a chip in the one she bit in the changing room. 'Clare, will you come here for a minute?' She taps the cushion beside her and puts her tea on the table.

I put my cards down and go over and sit down on the cushion next to her, even though I don't want to go near her or talk to her ever again.

'I'm sorry about yesterday.' She takes my hand in her shiny-nailed ones, and one of the edges is sharp and scratches me. 'I shouldn't have said what I said at all.'

I nod, trying to get pictures of maggots out of my head. I remember her telling us once that you should be careful what you say, because you can never take it back. Once words are spoken, she said, that's it, there's no going back. I think about that now and wish I could take my hand out of hers. After she said that, she said you should also be careful what you wish for – that it might just come true. I wanted to ask why. What on earth could you wish for that, when you got it, you wouldn't wish for it any more?

She sighs and takes a gulp of her tea, then shakes her head. 'I shouldn't have said that. I'm sorry.' Her eyes are dark. She has been dimmed, like the light in the sitting room that you can turn up and down and was left on low for me last night. I like it much better when she's shiny and sparkling.

'It's okay, Mummy.'

She pulls me towards her and I hug her, and she starts crying and holds me tight. When I feel her hair tickle my face and mouth, I remember the nightmare. There were snakes crawling out of my hair and down my face and I was screaming for Mummy, but she was in a boat in the sea, sailing away. The snakes jumped out of my hair and into the sea and I screamed, as loud as I could, because I knew they were going for her.

We're allowed to keep our clothes on this once, but we have to change our shoes for our polished black ones.

When we pull into the car park, everyone is getting out of their cars and walking towards the steps up to the church. I watch them all. The girls in their shiny shoes, frilly socks and dresses with belts on, and the boys in shirts and trousers. I'm happy I got to choose what me and Thomas are wearing, and I wonder why everyone always has to dress up on Sundays anyway. It's only to go into Mass and sit on a bench and listen to boring Father Feathers go on about something I can't even understand. His accent is so strong I don't know if anyone can understand him, even though almost everyone is Irish, like Mummy and Daddy.

We go in, walk three-quarters of the way up like we always do, apart from when it's really busy and we have to sit further back. Today Daddy sits between me and Thomas, and Mummy sits on the other side of Thomas, and on my other side is a gap and then another man.

Everything happens as it always does. Standing up, sitting down, kneeling, praying, queuing, bread on tongue without touching my teeth, more kneeling and more praying.

Father Feathers stands at the altar and crosses himself and we all have to stand up at the same time, then sit down at the same time and kneel at the same time. I know it all off by heart and try to do it a second before everyone else, just to show off. It's the only thing I can do to have fun when we're at Mass. I'm not allowed to sit next to Thomas because Mummy says we turn into giggling hyenas. Then we all get up and stand in a line and go up to the altar, and Father Feathers puts bread in our mouths. Only it's not really bread. It's a thin round wafer like the one you have with ice-cream, but it dissolves on your tongue and doesn't taste nice. He always puts it on the tip of my tongue. I have to make sure it doesn't touch my teeth or I'll go to hell. His name is Father Francis, but we call him Father Feathers because he has these little wisps of hair that fly around over his head like feathers. Mummy says he really should get it cut off. She remembers when he had more hair, years ago when she first came over to London and met him. But she thinks he wants to hold on to the last little bits he has left. I think he should wear a hat to cover it all up. A baseball cap, to show everyone that we don't have to dress up. Because all we do is go in and listen to him, and he doesn't even tell us good stories – not like Daddy's, which make me and Thomas giggle for ages.

When the old lady comes round with the basket, I get to put the envelope in. This is our donation. It says 'Mr and Mrs Michael Reilly' on the front, so that Father Feathers knows we gave money to the church. I think about putting it in my pocket and saving it for milkshakes for me and Thomas, but Mummy is looking. At least it looks like she's looking, but her eyes are dark and shiny and I'm not sure if she's looking at me. I don't keep it, just in case. Anyway, that would be so naughty I wouldn't be able to sleep tonight.

A really old lady at the end of the bench in front falls asleep and I catch Thomas's attention and point her out by nodding my head in the lady's direction. Then the bell rings and she jerks awake, and Thomas wants to laugh so hard that he sits back so he can't see me. I giggle inside and have to cross my legs, otherwise some wee might come out.

When Mass is finally over, we're almost free until next week. All we have to do now is queue to leave the church, while everyone shakes hands with Father Feathers and says their goodbyes. It goes like this:

'Goodbye, Father.'

'Goodbye, now.'

'Goodbye, Father.'

'Bye, now.'

'See you, Father.'

'Bye, now.'

I don't know why everyone calls him Father anyway. Daddy is right beside me and I don't need another one. This is what I'm thinking when I reach the door with Father Feathers looking down at me.

'Clare, say goodbye to Father Francis,' Mummy says, pulling me forward by my elbow. She says it in a funny voice, and it doesn't really sound like her. It's high and kind of empty. I wish then that I'd put on frilly socks and a lovely dress and a ribbon in my hair, because Mummy likes me to look beautiful, and Thomas to look handsome. She says that her and Daddy didn't get to dress up in nice things and play with nice things like us, and that we don't know how lucky we are. I look at my nails, but the paint has almost come off from the bath. I wish I was all beautiful. Maybe then she would be smiling at Feathers, and wouldn't care that I didn't call him Father.

'Goodbye,' I say.

'Goodbye, *Father*,' Mummy says. She looks at Feathers and laughs.

'Hello, Josephine, how are you keeping, my dear?' he says to Mummy.

'Hello, Father! Very well, thank you.' She smiles like she just won a prize. 'Getting ready for the holidays, now, for going home.'

'How lovely,' says Feathers, smiling.

She smiles back at him. She loves Feathers. She says he was like an angel to her when she was all alone and didn't have anyone, all those years ago.

I can feel Feathers's eyes on me. I'm holding up the queue – and everyone's freedom – until next week. Next week! Maybe we won't come because we'll be packing and getting ready to go. And the week after that we'll be at home in Ireland, and the week after that, too. I think of the crosses on my calendar and my heart beats quick. I'm dying to run down the steps and I suddenly realize we might get another milkshake for being good at Mass.

He smiles down at me, teeth twinkling in the sun, the wisps of his hair glowing, and I imagine him talking to God and doing all God's work, and I wonder if he really is an angel. In my head, I ask him that the next time he talks to God, it would be good if he got God to look after Mummy, to keep the snakes away, to make everything better. I tell him that I don't want more hot chocolate during the night, because then I have bad dreams and can't sleep.

'Goodbye, Father,' I say, hoping he has heard the rest of it, even though I haven't said it out loud.

'Goodbye, now, Clare.' He rubs the top of my head.

JOSEPHINE

19TH JUNE 1980

When I've finished doing myself up, I practise my smile, showing my top teeth but hiding the lower ones.

My stomach churns with hunger. I head downstairs with my passport and some money in my purse and sign the guest-book on the reception desk. Your man is awake now and dressed smartly in a shirt and trousers. He takes my passport and asks for ten pounds as a deposit for my stay, which I give him. He tells me his name is Mister Vish.

'Thanks, Mister Vish,' I say, and wave goodbye as I leave. He seems like a nice man, but I remind myself this is a foreign land and I will be cautious with all the men I meet.

A gush of wind takes my breath away when I step onto the street, the grit in the air slapping my face and the fumes making me cough. I contemplate the people rushing past in both directions, the cars and the red buses driving by in both lanes. What was deserted last night is now buzzing with life. The sky is blue, with clouds like cotton wool dipped in paint. Women rush along with small children in shirts and gold-and-blue striped ties, and grey trousers and skirts. I smile at the mothers, but they are in a hurry and don't smile back. I check my watch; it's a quarter to nine.

I turn right as if I know where I'm going and walk past several shop fronts, past a flower stall and a furniture shop and more bric-a-brac shops, and still the road doesn't come to an end. The noise, the commotion, the contamination are everywhere. I keep my elbows close by my sides, so as not to hit the people walking so fast they're almost running. It's cool and I have no jacket; I hold my arms across my chest to conceal my nipples, which I can feel start to poke out. A nervous shiver runs down my spine.

There's a market on the left-hand side, so I wait with other people gathered, until the lights change, and I cross the road and walk through the middle. It's lovely, with flowers lined up in pots and fruit piled neatly on top of each other. Then there's the butcher's and fishmonger's, and the smell on an empty stomach drives me out the other side.

A green shamrock light over a café makes me laugh and I find myself walking towards it. A little bell over the door goes 'ding-dong' when I go in, so that everyone turns round to look at me. 'Didn't expect that, now,' I mutter and smile, willing them to look away. I take a seat at the table in the far corner.

It smells of rashers and sausages and eggs and is strangely comforting. That's what we'd have on special occasions, and if Daddy came into some money or it was his birthday. On our own birthdays we would have a boiled egg and toast, and that was treat enough for us. I would chop the top of the egg off carefully with a knife and pour in loads of salt and put lashings of butter in, and mix the egg all around in its shell. Everyone was quiet round the table then, eyeing your egg, and you'd have to be careful not to leave the table or look away, in case your egg was snatched from under your nose.

One year, I remember, Siobhan shared her egg with me. That must have been when we were very little and still close. Before there were favourites and we were pitted against each other. Mammy always hated me, and adored her. I never knew why. Siobhan'd be mean, copying our mammy, and of course I resented her for it. I was only young myself – sure, I didn't know any better. So I'd be mean to her and wouldn't let her come and play with me and Bernadette. Feck off, I'd say when she'd go to follow me through the hole in the hedge. You feck off, she'd say in a low voice, you dirty tinker, you.

It seems appropriate to treat myself to a full breakfast and a cup of coffee, like I'm on holiday. I have some money to keep me going for a few days, maybe even a few weeks; I haven't properly worked it out.

A girl comes over and I order. She's very beautiful, with her auburn hair in waves and black liner around her eyes. I feel silly, now I've seen her.

She comes back with my coffee. 'There you go, now,' she says, and I'm sure she has an Irish accent.

'Was that an Irish accent?' I ask her, blushing.

'Yes, it was indeed,' she says, and she smiles at me.

It turns out she's from Wexford and has been here for six months. Her name is Joyce and she's twenty-three. I like her immediately. She's everything I'd love to be.

When she comes back with my breakfast she asks where I'm staying, and then she says she'll leave me to eat in peace. I would love for her to stay and keep me company, but I don't tell her that.

I wolf down my breakfast, adding plenty of ketchup and buttering the toast generously. As Mammy would say, I could eat a horse.

There's an Irish paper on the side. I get it and have a flick through, and then I go to pay the bill. Joyce tells me her boss is looking for another girl because someone just left. 'He'll like you,' she says, 'a pretty young thing. And he likes the Irish because he says, despite what everyone thinks, we're hard-working.'

'Thanks so much,' I tell her, 'but I'm hoping to get some secretarial work.'

'Well, good luck with that, but if you want this you'd have to be smartish about it, because it won't take him long to find someone.' Then a group of lads comes in and she has to get back to work.

I thank Joyce again for her kind offer and leave, the ding-dong of the bell sounding as I go.

Then it hits me like a hurricane. Doubt. I go towards the market, but my head is swirling like the eye of the storm. Go back in there and ask her to speak to her boss. Tell her you'd love the job. But you didn't come here to work in a café. But you need a job. But they'll laugh at you. But isn't it better than nothing? They'll all be laughing at you.

My head goes round and round until I'm dizzy and have to stand against the wall to let everyone rush by.

When it has passed, I buy a bunch of grapes and five oranges from a man at a fruit stall. Then I find a shop where I can buy a pen, paper and envelopes.

'Hello,' I say to the girl at the till, but she doesn't look up at me.

She puts the things into a bag and takes the money, without

so much as a word or a glance in my direction, then drops the change in my hand.

'Bye,' I say to her, but she makes herself look busy and doesn't answer.

Outside, I wonder if it's because I'm Irish. I hope I didn't offend her in some way.

Doubt still claws at me, but I try to focus on the positive: I could have just landed myself a job. That's great news, Josephine. Well done, you. I look at the rows of buildings on either side of me, running on and on and on. Their fronts are made of brick and their doors have round glass panels in them and brass knockers. I wonder who is behind them.

Mister Vish is sitting at the reception desk when I go in. I had hoped he wouldn't be there.

'Hello!' he says. He's all sprightly. 'You like Shepherd's Bush?'

'Yes!' I say in my high-pitched everything-is-great tone, and smiling as brightly as I can manage. 'It's very nice.'

'What will you do here?'

'I hope to get a secretarial job,' I tell him. 'I got the cert a couple of months ago.'

'Cert?'

'Certificate,' I explain.

'It's hard to get job,' he says, tutting and shaking his head, 'very hard.'

I nod.

By the time I'm in my room, I am sick to the stomach. I have made the wrong decision. If there was the opportunity of a job, I should have taken it. What a fool, I tell myself. A stupid, good-for-nothing, worthless fool. Daddy was always right.

I wipe my face with the dry facecloth. It scrapes the lipstick off me and, when I look at it, it's streaked pink and speckled black from my mascara. I sit on the edge of the bed and look around the room. My yellow dress is still hanging on the back of the chair. I pick it up and a moth flies up into the air. I go to the bathroom to wash it, together with my underwear. I use the soap sparingly, on the crotch of the knickers, the under-arms of the bra and the dress. I wash them in the sink and rinse them in the bath, then wring them through.

In my room, I take some hangers from the wardrobe and stand on the chair to hang them on the window rail. I wonder where I'll be hanging my clothes in the future; if it'll be a rose garden or a little patio, or in the window of a nice room. The thought of hanging my clothes to dry somewhere else other than Mammy's back yard fills me with hope, and I decide I'll go back to the café first thing in the morning. I fasten my suit-case closed, so the moths don't get in.

After a snooze, I set the fruit and the pen, paper and enve-lopes down on the table. The rooftops are getting darker now that the sky has clouded over and my dress hangs there in the middle, limp and dripping into the metal bin. The sky is purple like a bruise, and the pink blossoms whisper in the breeze outside the window.

I take out one of the oranges and peel it over the bin, licking the juice off my fingers. It is sweet and perfectly ripe, and the segments come apart easily in my hands. I eat it slowly, savour-ing it one piece at a time, having it all to myself. The smell of orange fills the room and a slice of sunlight breaks through the clouds and shines through my dress onto the floor.

CLARE

12TH JULY 1997

Faces smiling. Eyes twinkling. Mouths open, laughing. I want to jump in and be there right now. I would be in any one of the photos if I could, even the black-and-white one – the only one of anyone from Mummy's side of the family, the great-granny I've never met, and won't meet because she already died. I'd like to have met her, because Mummy cries when she talks about her. I know she's crying out of sadness and love, because she pulls me and Thomas to her for a cuddle, and kisses our hair and rubs our backs. I can tell when she's crying out of hate and anger, too, because she curls her lips into a horrible shape and shows her teeth.

I smile back at all the faces. They've been watching us ever since I can remember, from inside the frames. I took one down off the wall once to look at it close up and there was a white square on the wall underneath, like an open door waiting for me to jump through, eyes squeezed tight shut and hand holding my nose.

The last week of school has finally arrived and there are six little days to go. Tick-tock, tick-tock. Time flies when you're having fun. That's what they say, Mummy says. I don't know who *they* are, but whoever they are, that's what they say. I am happy. It's just in quiet moments, when I'm in the loo, or when no one's talking at dinner, or when I'm doing my hair in the morning, that I see snakes crawling around in it, and fat worms with big, round black eyes coming out of my ears.

Last night I weed in my bed without meaning to. I woke up every time I touched the wet patch because it was so cold. I pressed myself up against the wall as much as I could, and put the pillow right behind me, so I couldn't move back one little bit. Mummy doesn't know and I'm not going to tell her. She's still in bed anyway. I woke up all by myself, because she didn't wake us, and Daddy's not here because he goes to work when it's still dark and we're fast asleep. I'm ready and so is Thomas. I'm in the sitting room, looking at the faces smiling and their eyes twinkling, wishing I was there. This is the third day in a row that Mummy has slept in. I've woken up all by myself and got dressed and then I've woken Thomas, taken him to the toilet, got him dressed and brushed his hair, which takes ages because he always has electricity in it that gives me a shock. When he turns round and goes back to sleep, I've learned to pull the pillow from under his head. Then he's got nothing to snuggle into and cries until I pull him out of bed.

The only thing I keep forgetting is to change our pants, and then I remember when it's too late and we're already dressed. I haven't said anything because Mummy isn't good and hasn't even noticed. Sometimes I'd rather wear no pants anyway. Maybe tomorrow. I just hope Thomas doesn't say anything, because then I'll be in BIG trouble. I can't tell him not to tell, because if I do that, he'll definitely tell. Not to get me into trouble, just because then he'll remember it even more and he doesn't understand, like I do, that it's better not to say some things. I'm like a fairy, I watch everything and you don't hear a peep out of me.

Mummy walks around like she's playing a zombie in a film. Her hair sticks up almost as much as Thomas's and she doesn't talk to us. Just says her head hurts, and what in the name of God will she do?

'What do you mean?' I ask. And she turns to me, with her big black eyes that look nowhere, not wanting to dance with Daddy and not wanting to hear a squeak out of us or play with us before dinner, and walks straight past. I miss Mummy.

There's one big photo on the wall in a really fancy gold frame, so you can't help but look at it first. It's of all of us, at the altar. Mummy and Daddy are standing with a font between them, the round top filled with water. The water is holy, and was poured over my little brother's head just before the photo was taken. Thomas is the baby in Mummy's arms, in a huge, white gown that flows down past her waist. You can't see Thomas's face, just the blondie curls of hair on the top of his head. I am standing in front of Daddy, one arm up in the air; holding his hand. I am wearing a flowery dress with a pink sash round my waist, and my reddish hair curls around my face. My eyes twinkle and my mouth is wide open because I'm laughing. I think that was when we were happy.

Daddy is tall and handsome in a navy suit. He is looking at the camera, smiling so you can see his white teeth. His fine set of white teeth, as Mummy says. She says they were one of the first things she noticed about him. It's hard to come across in an Irish man, she says. The other thing she noticed was the scar on his forehead, which she liked because he told her a funny story that made her laugh, and his lovely blue eyes. I don't have them, but Thomas does. And Thomas has his blondie hair and his button-nose. He is Daddy's mini-me and I am Mummy's. I have her big brown eyes and her auburn hair that is a reddy-brown and goes really red in the sun. Mummy says Thomas takes after Daddy's side of the family, and I take after her side, but I'm not sure I want to take after her side because they don't sound very nice.

Mummy is wearing a navy dress that goes to her knees, with a cream belt pulled round her waist. It's one of her favourites. She keeps it in the wardrobe even though she doesn't wear it any more. She is looking over the font at me, so you can see the side of her face, her pretty nose, her eyelashes curling upwards with mascara. She is so pretty, all made up. If I ask really, really nicely she puts a splash of colour on my cheeks, and dries my hair so it's big and fluffy, and I look like her.

Sometimes, when we're all done up, we pose in the back room for photos, and I hug Mummy and smile for the camera, wondering if this one will be pretty enough to put up on the wall. I wish now I had chosen nice outfits for me and Thomas to wear on Sunday. Maybe then Mummy wouldn't be so sad.

There are so many photos. They're on the mantelpiece and the side tables and on the wall of the sitting room, all the way to the French doors that we open after school, now that it's warm and I can wear my summer dresses and Thomas can wear his shorts and vests. That way we can run in and out of the sitting room to the garden, and along the side of the house and in the back door and through the kitchen, then back through the sitting room and out through the French doors. We do that for hours.

One of the photos is of us sitting on the grass in the park down the road, where we go all the time with Daddy. It's the day Daddy taught us how to play with shuttlecocks, and I'm blowing a kiss at the camera and I have buttercups in my hair and Thomas has one behind his ear, which I put there. First I showed him what you have to do with buttercups. I held one under my chin, so he could see the colour of butter spread onto my skin. He held one under his chin and it went yellow like the sun and I told him so. Then I put mine in my hair and Thomas's behind his ear and Daddy called us and said to smile, and we did. That was last year. We haven't taken any from this year yet. Maybe when we're at home-home. It will be brilliant and we'll have a great time.

There's one photo in a wooden frame – each one is in a different frame – of me and Thomas with our cousins. We're kneeling down in a row, filthy dirty from rolling around in the sand, our hair falling into our eyes. I'm on the end and next to me is Thomas, and next to Thomas is our older cousin John and next to him is our other cousin Mary and then beside her is Sarah, their little sister. Mary is my age and Sarah is the same age as Thomas. Their dog is digging a hole in the sand, splashing us all, and John is about to hit her around the ear. That's Pretty Lady, she's lovely and soft and cuddly. That photo was taken by Daddy when we were playing at home in Uncle John's. We go there every year and spend all summer there and, except for when it rains, we spend every day out playing in front of the house, or on some days when we are really adventurous we make our way out the back and in through all the trees. That's where we're going in six days, which will be five tomorrow, and then bang on my favourite number – four – days the day after that. Our cousin John got his name off our Uncle John. Mummy said it's traditional for people to call their baby boys the same name as their dads, and when I ask why Thomas isn't called Michael, like our dad, she said it's because we're not that traditional.

When we go to Uncle John's we see our Aunty Joan, because she's John's wife, and we see Aunty Anne. She doesn't have a husband, so we have no cousins in her house, not like at Uncle John's. All of them are in photographs on the wall, too, but there are none of Mummy's brothers and sister or her mummy and daddy.

We're late for school. I go upstairs quietly, along the landing and to the front room, which is Mummy and Daddy's room, but where only Mummy sleeps lately because Daddy gets up so early to go to work that she doesn't want him waking her. I listen. The door is closed and there isn't a sound, only my heart going bum-bum, bum-bum. I don't know what to do. I could just go downstairs and put the TV on and sit down and watch it with Thomas. But then Mummy will stay up here all day and forget about us. Better to go to school and see Mandy and Hannah, and eat lunch made by the school cooks. There's nothing to eat in the kitchen, anyway. Me and Thomas have finished the last bit of cereal, which is my favourite bit because it's all sugar crumbs. I have PE today as well, which means we'll play games. We always play games in the last PE class before holidays.

I knock on the door as lightly as I can. I wait. Nothing. I hold my breath and knock again. 'Mummy,' I whisper. 'We have to go to school now.'

I try to turn the golden knob, but my hand is sweaty and it slides without moving anything. I wipe it on my sleeve and try again. I edge the door in a teeny-weeny bit, so that she won't hear or notice it, and if she's really mad I can run away and get down the stairs before she throws anything at me. Through the small gap I can see the darkness in the room. The curtains are still closed. I squidge my eyes together and see her dresser over in the far corner, clothes over the back of the chair, the drawers open. It looks messy. So does the kitchen. Mummy hasn't cleaned for days, and Daddy gets home late and by the time he makes us beans on toast we have to go to bed. Then he washes the dishes, but I don't think he's doing a very good job because there was hard cereal on my bowl this morning.

I move the door in a teeny-weeny bit more and push my forehead right up to the gap. I bet I'll have a line down my forehead afterwards. 'Mummy,' I whisper. I wait. 'Mummy.' I push it in more, but it knocks against something. I poke my head round the door and look at the bed. The sheets are pushed back and Mummy's not there. I scan the room and try to push the door in more, but it won't budge. Stubborn as a mule. I look down and there she is, in a ball on the floor. I scream as loud as I can and turn and run away, along the landing and down the stairs, one-two, one-two, and I slip and fall down the last few steps and land at the bottom with my leg twisted up behind my bum, but even though it hurts I get up and run through the kitchen and into the sitting room, to where Thomas is sitting on the sofa watching the cartoons on TV really loud. He turns and smiles at me and I stand there and breathe in and out and I want to scream and cry to Thomas, but what will he do? I can't tell him Mummy is dead upstairs because he'll scream even more than me, and that would ruin him for ever. I go over and sit on the sofa next to him and rub his hair.

'What's wrong, Clare?' he says.

I breathe. My chest is going up and down. 'Nothing,' I say.
'Is Mummy coming down?' he says.

'In a minute,' I say. My head is flying like a plane in the clouds and I'm trying to think of what to do. My chest pops in and out with the short, sharp breaths that hurt. I know what this means. It means I'm having one of those attacks like I had once when I ran around too much and I couldn't breathe. I go to the front door to get my inhaler from the drawer, holding on to the wall as I go, my fingers rubbing against it. I wonder if there will be a stain afterwards.

I open the drawer and take out my pump, unscrew the lid, and I breathe in and hold my breath. I do it again. I hold my breath as long as I can, and then everything goes grey and I fall to the floor, but it doesn't hurt because I can't feel anything. I can't see anything, either. Just grey like the sky from my bed. A square of grey clouds.

JOSEPHINE

10TH JULY 1980

Dear Granny,

London is wonderful, just like something out of
the pictures. There are the red double-decker buses
everywhere and people rushing around all the time.
It's gas altogether. When I have enough money I'll
buy you tickets to come and visit and we'll go for
walks and see Buckingham Palace where the Queen
lives and shop in London's shops and eat scones with
cream and jam and drink tea like the posh ones do
in the films. I keep thinking that any minute now
I might see the Queen and her corgi dogs, would you
believe it? She has loads of them, they say. I met a
lovely Irish girl called Joyce who got me a job doing
bits and bobs until I find something else. A girl from
her flat is going back home so I'm moving in with
her at the end of the week. We're going out on Friday
night to a dance in the church hall. I'll have a dance
for you.

I'm grand anyways, so don't be worrying about me now, will you. I have Saint Christopher watching over me and I don't take him off.

All my love,
Josephine

Dearest Bernadette,

How's your father? Have you had any luck finding a job? Here I am in the big smoke. (I know that's New York but this is my big smoke.) I've got a job in a café with another Irish girl called Joyce. She's lovely and has lots of friends she's introducing me to on Friday. She loves your lipstick, and she's teaching me how to make my face up properly. You'd like her. Everything is really fantastic, I'm having a blast. Are you sure you won't come out and join me? We'll have an absolutely gas time. Everything here moves so fast, I don't have a moment to think. Running, running, running, that's how it is here. The English boys are lovely, you'd love them. They're real gentlemen and open the door for you when you leave, not like at home. Have you seen Siobhan? Don't forget to keep an eye on her for me, will you?

Love,
Your good friend Josephine

P.S. Tell your mother I arrived safe and sound at the address she gave me. Please thank her for me. The owner is very nice and had a room for me without a problem.

Dear Mammy, Daddy and ye all,

I hope this finds ye well. I am well and everything is going fabulously. I've found a job doing secretarial tasks in a restaurant and have a local church where there is a nice Irish parish priest called Father Francis who I've already been to see. He says I can help out at Mass and do the flowers on the altar. I might be moving in with a new friend I met at work soon, fingers crossed. When I get my pay cheque through I'll send some money.

Love, Josephine

It takes me several attempts to get the letters right. I didn't think of buying a notepad with a page of black lines, so my writing slants upwards and looks untidy. When they are presentable, I put them in their envelopes and lick the seal closed, careful not to cut my tongue. It tastes of melted rubber. I put the letters in my bag until I can buy stamps at the post office later.

I get in early and Mister Cohen is there, with his yellow skin and bald top and small, glistening eyes. I thought he might be Irish because of the shamrock, but he says that's just to attract the Irish. He is Jewish himself. A shrewd businessman, the girls say.

When the café empties out after the morning rush, I move in and out of the tables, wiping them clean, taking away dirty plates and cups and saucers with baked beans and eaten corners of toast and bits of congealed egg, smiling as I go.

During my afternoon break I go to the post office for the stamps and send the letters.

*

Time flies and before I know it, it's Friday afternoon and myself and Joyce are walking to her flat, and I'm taking some of my things.

Joyce's flatmate is having a gathering before she goes on Sunday, so when we arrive, the sitting room is already full of girls standing together and talking, with drinks in their hands and music playing in the background. We go in and no one introduces themselves to me, so I pretend I'm busy looking out the window and playing with my fingernails, going red in the face while I do it. I am grateful when Joyce gets me a drink.

I watch them and they all look so confident and sure of themselves, with their little fingers sticking out from their glass and throwing their heads back when they laugh. Their confidence only makes me feel worse. I am the one fresh off the boat, and surely they can tell. One of them offers me a cigarette and I nod and take it, shaking a little bit as I light it.

A girl with light-brown curly hair and pale skin and blue eyes in a glamorous dress with polka dots goes over to the record player to put on a new record. She is the girl who's leaving, because the boy she left behind wrote to her and asked her to come back and said he wants to marry her. I would congratulate her, but I worry she will think me false and wonder who am I to congratulate her. She calls over to another girl called Maura.

It wouldn't be Maura from the boat? I wonder. Joyce, who was called away, comes back. I ask her if she knows her, and she tells me Maura has come over recently. I explain what happened on the boat and Joyce calls Maura over to us.

'Maura?' I say to her. 'You didn't come over on the boat last month?'

'I did,' she says. 'You're not...?'

'I am!' I say.

We erupt in laughter and all the others watch us, wondering what's going on.

She turns to them and explains what happened, and now everyone is laughing at the wonders of London and I already feel more at ease.

Maura is funny as she tells the story of her vomiting on the boat the whole way over and that I was the only one to ask if she was okay. Then she tells me about herself. She is from Kerry and is twenty-three, and is staying in a motel down the road and hasn't got a job yet, but she's all right because she comes from money. She has a nice gold necklace around her neck and a pair of sparkling earrings.

Joyce puts make-up on one of the girls in front of a mirror propped up on the table while we talk. When she's finished, she asks who wants to go next. I look around and everyone is distracted in conversation, so I ask if she'll do me.

Sure, she says, patting the seat of the chair in front of the mirror.

I sit down and hold my glass on my lap.

'Close your eyes,' she says.

I do. The girls behind me are laughing and someone puts on a record. It starts up and at first I don't think I know it, but then I realize I do: it's 'Walkin' Back to Happiness' by Helen Shapiro. They're all singing along and I hum along myself as Joyce wipes cool, wet cotton wool over my face, before patting my skin dry. Then there's another layer of something wet being spread over my skin: a mask. Next, she tickles my eyelids with a brush and then she draws a line along the rim of my eyelashes.

She tells me to open my eyes and look downwards and she pushes the mascara brush up through my lashes several times on both eyes. Then I look up and she does the bottom.

She puts lipstick on my lips and says I can look.

A face has been painted onto mine, and it is quite beautiful; the eyes are big and sparkling with long black lashes and the lips are red and shiny. The skin is peach-coloured and silky-looking. I look sophisticated and worldly.

'Make sure, when they invite you for a drink, that you get me one, too!' Joyce says, and all the girls laugh.

I smile, hiding my lower teeth the way I have practised.

I would say I have a nice smile, and nice teeth, as long as I only show the top row. The bottom ones are all different lengths, from when Daddy filed them when I was small. Dear Jesus, the pain. He came home one day and told me to come here. He sat me between his legs, his knees clamped into my sides, and told me to open my mouth. I did. Then he stuck his fingers deep into my mouth and I heaved to be sick.

'Stop it and sit still,' he said.

My eyes streamed with water as I kept the vomit down and held my mouth open, and he reached for a tool on the arm of the chair. I wanted to ask what it was, but my mouth was wide open and his hand was inside and I was about to be sick and I couldn't risk trying to speak because I would get a belt around the face. He told me he was going to make me look right, that the dentist was too expensive. He pointed the metal tool into my mouth and slid it outwards. A pain as hot as the poker from the fire shot through my head and down my back. It was a chisel he was using to file my teeth. Since then my bottom teeth have been all different heights and slanting up and down, like see-saws with one end held to the ground by a heavy child, the other one skinny and light, the end high in the air. I still get shooting pains through my mouth sometimes, and can hear the scream of the chisel scraping my teeth away.

Not long after that, my poor brother Brendan started complaining of toothache. I tried warning him to keep quiet, but he couldn't. Sure enough, Daddy removed the rotten tooth with a pair of pliers. Brendan couldn't eat for a long time after that.

I thank Joyce and tell her I'm not going to move my face all night.

Maura says now they need to sort out my hair, which, they say, is beautiful but unkempt. Is it dyed? she asks me, and is very impressed when I tell her it's not.

In the bathroom, she gathers it up into a bun with wisps falling about my face. Then she closes the door and goes to the toilet to wee and laughs that we've been through it all now.

I laugh and take a sip of my drink. 'I need to go after you,' I tell her, and I put my drink down and hover over the toilet, giddy and hot. 'I can't believe we've met again!' I say, unable to wipe the smile off my face, I'm so happy.

'I know! Crazy, isn't it?' She laughs and so do I, and it feels like we've been friends for years.

Joyce knows your man on the door, so we get in for free. Inside, the place is alive. The band is going and the beat bounces through the air and the floor, through the men's feet and the women's hips. I stay close to Maura and Joyce and the others lead the way.

'Jesus, this is wild, isn't it?' Maura whispers in my ear.

'It is,' I say.

Her eyes are shining and I'm sure mine are, too.

'Come on,' says Joyce, 'let's go and get a drink.' She goes through the crowds and we follow, inching through, turning sideways and being jabbed by shoulders and elbows. It's like home, only more. I think of a night out with Bernadette, when we got the bus into town with all the lads and there was one smiling at me. I think of them, moving through the crowds where I know no one – only these girls I've just met. I think of the girl going home to get married and I am jealous of her having her whole life mapped out before her. I wonder if someone will ever tell me they want me for themselves for ever. A dirty little whore like me? I doubt it.

I brush off the thought as I wipe some loose hairs away from my face and tell Joyce I'll have what she's having.

'They're called the Irish Tunes,' Joyce shouts over the music, nodding in the direction of the band when we make our way back to the others with our drinks.

'They're great!' I shout back. I tap my foot to the music and take a drink, then I get my cigarettes out, offer them round and light one for myself. I catch a glimpse of myself in a pane of glass as I take a puff and, feeling confident all of a sudden now that I've remembered how I look, I blow the smoke out in small clouds.

We watch everyone dance. Someone Joyce knows comes and takes her out for a number, so I hold her drink while Maura and I watch. All the others are dancing with fellas too.

When the set finishes, it's my turn to get the drinks. I head to the bar on my own, brave now with the alcohol on me.

'Hello,' says a man's voice from behind me.

I pretend not to hear it and look busily ahead to get the bartender's attention.

'Hello,' he says again. He taps my arm.

I turn round and have to lift my head up, because the man speaking to me is more than a head over me. He has wide shoulders and is wearing a shirt open at the collar. He has a big, open kind of face, with blue-grey eyes and a dimple in only one of his cheeks, now that he is smiling.

'Would you like to dance?' he says in an Irish accent that is soft, like he's been to college.

'I'm just getting drinks,' I manage.

'When you've got your drinks.' His dimple goes deeper.

'Sure, all right,' I say, conscious of sounding like a country girl. I turn back to the bar and the jitters in my chest put me on edge.

He moves into a gap beside me and asks my name.

'Josephine,' I tell him.

'I'm Michael,' he says, holding out his hand in the cramped space to shake mine. 'Lovely to meet you.' He smiles and his dimple is back and his eyes sparkle.

I remember fleetingly a little sister I had once who had a dimple. She died when she was very small, and we were prohibited from speaking about her ever again. There were so many things not spoken about in that house.

'And you,' I say.

'I've seen you at the café,' he says.

My heart goes. I would have liked to say I worked in an office, or that I was looking for a job. I tell him it's temporary and he tells me he is a navvy. What's that? I ask, and he tells me it's short for Navigational Engineer. Sounds posh, I tell him.

I order the drinks and pay. The girls come to help me and I am both glad and regretful. I say goodbye and follow them.

I don't think he'll seek me out, but he does, a few songs later. I don't have the chance to ask how my lipstick is, or if my hair is in place. I flatten my navy skirt down with my free hand and he takes me by the other.

It's a quick song and he takes me round the dance floor, twisting me this way and that. It's exhilarating and I let out a laugh. He spins me round. He gently tugs on my arm and I know to turn, he flicks his wrist and I know to go the other way. He is a puppet-master and I am his doll. He turns me round and round and, just when I think I'm going to lose my footing, he whips me back so I'm facing him. There is something about him that has my heart beating in my ears, and me picturing myself waiting for him to come home at the end of a long day, all tired and his hair and clothes scruffy from a day's work. I would meet him at the door and throw my arms around his neck like it was the first time I saw him.

We dance a second dance and every now and then I look up at him, until my shyness and his warm gaze force me to look away. Eventually I pluck up the courage to look him straight back in the eyes.

You're lovely, they say. Don't worry, I won't hurt you.

I believe them, and my legs go heavy with the emotion of it all, as if I were dancing underwater.

In bed, I relive it over and over. I am dancing with Michael, spinning round like a fairy, and the music is going and he is smiling away at me with his one dimple and his sparkling eyes.

One second Michael is twirling me round, and the next I am across the water again, back home in Ireland. I'm lying in bed in my thin white nightie to my knees. It's the night Sean was born. Mammy is in bed with the new baby and Daddy is in the front room celebrating with Bernadette's father and Uncle Patrick.

I am asleep and then I am awake. My eyes are open, but the room is black, there is just the sound of raspy breathing and the stink of whiskey and cigars. 'Daddy?' I whisper. He must have drunk too much and come into my room by mistake.

Footsteps on the floor, coming towards me. A belt being unbuckled.

'Daddy, is that you?'

The pain sears through my right shoulder when he yanks me out of the bed by my arm. Hail Mary, full of grace, the Lord is with thee. The cold floor cuts through my nightie. The sweet, sickly smell of whiskey makes me want to be sick, the quick short puffs from his round belly force the breath out of me. My mind flicks through the men in the front room. Bernadette's daddy is skinny from illness; it's Daddy and Uncle Patrick who have the bellies. Blessed art thou amongst women, and blessed is the fruit of thy womb, Jesus. The burning, like the poker straight from the fire, between my legs. The weight on top of me, so heavy it's crushing me into the floor and all the way down to hell.

I want to scream, the way Mammy did yesterday, when Sean and his dead little twin sister were coming and we weren't allowed in the house but could hear it all through the window, but it's as if Daddy is chiselling my teeth again. I can't form the sounds with my tongue. I want to scream for Mammy, for her to fling open the door and let light into the room and put a stop to this pain. I want to see who is doing this to me. Holy Mary, Mother of God, pray for our sinners, now and at the hour of our death. My legs wide open, my nightie high, my eyes squeezed tight shut. God forgive me. Amen.

JOSEPHINE

9TH AUGUST 1980

I look out for him every day, desperate to see him and dreading it at the same time. Each day that passes confirms it was nothing, and I am disgusted at how pathetic I am. What a preposterous idea that a young, handsome, educated man like that would be interested in a girl like me.

Joyce and Maura keep on at me, saying your man will be in any day now. I tell them to stop, but they think it's gas altogether.

I try to concentrate on work and making the flat homely. I clean it top to bottom and buy flowers to put in a vase and a picture of the London skyline for the sitting room. In desperate moments, I wonder if I shouldn't just join a nunnery and be done with it. I could shut myself away from the world and repent for the rest of my life.

'I'm going to join the nunnery,' I tell the girls one night when we're sitting in the kitchen, drinking. Joyce has cleared out the small room that was full of junk and Maura moved in a couple of weeks after me. Since then, we've been partying in the kitchen almost every night.

They burst into fits of laughter like it's the funniest thing they ever heard.

'I'm serious,' I say. 'I'm considering it.' There is something terrible about being tortured by the absence of someone you don't know, but have fallen madly for, knowing full well they will never want you, I tell them.

'Sure, Jesus, what are you on about, woman?' Maura says, getting up and going to put on some music.

'No one will ever want me.' My body is so heavy it has me slouched over the table. I go swaying to the toilet and hit the wall with my shoulder.

When I come back, Joyce points out that I've danced with several men every Friday and Saturday night for the last three weeks.

'That's because they want a dance.' I top up our glasses with a splash of brandy and ice. 'They don't know me. Nobody knows me.' And then it occurs to me that what they wanted was a leg-over, and they saw me coming.

'You're raving, woman,' says Joyce, and they cackle loud the way they do after some drink. 'They're all after you.'

'They're after *you*.' I point at her. 'And you.' I point at Maura with my finger. 'Because ye are both beautiful, inside and out.'

My head is going to split in two. It's hot and my stomach clenches, pushing up cloudy yellow bile. The nuns would love this: me, self-purging. Sister Mary, with her habit and her rosary beads draped over her skinny knuckles. How she would dig them into my back if she saw me now.

It's Sunday and for the first time I'm on my own. I decide I'll go to Mass; that it'll be the best place for me. I get dressed into my good clothes and do my face to make myself look decent.

The smell of incense hits me at the entrance. I dip my fingers into the font and bless myself; the holy water is cold and I shiver when it touches my forehead.

I walk up the side of the church, slowly and carefully so as not to make a noise, but each step creates a loud tap that bounces off the walls. The two people kneeling up ahead turn to look at me and I quickly mock-kneel at the end of a pew and bless myself, before kneeling to say the 'Our Father' and nine 'Hail Marys'. I shut my eyes tight and mutter the words under my breath, skipping over them, leaving their ends unfinished, I know them so well.

My head is reeling with holy words and the guilt I suffer the day after a few drinks. I think of Granny and Bernadette and their letters I've saved under my bed, and I think of Mammy and Daddy, who haven't said a word about my letters or the money I send. I try not to hope, but every time there's an envelope on the mat and it's not her writing on it, I hate them a little bit more.

Father Francis comes out from the room behind the altar and walks down the steps to the confessional box. Myself and the other two people move nearer to the box; one of them goes inside, and myself and a haggard-looking man sit on a pew nearby.

A good half-hour later it's my turn; I go into the box and kneel facing the grille. 'Hello, Father Francis,' I say. 'Bless me, Father, for I have sinned.'

'Tell me, child,' he says. It's always the same rigmarole. The nuns prepared us for our first confession and told us all the lines and how they went. We had to think of our sins before we went into the room, where the priest was sitting on a chair and you had to sit down and face him. I told him the same thing we all agreed to say in class: that I had said bad words, I'd had bad thoughts about my brothers and sister, I had talked back to my mammy.

'How long since your last confession?'

'Two weeks.'

'Tell me,' he says.

'I have bad thoughts, Father.'

'Yes.'

'Dark thoughts.'

'I see.'

'I wish ill on people.'

'Why?'

'Because they deserve it, Father.'

'That is not for you to decide, my child,' he says.

'No, Father,' I say. 'I have troubled thoughts.'

'Lots of us do,' he says. 'What are your troubled thoughts, my dear?'

Waiting outside has built it all up and I'm shaking with nerves and anger. I start to cry. 'I worry that I'm not good enough.' *I want to join the nuns, Father.* I will myself to say it.

He waits quietly for me to say more.

'And that I don't deserve happiness.'

'How long have you been here?'

'Seven weeks.'

'Give yourself time – it's a big thing for a young girl like yourself to leave home and come to a new place where you know no one.'

'Yes, Father.'

'You haven't come to arrange the flowers. Maybe it would be good for you, Josephine.'

'Yes, Father.'

'Were you praying when I came in?'

'Yes, Father.'

'What did you say?'

'Nine "Hail Marys" and an "Our Father".'

'That'll be all for today, then.'

'Okay, Father, thank you.'

'God bless, my child.'

I go out and sit back where I was, and say the Act of Contrition. The painted angels overhead have strange smiles that make them look old and evil. On my way out, I fill a small plastic lemonade bottle with holy water to take home.

The girls come back in the afternoon from their mad antics with two lads from last night, and they're raring to go all over again. We get dolled up and head down to O'Conner's at the end of the road. There's a band on and everyone is happy and drinking and smoking, and soon I've forgotten my desperation and I'm laughing and listening to them tell their stories, holding my cigarette high in the air with my arms crossed. Everyone's eyes are glassy with drink and I know mine are, too.

I'm watching the band through the crowd when I see him leaning on the bar. I swing round so he doesn't see me, and when Joyce asks what's wrong I tell her it's nothing.

'Why don't we head back and put on a few records?' I tell them, and they love the idea.

On our way back to the flat, everyone is happy and singing, delighted to keep the party going.

My heart is thumping with the relief. Thank God I didn't have to suffer the humiliation of watching him with a girl, in front of everyone.

*

A few days later I am walking home, looking at the paving stones as I walk, careful not to stand on the cracks because that would mean bad luck. I stop at the lights and there he is, standing on the other side of the road. I go to turn round, but the lights change and he has already seen me, so I cross the road, focusing straight ahead as if I hadn't seen him.

He waits for me, so that when I reach the other side he is standing in front of me.

'Hello, how are ya?' I say in the way everyone does at home, which means you don't have to stop or answer.

'Hello, Josephine,' he says. He is in a T-shirt and shorts speckled with splashes of white paint and black drops of tar. His hair is falling into his eyes, which are pink, with irritation or maybe tiredness. 'How are you?'

'Grand,' I say.

'You left the pub early the other night.'

My face burns. I think I might cry.

'I'm just on my way home,' he says.

I nod. He looks lovely, with his pink eyes and his messy blond hair. He smells of tarmac, when it's been burning in the sun and, if you stepped on it, you'd leave a footprint. It stinks and the smell makes me high. If only I could say something, but the whole of me has gone numb.

'Listen, would you like to meet later for some dinner?' he says.

'That's very kind of you,' I tell him. 'But there's no need.'

'Have you got plans?'

I tell him I haven't.

'Well then, I'll take you to my favourite spot.'

'Really, there's no need.'

'Sure, we've all got to eat,' he says, chuckling. And he says he'll meet me at the same corner at seven o'clock.

I nod and continue the walk home. I am sick with delight and anxiety.

CLARE

12TH JULY 1997

'Clare! Wake up, Clare! Mummy! Mummy! Clare's gone asleep!' Thomas screams. He runs upstairs, on his hands and feet to go quicker, and I can hear his pitter-patter and I want to shout, 'Thomas, don't go; don't go, Thomas, she's dead', but I can't speak. I'm there but I'm not; I can see the round panel of coloured glass in the front door and the walls either side, but even though I know there are colours in the glass, they don't have colour now. Maybe we've all gone to heaven. Maybe this is it. I can see the white hairs of Father Feathers shining in the sun, an angel come to take us away. I hope he doesn't take Thomas. He's so lovely and happy, he should get more time on earth. It's okay to take Mummy because she's not happy here, and I don't mind going with her, because I don't want her to be on her own, because I love her all the way from Australia to here and back. I'll be able to watch Daddy and Thomas from the clouds anyway, won't I?

Thomas's scream is loud, short and sharp, like the pain of a plaster being ripped off. I try to breathe properly – in and out, pause, in and out, pause – but it just makes me worse and my chest goes faster. I told you not to go, Thomas! I want to shout at him and slap him on the bottom, the way Mummy does. He comes down the stairs, past me, down the hallway and into the sitting room. He's going to watch cartoons. I try to open my eyes, but I can't tell if they're open or not because everything is grey.

He comes back and kneels beside me and puts his head on my tummy and cries. I lift up my arm and put it on his back, even though it's so heavy and feels like a tree trunk and not even my arm.

Neeee-naaaaw, neeeeeee-naaaaaw, neeeeeeee-naaaaaaaw. More screams through the house. There must be a fire nearby. Then the glass circle in the front door is black and people are talking and saying to open the door. 'Don't do it, Thomas, we can't open the door to strangers,' but he gets up and stands on his tiptoes and a ray of light rushes in before the shadows, and they're all around me and then running upstairs, making loads of noise, and they haven't even wiped their feet on the mat and Mummy would be so mad if she wasn't already dead.

More sirens. But now I have my eyes open and can see colour and lines and faces and the inside of the ambulance, where I am, with Mummy lying on the bed beside me and Thomas strapped into a chair, crying. I have a mask on my face, which is digging into my cheeks, and it's tight and hurts but I don't dare say anything. I'm just glad I can breathe again. In, out, in, out. It's so nice.

We get to the hospital. They wheel Mummy away and then put me into a wheelchair and take Thomas by the hand and bring us inside. I close my eyes because I'm so tired and they're holding Thomas's hand, so I can rest my eyes for a minute, like Daddy does when he gets in from work and sits on the big comfy chair.

They put us in a nice room with Disney characters on the walls, and toys. A woman with hearts on her cardigan talks to Thomas. I realize she's telling him Mummy is dead and I start crying. The tears fall down the mask like the rain drips down the windscreen.

'Hello, Clare,' she says. 'How are you feeling?'

I cry more. 'I want my daddy,' I say, but the sound is all muffled. I take the mask off; 'I want my daddy.'

Thomas runs over and tries to climb up onto the bed, but there's a bar in the way, so the woman lifts him up and he lies down next to me and snuggles up.

'He's on his way,' the nurse says.

I know she's talking in an extra-soft voice because my mummy's dead, but I don't care. I don't like her. My mummy wouldn't like her, either, with her bad teeth and dirty-looking hair and stupid hearts on her wrinkled cardigan.

'You've had an asthma attack,' she says. 'Your mum is—'

'Dead.' I howl like the fox I've heard in the garden at night.

'No, sweetheart, she's not dead, she's with the doctors, that's all.'

'I thought she was dead,' I cry, and I hug Thomas and cry into his hair.

She's alive, I think. We haven't gone to heaven. We have another chance. We can still all be together.

I don't know which one of us falls asleep first, maybe it's Thomas, maybe it's me, but we hold each other tight, knowing the bars won't let us fall out.

*

The door opens and Daddy comes in, with small red eyes and a white face. I think maybe the lady lied and Mummy is dead after all.

'My darlings,' he says, and a tear falls out of his eye. He wipes it away quickly before we can see it, but I already have. 'My poor little things.' He reaches over the bar and hugs us, pulling us close so our faces are pushed against his jacket and his T-shirt. The zip of his jacket is cold against my cheek. Then he pulls away and kisses us hard, and I can feel his face is wet.

'Don't cry, Daddy,' I say.

'I'm not crying, Clare,' he says, but I can still see the tears stream down his face.

'Is Mummy—?' I can't say the D word.

'She's okay,' he says. 'She hit her head and went to sleep for a while, but she'll be fine.'

'I thought she was dead,' I start, but then the upset comes and my throat closes up tight.

Thomas starts crying then, in quiet sobs that make his shoulders jerk.

Daddy lifts him up onto his lap and rocks him from side to side. I push back the blanket and move closer to him, and he lifts me up over the bar with his other arm and I sit on his other knee. He rocks us both from side to side. Thomas whimpers quietly until he's so tired he falls asleep again.

'It was horrible, Daddy,' I say after a while.

'I know, honey, I know. I'm so sorry. It will never happen again. We'll go on holiday and have a break and when we get back everything will be different, everything will be better, you'll see.' He puts Thomas into the bed and pulls up the blanket, and takes me back on his knee. 'You'll see, everything will be better.'

'You promise?' I say into his T-shirt.

'I promise,' he says.

I sniff some tears and snot up my nose, feeling a teeny-weeny bit better.

Daddy rocks me back and forth, like the way he painted the fence with a paintbrush a few weeks ago, so the garden would be lovely for the summer. He sniffs, too, so I think he must be feeling a teeny bit better as well.

He puts me back into bed with Thomas and I rest my eyes again. When I wake up, it's dark outside and the bright white lights are on. The woman with hearts on her cardigan comes to see us again and asks us what happened. She asks us some questions and then we're allowed to play with the toys while she goes out to talk to Daddy. Nosy parker, asking all those questions. They stand outside the door with glass in it and lots of little squares, looking serious and talking hush-hush.

A little while later Daddy says it's time to go and he'll be back in a minute. The woman puts the bar down and I sit on the chair at the side of the bed, with Thomas on my lap and my arms around his waist, and we wait.

Daddy pushes Mummy into our room in a wheelchair.

'Mummy Mummy Mummy!' we squeal, and we run to her and Thomas jumps on her knee, but Daddy says to take it easy and settle down.

I hug her and hold onto her and rub her hair with my hand. I want to stay like that for ever. When I pull away and look into her eyes, they look so sad and tired that I want to cry all over again. She needs a little break at home in Ireland, with the green fields and the sea and the sand. That's what she needs. And we're going to see her family this time, for the first time in so long. She's probably nervous, but once she sees them I bet it'll be the best thing ever. Then she'll be happy and laughing, and her eyes will be big and full of life again.

On the way home we stop to get chicken and chips because there is no food at home and it's late. Daddy goes into the corner shop first, to buy breakfast and lunch for tomorrow, because we don't have time to go to the supermarket and do a proper shop. Then he goes to the chicken-and-chip shop and gets a family meal, even though Mummy says she's not hungry. Everyone is quiet. Daddy hasn't even told us to put our seatbelts on.

'Does your head hurt, Mummy?' I ask.

'Yes, darling,' she says in a floaty voice, 'it does.' She keeps looking forward. 'You were both so brave today,' she says. 'I'm sorry you had to see that.'

Thomas sits forward. 'You couldn't help hitting your head, Mummy.' He cups her face in his hands from behind and kisses her neck.

'Thank you, sweetheart.' Mummy takes one of his hands in hers, and reaches her other arm back to look for me.

I reach out my hand and we hold hands.

'I love you both so much,' she says, and she starts crying.

I get up and hug her as best I can from the back seat, my head on her shoulder. 'I love you, too, Mummy.' I cry as well, and so does Thomas. We stay like that until Daddy gets back, and Mummy sniffles and wipes her face and says, 'Now, now, let's head home.'

We each give Mummy a kiss on the cheek, being careful to be as soft as we can, and then Daddy takes her upstairs to get some rest and comes back down. We eat our chicken and chips in the sitting room in front of the TV, which we're never allowed to do.

We eat quietly, watching the telly. When we've finished, Daddy puts us to bed and tells us a little story so we have sweet dreams.

When he's finished and he's switched the light off, he says, 'Night-night, sleep tight, don't let the bedbugs bite.'

'Daddy?' I say when he's walking out.

'Yes, sweetheart?'

'Can you leave the light on?'

He clicks the switch and the light comes on with a flash, and then he turns the little knob until it's a golden glow.

'How's that?'

'That's okay.'

The next day Daddy gets us up for school and makes us breakfast and does our lunch boxes. He tells us to be quiet because Mummy is resting and needs to get her energy up for Ireland, so we're really quiet and every time we have to say something, we whisper it.

When I stand beside the car, waiting for him to open the door to take us to school, I wait for a minute even though he's unlocked it from inside, because the cold wet of the drops on my face is so nice. The sky has opened up and the storm has passed – that's what Mummy always says when it rains. And she says that the angels have been having an argument. I wonder what the angels were fighting about, and if they've made up.

I ask Daddy if we can stay at home, but he says no, it's better that we go to school because we only have a couple of days left. He asks, don't I want to be with my friends, because after Friday I won't see them for a while? But I don't feel like it today. I don't feel like talking. When Daddy stops at the gate, I undo my seatbelt and kiss him goodbye on the cheek then lean through the gap between the seats because I'm in the front, and kiss Thomas goodbye. I walk slowly up the path, kicking the ground with the toes of my shoes like I'm not supposed to, because it ruins them. I keep my head down so I won't see anyone and go and sit on the bench in the wilderness, where nobody will find me. When the bell rings, I think of staying there, but I'll only be found out when everyone comes out at break and for P.E, and what will I do then? I climb over the wall and walk along the playground until I get to my line and stand at the back. I keep my head down and follow my class inside. I sit down at my desk and put my head in my arms, facing the window, so no one can see me. Everyone stays away. When my name is called I say, 'Here', and Miss doesn't even stop, she keeps reading through the register. I say the names in my head with her, and keep my eyes closed.

When class starts, I sit up because I don't want to get in trouble. I pretend that I'm listening, but really I'm looking out the window and thinking of Mummy nearly being dead, and Father Feathers being an angel here to take her away, and the snakes swimming through the sea, getting nearer and nearer, and me screaming to warn her.

I close my eyes to shut out the snakes, and cross my fingers that Ireland will be good for Mummy, like Daddy says.

JOSEPHINE

22ND OCTOBER 1980

I see Michael on nearly all my evenings off. We walk through Holland Park, going off the main path and getting lost in the trees, coming across the most beautiful pond that looks like something out of the pictures, it's so idyllic. There's no one else, just us, wrapped up in gloves and scarves, and I feel like one of the wealthy women who live in the big houses we've passed, going for a walk with my wealthy husband. Who needs money? I think. I don't need anything else. I've got who I need right here. Everything is so sweet and pleasant with Michael beside me. Sometimes he brushes his fingers against mine, other times he puts his arm right round my shoulders and I feel like I'm someone special.

He takes me to his favourite parks and pubs and the cinema and for dinners, and on a Friday night we go out with the girls and a few more lads to the dance in the church hall, or a ceílí. On Saturdays one of us is usually working, and on Sundays I might make us a nice meal and we'll drink a bottle of bubbles. If it's nice we'll go to the park and eat a ham-and-cheese roll and a choc-ice. Life takes on a nice rhythm and

I am optimistic about it all. I even sign up to an evening class in accounting, to complement my secretarial cert. That way, I might get another job on the side and maybe even leave the café. The way Michael looks at me makes me believe in myself. He makes me feel beautiful and sure of myself and able to do things.

On our first Saturday off together since we've been going strong, we're going on a day out to Buckingham Palace. I'm supposed to be leading the high life over here, so I should at least go and see the palace. We're going for tea and scones afterwards. Michael has the name and address of a nice place and we're going to have a lovely day.

I have a while before he's coming over. I take out my pen and pad to write some letters home. In Bernadette's, I insert the Mass card I got from Father Francis this week and tell her I'm praying for her and her mother and send them all the love in the world. Then to Granny; I ask how she is and give her an update on the girls, the flat and work. I tell her that Michael and I are going to see the guards change at Buckingham Palace and that afterwards I'll tell her all about it. I tell her I'm in love, and I think he is the man for me. My last letter is for Sean, because it's his birthday next week and I'm sending him a red double-decker bus as a present.

I put the letters in their envelopes and wrap Sean's present. I insert the money for Mammy and Daddy into a separate envelope and put it inside Sean's, and put some more inside Granny's.

Writing the letters has lowered my mood. I hum a tune to distract myself; to stop me going round and round in circles inside my head. I still can't get over them not writing me a single letter. I still can't get over any of it.

I consider getting back into bed and beating the pillow with my fists and not answering the door when Michael comes. The best place for me would be in bed, with the curtains drawn and the door closed and no one to disturb me.

Don't be a fool, now, Josephine. You're off to Buckingham Palace to see the guards change with a fine, handsome man you're in love with.

Joyce is sitting at the kitchen table filing her nails. 'Morning, petal,' she says. She has a habit of calling everyone something related to flowers: petal, blossom, clover. I envy her upbeat attitude and sing-song way of talking.

'Morning!' I breeze in and switch on the kettle, determined to shake the divil. 'How are you?'

'Grand, now,' she says, pushing an emery board across her index fingernail. 'I'm going to have a nice, lazy morning for myself.'

'Good for you. Will you have one?' I put a teabag in the mug and pour in the boiling water. Joyce nods, so I get another teabag and pour her a fresh one. I add the milk, making hers milky and mine strong, the way we both like it.

'And where are you heading today with lover boy?'

'Buckingham Palace, my lady.' I bow my head and put the milk bottle back in the fridge. 'We're going to see Changing the Guard.'

'Are ye now?'

'We are indeed. Have you seen it?'

'Yeah. It'll be good, now. Something to see, that's for sure.'

'I can't wait.' I sit next to Joyce at the table and watch her paint her nails. 'I have to get myself dolled up. Can I borrow your make-up?'

'Help yourself.'

'Thanks. Where's Maura?'

'Early shift.'

I look up at the clock on the wall. It's nearly half-past nine, and Michael is coming at half-ten. I should get ready. I hold the warm mug in my hands while Joyce puts on the second coat. It looks grey outside. I hope it doesn't rain.

'Are you all right?' she says after a while.

'Yes, sure, I'm grand,' I say. 'It's just my little brother's birthday coming up, that's all.'

She sighs, and waves her burgundy-nailed hand in the air as if to say, Tell me about it. 'I know the feeling,' she says. She takes a cigarette out and offers me one. I take it, even though I try not to smoke so early in the day. I'm supposed to be cutting down.

We sit together, with just the tick-tock of the clock for noise. I inhale deeply, waiting for the nicotine to take the edge off my nerves.

I will need the full mask today. Beads of sweat break out above my top lip; I rub them away with a square of toilet roll. It's one of those days when it's hot and muggy and chilly, all at the same time. I dab the foundation onto my face and rub it in with circular motions, and then with a small brush, I rub light-brown eyeshadow onto my eyelids. I lean heavy on the eyeliner, making the line fat along the curve of my eyes, and thicken my lashes several times with mascara. Dark-red lips today: I start with the lip-liner, to stop them bleeding the colour, and then rub the lipstick around my mouth. I pull off another square of toilet roll and clamp my lips round it a few times to get rid of any excess.

I smile at myself in the mirror, but the darkness within me doesn't lift. I show my upper teeth, not the lower ones, and then I laugh as if I just heard someone tell a joke and I think it's really funny.

I get dressed in a pair of flared jeans and a soft pink blouse I bought in the sales, and brush and dry my hair. Eleven years. I think I might be sick. I concentrate on what I'm doing, pushing the ball of sick down into the pit of my stomach, the way I always do. I play with the idea of telling Michael the truth about myself. My head is light from the cigarettes and the thought.

How could he ever love me? I mean, really love me? Wouldn't he look at me and see something horrible and disgusting? Michael, with not a secret to hide or a bad word to say about anyone. With his soft voice and his gentle ways, his college friends and his love for long walks and words. Wouldn't I destroy myself for him, with the idea of a fully-grown man coming into my room the night my little brother was born?

Who was it? he'd ask, angry, or maybe crying.

I don't know, I'd have to reply, I'm not sure.

Him, incredulous: What do you mean? How could you not be sure about something like that?

I didn't see him. It was dark. Pitch-black.

He wouldn't believe me. Sure, who would? My own mother didn't want to know.

My breathing is quick and shallow as I imagine taking off all the faces I've ever worn and showing him my own, raw, swollen face and pink, puffy eyes, which Mammy saw that night when she called me to help her to the toilet, a few days after Sean was born.

'What's wrong with you?' she asked, irritated, thinking I was feeling sorry for myself because I was doing all the housework.

'Nothing,' I muttered. Then when she was on the toilet, I started crying. She told me to stop acting the fool and demanded I tell her what was wrong.

'I'm going to hell,' I sobbed.

'Don't be an eejit.'

'I am. Something terrible has happened, and I'm going to hell.'

'Such a drama-queen. Now help me up.'

I got hysterical and my legs gave way, with the pain and the weakness in my body. I cried in a pile in front of her.

'How dare you?' she snarled. She grabbed the hair on the back of my head and pulled me upwards. 'I have just lost a baby, and I have her little brother in the room to look after, and here you are, feeling sorry for yourself, like a spoilt fecking madam.'

I cried out and she pulled my hair harder. 'But, Mammy...'

'Now help me off this toilet. You are to keep this house immaculate, cook for your father and your brother and sister, and keep your head down. I don't want to hear so much as a word from you.' She gave a last tug to my hair, jerking my head towards her. 'Do you understand?' she said, her lips thin and her teeth glistening with spit. I swear I've never seen anything that looked so much like a rabid dog before or since.

'Yes, Mammy.'

She let go of my hair and I stood up, wiped my face dry and helped her back to her room. In bed, I cried myself to sleep. I was already in hell.

*

I'm trembling when the doorbell rings.

'Josephine, it's the door!' calls Joyce.

'Coming!' I wipe my face around the eyes and go downstairs.

Michael is standing in the middle of the doorway with a single red rose in his hand. I fling my arms round his shoulders and start crying.

'Whoa!' he says, untying my arms from around his neck. 'What's the matter?'

'I'm sorry,' I tell him. 'It's just so lovely.' I take the rose and hold it in my hands. A thorn pricks my thumb and I lick it.

'If I'd known it would've got that response, I wouldn't have got it.'

'It's lovely, honestly,' I tell him. 'It's just that, it's my little brother's birthday next week and it's got me thinking.'

'That's Sean, is it?'

I nod.

He pulls me to him for a hug. 'When I get homesick I try to focus on what I've got, and what I'm building, here with you.' He takes my hands and kisses them.

I swallow back the rest of my tears, seeing myself curled over on the toilet, flowing away from myself. 'You're right, I'm sorry.' I lean forward and let him hold me in his arms, where I am safe and the world is in order, even if just for as long as the embrace.

He looks down at me and I kiss him deeper than I ever have before, and he is warm and gentle.

When I pull away, his face is red and I have to wipe his mouth dry. I give him a kiss on the cheek and tell him I'll get my bag and be down in a minute.

*

We stop off at the post office, where I send the package and letters, and we get on the first bus into town.

'It looks like it'll rain,' says Michael.

'It'll hold out,' I tell him, holding his hand in mine, but just then the sky breaks and large drops fall like pellets on the roof.

'Do you still want to go?' His face is all honest and open.

'I most certainly do!' I have perked up suddenly and Michael tells me he's glad, and kisses me on the forehead.

I get off the bus first and run through the rain, holding my jacket over my head like a blanket, not caring about the cold water seeping through my blouse. Michael is behind me but I don't turn to look for him, I know he'll come after me, and I run across the road and through the crowd. I jump over a puddle and nearly fall over. Michael catches up with me and we laugh and run together, side-by-side, our faces shiny with water. My make-up must be in streaks down my face.

'This is crazy!' he calls over the crackle of the rain and the cars swishing by.

'It's brilliant!' I tell him, and there, in the park, I put my arms down and hold my hands palm-up to the sky and let the water soak all over me. I tilt my head upwards and my hair hangs like a drenched sheet in the back yard. Sometimes I am so tired of playing a role that I am sure I could lie down and just die right there. 'Michael,' I say. I take his hand.

'Yes?' He looks concerned.

'There are things.'

He steps towards me and wraps me up in his arms, as if I were a little girl and he was a bear, come to save me from the wolves. He rocks me from one side to the other and I hold him tight.

'Come on, we're going to miss it.' He takes my hand and leads me through the dripping trees towards the palace.

The gilded gates run on, bar after bar, and we join the crowds peering through them at the small, dark windows. Soldiers in red uniforms and huge black furry hats stand dead-still, staring ahead.

A flag billows high in the wind, heavy with rainwater.

'That means the Queen's in.' Michael points in the air.

'Does it?'

'It does.'

'Well, then I'll have to wave to the Queen,' I say, waving my hand madly.

We wait with the people gathered with their cameras and their umbrellas, but after a while we're told that Changing the Guard has been cancelled, due to the weather.

Michael looks disappointed, but I think it's hysterical and can't help laughing.

The rain calms to a gentle drizzle and Michael keeps an arm round me as we walk back through the park. He stops at a bench and tells me to sit down, and then he gets down on one knee and says he knows it's soon, but I'm the most beautiful woman he has ever seen.

I put my hands to my face; mascara comes off on my hands. 'But I'm a mess,' I say, 'look at me.'

'You're beautiful,' he says.

'Am I?' My lips tremble.

'Of course you are.'

'But—' I begin, wanting to ask if he doesn't see the black holes in my eyes.

'Josephine, you would make me the happiest man alive if

you would marry me.' He takes out a box and inside is a gold ring with a small, shining diamond. He slips it on my finger. It's big for me, but I couldn't care less. It's the most beautiful thing I've seen. Nothing could spoil this absolute joy that I'm feeling, and which I want to hold on to for ever.

I take his face in my hands and kiss him. 'Yes, yes, yes,' I say, kissing him once, twice, three times.

He lifts me up and spins me round. All I can see is his hair that's gone curly in the rain, and the make-up that has rubbed off onto his face and his dimple, deep now as he smiles at me with loving eyes.

The flat is empty when we get back with a couple of bottles of sparkling wine and crisps and olives, already giddy from the glass we had with our tea and scones. I have a shower and then Michael goes in after me.

I am drying my hair when he comes into my room with a towel around his waist.

He looks at me with those sea-blue eyes of his and his tufts of blondie hair curling towards his face and I smile shyly, but then he walks towards me and the room is too small and I run away to the bathroom.

He knocks on the door and says he is sorry and that he has ruined everything. No, I want to say, but the words won't come out. All I can do is shake my head that no, he hasn't ruined anything; that I am the one ruined.

I can picture him on the other side of the door, his forehead all creased with concern, and I want to set him free. He deserves someone clean and uncomplicated, not like me. I swallow the lump in my throat. 'Michael, you should go. You don't want me.'

'I do, though, I do,' he says.

'You don't, believe me.'

'I don't know what has happened,' he says, 'but I'm not going anywhere.'

I let out a deep breath of air, realizing that he means it. 'There are things...' I say, 'things... that were done to me. I was a little girl...' I want to tell him everything, but my throat has already closed up and all I can do is cry quietly because it hurts.

Eventually I open the door and he sits with me on the floor and rocks me in his arms. I fall asleep like that, half on the bathroom mat and half on the cold linoleum floor, and when I wake, he is stroking my face, and peeling off my skin the hair that has stuck to my tears. I have never felt so loved.

'Who?' he says after a while.

'Someone from the town,' I say, thinking of the belly that pushed down hard on me and stole the air, and so much more, from my body.

I think of the breathing and the footsteps and the smell of whiskey and cigars, the sound of the unbuckling of the belt. I think of things on other days, like when I was pouring them drinks and Daddy said, 'Look at the arse of it, bigger by the day,' and Uncle Patrick laughed and slapped me across the backside. 'She'll be a fine woman, all right,' he replied, winking, and I went red with humiliation and the shame and ran out of the room and the house, over to the stream to cry. Or when we were all at the pub one day and Uncle Patrick questioned me in front of everybody about having a boyfriend and how I must have a boyfriend, and Daddy said I better not have a boyfriend, if I knew what was good for me. But that I was so bold he wouldn't put anything past me. Ah, no doubt she has one hidden somewhere, said Mammy, curling her lips, with all the flirting she does. Or when Daddy clamped his body around mine to file my teeth, digging his knees into me and forcing my mouth open as he breathed into my face.

I relive it all, as I have so many times, trying to find something that gives him away. What I would give to know it wasn't my daddy. What I would give to undo it altogether.

Michael holds me and doesn't let go. I never want him to let go. I feel as raw as if I had been turned inside out, at the same time as feeling an odd sense of calm, for the first time in my life.

CLARE

Thomas climbs to the top and we jump up and down on my bed until we're out of breath and he has snot running all the way down to his top lip. Then we climb down, me first, then him, so I can hold his bum, and we go over to my calendar. I get the marker and take the lid off and show Thomas which square to write a large X in. He does it big and it goes outside the box, but it doesn't matter, because the countdown has finished and we're all going on a summer holiday – like Cliff Richard sings. I sing the words and Thomas joins in and then we jump up and down on the spot. I feel a flutter inside because we're going to have so much fun and so is Mummy, and that is obviously just what the doctor ordered, Daddy says. I think she just needs a good cuddle from her own mum and then she'll be as right as rain. That's what I tell Thomas, but that means I have to explain that 'as right as rain' means good and back to normal, not cold and wet in the rain. He doesn't get it, even though I explain it to him three times.

We're going to go to the beach to swim in the sea, eat sausage and chips on the pebbles and see our cousins who we haven't seen for a whole entire year. I'm so excited I could burst and splatter all over our pink room. Our room is pink because I'm a girl and, even though I share with a boy, I'm the Big Sister so I got to choose. When I'm a little bit older I'll be getting my own room all to myself, and it'll have even more pink and no boys.

We go through our fluffy rucksacks that look like bears and check we have all our emergency items. Teddy, blanket, reading books, drawing books, felt-tip pens and pencils, and our bottles with the twirly straw that circles all the way up to the top, where you suck from it and watch the drink go round and round, up and down.

Daddy dresses us while Mummy makes sure everything is packed in the big suitcases. Daddy has been staying at home since Mummy hit her head, to look after her and us. Her head is much better now. When we're at the door ready to go, Daddy brings down the cases one by one and Mummy gives the house a final once-over, making sure all doors and windows are locked, and that the light timer that comes on whenever you want it to is set. That makes it look like we're in the sitting room or upstairs in our rooms, even though we're not.

'Ready, everyone?' Mummy says.

'Ready!' we shout at the same time, jumping up and down. Since Daddy has been staying at home and Mummy has been taking it easy, she is much better and we can shout again.

Mummy pulls us towards her. Me and Thomas wrap our arms around her waist and our hands meet on her bum. It's so good to have her back.

'Ready?' she says once more, kissing me on the head and then bending down to kiss Thomas. She has her make-up on and her hair is all nice and big and wavy and she's wearing her favourite red mac. She looks like herself again. I squeeze her so tight, and then I check for the bruise on her forehead; it isn't there any more.

Me and Thomas climb into the back of the car and Mummy drapes the duvet over us, so we're warm and snuggly. We wiggle our toes until they touch.

Daddy loads up the car and Mummy gets in the front. Then Daddy gets in and puts his belt on. 'Buckle up, everyone,' he says, turning to look at us over his shoulder. 'Off we go!'

'Yaaay,' me and Thomas shout when he pulls out – well, I do first and then Thomas copies.

It's early in the morning before everyone gets up and has their breakfast and leaves their houses, so we're the only ones on the road. Daddy whizzes along like Superman. It's still a bit dark, not pitch-black but not bright like the day, either, but I'm so awake that Mummy says my eyes are like saucers. I watch the streets as we fly by and see people put up shutters of shops and others walking along the pavement. I wonder where they're going. Thomas falls asleep with his feet looped with mine; I stay still, so I don't wake him. We sail through the streets, and the sun starts to shine over everything, making it all yellow. Then we're on the motorway and going in one straight line and I gaze out the window at the green, imagining what it will be like on holiday. When my neck starts to hurt from turning my head all the time, Mummy tells me to lie down and get some sleep because we have a long journey ahead of us.

It starts to get bad when we're in the mountains. Daddy is curving his way through them and we're slithering like a snake, making S-shapes all the way. My tummy turns and I can't help it, I'm going to be sick, but before I can say anything, yellow liquid that tastes like old orange juice comes up.

Mummy says, 'Oh, shit!' and reaches down to get a bag, but it's too late and a little squirt goes on the duvet. Then there's another gurgle in my tummy and Mummy pushes a bag to me from her front seat and I get the next squirt in there.

'You're okay,' Mummy says. 'Lie down.'

I lie down and it feels a teeny bit better, but my tummy is moving around inside, like I'm on a ride at Alton Towers, one of the scary ones for big children that go round and round and round.

Mummy tells me to sleep. 'You're okay,' she says again.

I breathe in and out as slow as I can, and the last thing I see before I close my eyes are the tall, green mountains that fill my window like giants.

The next time I open them the huge ferry is right there in front of us and we're in a line of cars waiting to go into its belly. We drive in slowly. Men wave to Daddy to tell him where to go and he follows cars until a man waves him to stop and it's time to get out. We park and lock up, and me and Thomas take our rucksacks with us. We go up loads of stairs until we get to the deck. Daddy pushes open the door and we go outside where we can see the sea.

I run over to the rail and Thomas follows me. Daddy comes after us and holds on to the top of our coats so we don't fall over, even though the rail is so high. The big sheet of sea goes on for ever and ever. The wind blows and takes my breath away, and I remember my bad dream and the snakes in the sea going after Mummy. I shiver and hold on tight while I look out to see how far up we are. The snakes will never get Mummy all the way up here. I have to remember to keep an eye out for her just in case. I hope I can shout to warn her, not like in my horrible dream. No matter how much I squint my eyes, I can't see anything but the sea until it meets the sky, although I can't work out where. The swish of the waves hits off the boat's belly, and me and Thomas watch the waves break and the white froth bubble up. Daddy stands behind us holding onto our jackets like we're puppies and he's picking us up by our skin. I've seen on the TV how you can pick up puppies by their skin but it doesn't even hurt them.

When the boat moves, the air gets wet and smells of salt, and when I lick my lips they taste of salt-and-vinegar crisps. I take my ponytail out and my hair flies about like mad, and when I turn from one side to the other it swishes around my face. I take Thomas's hands in mine and we lean our heads back so the wind flies through our hair. Daddy puts his hands through my hair and ruffles it around. I breathe in deep. The snakes will never get us here.

Mummy stands over on the other side of the deck. I can see her back. Her hair sparkles red where the sun hits it and brown where it doesn't, and it's blowing in the wind. It must be sticking to her lipstick because she pulls it away. The belt of her red mac is blowing behind her. Just when I think she'll lose it, she reaches back without looking and ties it round her waist.

Daddy takes us by the hand to a bench and tells us to stay put, and I watch him walk over to her and put his arm around her waist. I wonder if she'll turn round and kiss him, like in a film, but she doesn't. She does turn, though, and I can see the side of both their faces while they say something. I decide that they look like the picture of love, right then. Looking at each other and saying something to each other while Daddy holds onto Mummy, protecting her from the snakes, and her hair tickles his face. If I took a picture of them now, it would definitely be one for the wall.

It's dark when Mummy wakes us up and says in a whisper, 'Clare, we're here.'

I've forgotten where we're supposed to be, and put my arms around Daddy's neck when he lifts me out of the car, and close my eyes as Mummy lifts Thomas out the other side. I shiver with the cold of the air and then we're inside and they carry us upstairs and put us on the bed, take our shoes off and pull the blankets over us.

'We're here, we're here,' I think in my head. I remember where we are and I smile and fall asleep, happy that I don't have to change into my pyjamas.

Loud shouts wake me up. I get a shock and wonder what's happened, if Mummy and Daddy are fighting, and then John and Mary and Sarah run through the door and jump onto our bed. I get up on the bed, too, and we all jump up and down like it's a bouncy castle. We hold hands and make a circle and Thomas gets up, too, wipes his eyes and bounces in the middle. When we're out of breath, we all bounce and then fall down on the bed, one on top of the other.

They all look the same as last time. Mary is so funny. She has mad blonde curls that spring right back to the way they were after you pull them. Kind of like Thomas's hair but even more springy. She has a button-nose and freckles on her cheeks. Sarah is little, like Thomas, but taller than him, like Mary's taller than me, because their mummy is tall and ours is short. She has curly hair, too, but not like Thomas's. They're bigger curls that bounce every time she moves. I want curly hair. Mummy says mine is wavy and wispy but I want it to be springy. John is the oldest of all of us. He's twelve and tall and has red hair like wood, much redder than mine and Mummy's, and bright white skin like the others. All their skin is as white as the tops of my fingernails, even Thomas's. It's only me that has darker skin and auburn hair, which goes brighter in the sun. Mummy says that's because I follow her side of the family. The cunty side.

'Wash yer faces and we'll show ye the pups,' says Mary in her high-pitched voice. She speaks so different to me and Thomas that I go a bit red and nod; I don't want to speak and for them to hear my voice is different to theirs.

Sarah pulls my hand and I follow; we go down to the bathroom to wash our faces.

Downstairs, Aunty Joan is in the kitchen with a tea towel in her hands. She puts it down on the table and comes to hug us. She kisses me and Thomas and grabs our cheeks and says how we've grown, and then Uncle John comes in and says, 'Look who's here,' which makes us giggle. Then he hugs us and ruffles our hair. He's tall and strong like Daddy, but he's thin as a beanpole, Daddy says. Aunty Joan gives us all a muffin each and tells us to get out of here, and we take it with us and run outside.

It's cold and the sun isn't even out yet, but I don't care. I love the cold air here, and the rush of wind that is so fast and noisy you can hear it at night as you snuggle deeper into bed. The smell is different to home. Here it smells of cows and their poo, and all the muddy grass and the trees that are round the back of the house. It smells good. I breathe it in deep and then cough, because I have some muffin in my mouth and a bit has gone down the wrong way in my throat. There's just grass as far as I can see, like yesterday there was just the swish-swosh of the sea.

John leads the way around the side of the house and now I see the trees for the first time, even though I already knew they were there. 'Wait till ye see this,' he says, and Sarah grabs my hand and I squeeze it tight with excitement. We go into the hayshed. We walk all the way through to the back, where there is a blanket and lots of newspapers on the ground next to the pile of hay. John puts his finger to his lips to say shush, and we all tiptoe after him. I turn round to look at Thomas and Sarah who are holding hands and giggling, and that's when I hear the little high-pitched whimpers.

Pretty Lady is lying on the blanket and beside her are lots of little balls of black-and-white fluffy puppies. I gasp, and Mary pulls me forward and we kneel down on the floor. I'm sure Pretty Lady knows me from last time, because she sniffs at my hand and wags her tail so it thumps off the ground, like she's happy to see me. I stretch out my arm and rub one. Then the teeny balls of fluff start getting up, but they can't walk much so they wobble around and we all start laughing. One comes over to me and I pick it up. It's so small and warm and fluffy, and I can hold it easily in one hand, but I'm scared to drop it, so I hold it in two. It licks my hands.

'He likes you,' says Mary, which makes me smile a big smile.

'Is it a boy?' I ask.

Sarah nods.

He is white apart from a black dot on his back and three black paws. He's the cutest of all of them because he's different. John shows me how to tell if he is a girl or a boy, and I turn him over and look between his legs and I can see he has a little willy like Thomas. We all giggle. I count how many brothers and sisters he has. Four. I nuzzle my face into his tummy. He's so warm. I decide right then and there that I love him. 'Do they have names?' I ask, holding him while Thomas rubs his back.

'Not yet,' says Mary, who is playing with the pup in Sarah's arms. John is holding another.

One is black, so we decide to call him Blackie. One is black and white all over and she's a girl, so we call her Fluffy, like the fluffy clouds in the sky. John wants to call the one he's holding Handsome, so it goes with Pretty Lady. Mary and Sarah call the one they have Freckles because it has lots of little brown spots. That leaves the one I have in my hands.

'Sooty!' It comes to me straight away, like it was meant to be all the time. It's like his paws have been dipped in soot from the chimney.

'Sooty!' says Thomas, rubbing him on the head.

'Sooty's for a girl!' says John.

But I don't care. Sooty, Sooty, Sooty. I say it in my head and rub him under the ears and on his forehead and his tummy. He touches my face with his paw and I wiggle my nose into his fur and scrunch up my nose. I love you, Sooty, I say in my head. I love you so much. And I remember what Mummy says when she swears to something and it's so, so true. I swear I love you, Sooty, I say in my head, God can strike me down if I'm lying.

We stay in the hayshed with the pups until Aunty Joan shouts for us to come inside for lunch. We eat cold ham, turkey, bread with thick, yummy butter that stays in lumps when you put it on the bread. Yum, yum, yum. Mummy takes the knife off me to spread it properly, but I don't want her to because it's so yummy like that. It's not healthy, she says quietly. Then I make an effort to spread it down better, because of the lips-and-hips rule. We sit around the table and gobble it up as quick as we can and go straight back to the pups. We crawl up to the top of the piles of hay and we bring the pups up, and Pretty Lady comes too, and we make sure they stay on our laps and don't go wandering over to the edge like naughty boys and girls.

'Let's go and show them the treehouse!' shouts John all of a sudden.

'Kewl!' says Mary.

'Kewl!' says Sarah.

The way we speak sounds so different to the way they speak and they laugh a bit at our accent, so I decide I want to sound like them. 'Kewl,' I say, and then Thomas says it too: 'Kewl!'

We climb down carefully, and I am so careful to keep Sooty close to my chest and not squeeze him against the hay or let him fall because he would get hurt a lot. My Sooty. My teeny-weeny, soft, fluffy Sooty. 'Can we take the pups?' I ask.

'Yeah! Let's take them!' shouts Sarah, and we go out of the hayshed with the pups in our arms and walk towards the trees. Me and Mary walk side-by-side through the trees and I am careful where I step and lift my feet high over the tree trunks and branches and things that get in my way. I lift Sooty up and whisper in his ear. 'Do you like it, Sooty?'

He squeals and I know he loves me as much as I love him. I decide now that I am having the time of my life. That's what Mummy says when she's having a really, really great time. I decide that if Mummy has even a little bit as much of a good time as I'm having when we're with her family, she'll be having the time of her life, too.

JOSEPHINE

10TH MAY 1983

I know something terrible has happened when I see Mammy's handwriting on the envelope on the mat inside the front door. It's the first letter she's written to me and I know her writing straight away; it's scrawly and the letters are all different sizes as if they belong to a child. I tear it open and am skimming the lines when the life is ripped right out of me and I slide to the floor and the pins of the doormat prick my skin. I fade in and out, my body heavy and hot and stuck to the bristles of the mat, the tears flowing from my face and down my nose.

She doesn't write to me for God knows how long, and then she writes to tell me that Granny is dead and it was three days until she was found and that the funeral will be in two. I want to run down the front steps of the house and all the way to the airport and get the first flight over. When the darkness with shooting stars has gone from behind my eyes, I sit against the wall and look at the stamp date; it was sent over a week ago, so the funeral will already have been held. Nausea comes in a tidal wave to drown me and I'm suffocating.

Michael comes running down the stairs, shouting, 'What's wrong, what's wrong?'

In a voice that isn't my own, I whisper, 'It's too late. Too late.' I'm tingling all over. Michael is shaking me but I can't see him.

'Josephine! Josephine!' he shouts, and it all sounds so serious, and I think, It is serious.

Then there's Joyce's voice calling from the top of the stairs: 'What in God's name is happening?' and Michael telling her to go for water.

'She's dead, Michael. Granny's dead. We're too late. We didn't make it. Just a couple of months...' I say it all with my eyes closed because I can't see, and I lay my head on the dirty floor because the world is rocking around me. 'She was three days dead before they found her, and the funeral's gone. It's too late.'

He rubs cold water over my face and it seeps into my blouse, and all I can feel is the trickle down my back and my teeth knocking off each other as if I was freezing cold. He carries me up the stairs and, if it was any other moment, I would think it was so romantic, like something out of a movie; but my arms hang limp and my jaw hurts and I'm rambling. It doesn't feel romantic. It feels like a piece of me has been cut off and is bleeding all the way up the stairs.

Michael lays me on the bed and the letter falls out of my hand. Someone puts a glass to my lips and whiskey soaks my tongue. I retch to be sick.

When the heaving is over, I say, 'We should've gone, Michael. We shouldn't have waited.'

'Shush,' they say, rubbing my face, which only makes me worse.

I turn my back on them and curl my legs up to my chest. It comes to me that I was on my way to my new job. 'I've got to go to work,' I start, 'I've got to...' I go to get up, but they push me back and say to lie down and not worry about that.

I close my eyes and drift off up the path to Granny's house, where the nets are clean and she's waving to me through the window. We're sitting at the kitchen table. I'm telling her a story about Bernadette getting a stick across the knuckles for talking back at school, and then she gives me a boiled sweet to give to Bernadette the next day when I see her. She has her back to me, but tells me she's still listening while she spreads hard butter over a slice of toasted soda bread. I am sitting on the small chair on the other side of the fire, getting hot from the blaze. My face burns just the way it did on those evenings, but now it's with fever. My eyes hurt and the sockets behind them feel like thumping, gaping holes.

Granny, I have someone for you to meet. His name is Michael and we're getting married. I have the polka-dot chiffon scarf I promised her; that'll have them all jealous when she wears it to Mass on Sunday, and she is squealing with delight.

Granny, Granny, I whisper in her ear. She's in bed lying on her back like a corpse, and I move her silver wisps of hair to the side and whisper again, Granny. She wakes up with a fright and says I scared the living bejesus out of her, and what time is it at all? It's the middle of the night and I have found my way to her house in the blue-black dark, in my nightie and shoes, because I know the road and its curves and the pebbled opening where you take the fork up the path to her house. I ask her if I can move in with her for ever, and she says, What on earth has come over you? And she lifts up the covers and

I climb into the warmth and cuddle her all night.

The next morning she asks me what's wrong, but, in the light of day, what can I say to her? How can I say such abominable things to my granny, who is the only one who loves me?

We walk back to the house in silence. When she leaves, I get the belt across the back of my legs and am told if I do such a thing again I will be marched straight to the asylum for bold girls like myself. Just one wrong step. One step and they'll have me locked up.

Granny, Granny, I whisper in her ear, and this time she is lying on the kitchen floor, face-down, blood running from her nose from the impact of the fall. The fire has gone out and her skin is waspish as a wire sponge. I carry her to the chair and light the fire with paper and a small square of carbon and throw in two sods of turf from the bucket, and I sit on the arm of the chair, putting my hand through her hair because touching her skin is like rubbing yourself against sand. I massage her cardigan over her chest to get her heart going again.

'How are you, Josephine?'

The voice breaks me in two, but no one sees because my shell of skin holds me together. I let go of my pendant and look up. It's Mister Cohen, looking at me with concerned eyes. I wonder if he is worried about me, or about the sad sight I must be, moping about in front of the customers. He puts his arms round me and my chest is pressed up against his, and I feel sick at the thought of him making the most of the opportunity. I would push him away but I can't muster up the courage.

He says he can see I am not well and I should go home, but I tell him I need the money.

He tells me not to worry about anything, that it'll all be okay.

Riddled with guilt for doubting him, I get my things and promise to be back tomorrow.

I visit Father Francis and give him an envelope with money in it, so Granny will be remembered in Mass for the next week, and I stay to help arrange the flowers for the altar. Someone told me once that cut flowers are already dead, so each stem I cut at a diagonal, smelling its sweet pollen smell, is a reminder that Granny is gone.

None of it matters, any more. There's no need to put on a show and force myself to smile when they kiss Michael and shake his hand and congratulate him. I picture Daddy patting him on the back and asking what he'll have to drink, and my skin crawls with maggots that aren't there.

'We won't be going home,' I tell him when he picks me up from work on Saturday. He picks me up now whenever he can, and I know he has spoken to the girls to keep an eye on me.

'Oh, come on. You'll regret it if you don't.' He has his arm round me and he taps me with his hand, as if that will make everything better.

'I won't.'

He stops and turns towards me. When I don't turn, he takes my shoulders in his hands and makes me face him. 'Josephine, we've got to go – we've already got the tickets.'

'I'm sorry, Michael. You go to visit your family and get a ticket to come home. That way, at least you'll use one of the tickets.'

'But we were going to meet each other's family. That was the plan.'

'I can't do it now, Michael,' I say. 'I just can't. Maybe next year.' I know he is disappointed, and that this trip meant a lot to him. But he must see the look on my face because he puts his arms round me and rubs my hair with the palms of his hands.

'It's all right, it doesn't matter,' he whispers in my ear. 'Everything will be okay, you'll see.' He kisses me on the cheek, softly, in fear of hurting me, the way you do when someone is sick.

When I get home I write a letter explaining that things have changed and I can't get away from work. I enclose money for them to put towards the funeral.

Michael starts looking for a house and in a matter of weeks has put in an offer and it's accepted.

It's just what I need to bring me up again. Between the new accounts job in the mornings and the café in the afternoons, and now a house, I am kept occupied and my mind is busy. I put what energy I have left into throwing a party. I follow recipes in cookbooks to make canapés with cheese and pear and walnuts, and ham and roasted cherry tomatoes. I am the woman who can do it all.

When that's over, I am busy packing up all my things to move into the house. He borrows a van and the girls help us carry down the boxes. Joyce and Maura can't believe I'm moving in with Michael without getting married first, but what does it matter? Michael is a progressive sort of fellow, he doesn't believe in all of those rules that box us in, and I was never a pure woman, anyway.

For our first Friday evening in our new home I have bought a bottle of expensive red wine and a bottle of sparkling. I've set the table and lit candles and am preparing minted lamb with Dauphinoise potatoes and roasted carrots. I'm standing at the kitchen counter chopping the fresh mint when Michael comes in, smelling of shampoo and with his hair flopping around his face. He puts his arms round my waist and kisses me on the neck.

'I could stay like this for ever,' I tell him.

'Really?' he says.

'Yes,' I say. 'Truly.'

'You could stay like this for ever?' Sometimes he teases me and I call him a tinker and tell him to leave me alone, but I love it.

'I could.' I turn and look him in the eyes and he knows I mean it.

'So could I, my darling.' He takes my hands and lifts my arm over my head, twirling me round, and we have a dance, just the two of us, on the kitchen floor.

He kneels down on the old brown linoleum with diamond shapes and rips, from where knives have fallen and sliced it.

'What are you doing?' I laugh, pulling his hands for him to get up.

'I know I've done this before,' he says. 'But I want to do it again. Josephine, I want you to marry me. What are we still waiting for? Let's just do it. Life's too short.'

I kneel down on the floor in front of him and put my arms round his shoulders. Yes, yes, yes. I say it over and over again, kissing him as I say it. 'You're right. Life is short.' Tears stream down my face and my throat blocks up, but it's not with sadness. 'I love you, Michael, I love you so much.'

'I love you too, my darling.'

'Don't ever leave me.'

'I won't. Nor you, me.'

'Never. Shall we do it as soon as we can?'

'You'd make me the happiest man alive.'

I tell him I'll call Father Francis, and I run to the phone and dial his number.

'That's great news, now, Josephine,' he says when I tell him.

'Thanks, Father!' I squeeze Michael's hand tight. 'We're thrilled!'

He looks in his diary and tells me he has a free slot in two weeks.

I turn to Michael and he gives me a big grin, so I tell Father that would be wonderful, and to please note us down.

I am so light with happiness that I am floating on clouds.

For dessert we have meringue with strawberries and cream. 'I suppose I'll give up my jobs once we're married,' I say, pouring us a glass of sparkling wine to go with dessert.

Michael rests his hands on the table and watches the bubbles fizz in the glasses. 'Whatever you like,' he says.

'Then I could concentrate on making more nice dinners like this, and decorate the house, and we'll have babies...'

He picks up his glass. 'Cheers,' he says, 'to dinners, decorating and babies.'

I clink my glass with his. 'Cheers!' My cheeks flush red.

We carry on eating. After a while Michael says, 'Of course, we have plenty of time. Don't rush anything, just for me.'

'I won't,' I say, feeling like a fool.

We finish off the bottle and curl up on the sofa with records playing softly on the record player. I look around the bare room, with a sealed box still in the middle of the floor and nothing else, apart from a lamp I brought from the flat and a small coffee table of Michael's, and I try to get back that happy feeling I had when he was kneeling on the kitchen floor, telling me to marry him, and I was saying, Yes, yes, yes.

I mentally draft the letter to my mother informing her of our wedding. I will invite them, but I know they won't come, and I am glad.

JOSEPHINE

Missus Michael Reilly. Missus Reilly. Missus Josephine Reilly. I never get bored of it. It has a lovely ring to it. Missus Michael Reilly. 'Hello, Mrs Reilly. Goodbye, Josephine Callahan,' I say into the mirror. I say it smiling, as if I'm announcing my new name to friends. Then I say it officiously, pretending I'm in the bank, telling the woman behind the counter who I am. I'm bursting with pride. I'm a new woman. From now on, everything will be different. I can feel it.

'Josephine, come on!' Joyce calls from the hallway. 'Today, woman – today! Or you'll miss your own wedding!'

'I'll be right out.' I sit down to do a piddle. I look around the bathroom. The paint has begun to bubble from the damp and it's turned a mottled-yellow gungy colour.

'Ye'll have to ring the landlord, over the damp in there,' I tell them when I come out.

'Ah, sure we will, one of these days,' says Joyce.

'Listen to her ladyship, now that she's got her house and her man!' says Maura.

I laugh, but the comment comes as a jab. I hope they don't

think me high-and-mighty; I was only thinking of them.

'Can I nick one off you?' I ask Joyce, picking up her cigarettes.

'You eejit,' she says, 'nick away.'

I join Maura at the kitchen table, where she is painting her nails. The smell of the nail varnish and frying rashers and eggs makes me smile. I light the cigarette and pull on it hard.

'Are you nervous?' asks Maura.

I fold my arms and hold the cigarette up high, so the smoke wafts above our faces. 'You know, I'm not.' But the truth is that, now she's asked me, I'm aware of a ball of heaviness in the bottom of my stomach.

'Crack open the Buck's Fizz,' says Joyce to Maura, but Maura's nails are wet, so I go to the fridge and take out the bottle and three tumblers.

I undo the plastic seal and turn the cork, but I'm terrified of it popping, so I turn it just the smallest bit. Joyce says we'll be here all day, so she takes it. I don't have the nerves for opening bottles of fizz. It puts me on edge.

She twists the cork and it pops with a big bang. I scream, even though I knew it was coming, and Maura and Joyce laugh at me and I laugh at myself because even I find it funny. The Buck's Fizz splashes onto the floor before Joyce gets the bottle to the glasses. I know it'll be sticky for days, without me around to clean it. I imagine my shoe sticking to it and it gives me a shiver.

'Cheers!' says Joyce.

'Cheers,' say Maura and I, and we tap our glasses off each other, making sure we're looking into each other's eyes. We take a gulp.

It's awfully fizzy and sweet and it hurts going down. I decide not to have any more; it'll only make me worse.

'How did you sleep?' asks Joyce. She's back at the hob, moving the sausages around. The bacon and eggs are already served on three plates on the counter. If she'd started with the sausages, everything would have been hot.

'Grand, now – grand.' Feck it, I think, and I take another sip of Buck's Fizz. It makes me burp. I had dreams last night, but I can't remember them. Probably anxiety dreams; that's what they call it when you're apprehensive about something important happening, before it happens, and you have strange dreams. I read it in a magazine.

I get out the knives and forks and clear the table.

'Will I paint your nails?' asks Maura.

'Do.'

The music's blasting. It's Crystal Gayle singing her heart out. 'Somebody Loves You.' The neighbours could come knocking any minute, but I'd tell them I'm getting married. That today is my wedding day. Part of me wants them to come, just so I can tell them. I want to tell everyone. I would parade myself down the High Road if I could, showing everyone what a fine husband I got myself. And they'd all say, Didn't you do well, now? How did you manage that, altogether? But I would be so proud I wouldn't even mind.

When my face and hair are done, Joyce and Maura help me put my dress on, so I don't stain it with make-up. I bought it from one of the shops on Oxford Street. It's cream and to the knee and it has embroidery across the chest and shoulders.

'It's perfect,' says Joyce when the zip is up.

'It's beautiful, Josephine,' says Maura.

I look in the dressing-table mirror in Joyce's room and remember the first night I came to this flat, when Joyce made me up and I looked like someone else. I look like someone else now, as well. Like an imposter. A pure, blushing bride. It's not enough that it's not a wedding dress. I should have gone for green, or red.

Michael's old flatmate Daniel comes to pick us up. He has even gone to the trouble of putting a ribbon on his car, an old white Ford with rust along the edges of the doors. You can see where he tried and failed to attach the ribbon, because it's stained on the bonnet.

We can't open the windows because the ribbon would fall out. It gets hot and stuffy on the way and I keep touching my face to check if I'm sweating. Beads of sweat will be breaking out above my lip, I know.

Joyce tells me off and lightly slaps my hand away.

'Do I look all right?'

'Of course you do. Sure, you look beautiful.'

'Do you promise?'

'I promise.'

The heavy purr of the old engine reminds me of Daddy's truck and I think I'm going to be sick. I picture the yolk of the eggs I had for breakfast mixing with the Buck's Fizz. It makes me woozy. I hum a tune from this morning in my head. I pretend the vibrations are coming from the record player and that I'm on firm ground and everything is all right. I'm stuck on the same line, the way the pin gets stuck on the record player and it goes on repeat.

Walking down the aisle, I'm sure my legs are going to buckle from under me, but they carry me to the altar and when I get to Michael, I clutch his hands and never want to let go. My mouth, my chin tremble. He blinks in surprise and I know it is because he thinks me beautiful, and he loves me more than I could ever love myself.

'I love you, Michael,' I whisper. He looks so handsome in his suit and tie, with his blondie locks shining in the light – more handsome even than the day I met him.

'I love you, too,' he says. He rubs my hands in his, then tries to release my grip. I don't let go. If I let go, surely I'll fall and ruin my lovely dress and my make-up and my hair, curling down my back.

My chest swells like the river behind the house at home after a downpour. I think of the river now, flowing, as I look into Michael's open, shining eyes. I think of them all, and it occurs to me that I am a stranger to them now. And that I don't know them, either. I wouldn't know Sean if he walked past me in the street. I will never go back. I have everything I need now.

The vast wooden doors close with a bang that bounces off the church walls like arrows. The sunlight is blocked out and we are left with the reds and yellows and blues of the coloured glass. New shadows are cast, as if my family were here after all. There go Mammy and Daddy, dancing on the wall behind the statues. They're laughing at me. *Who do you think you're kidding? Look at her, pretending she's Lady Muck. Who does she think she is?*

I want to scream, *Go away! Go away you dirty, rotten, filthy bastards!* They won't leave me alone. They will ruin everything for me. Even my sweetest, happiest moments.

'Josephine.' It's Michael. He is looking deep into my eyes and shaking my hands to bring me back to him. Father Francis is speaking. I smile at Michael and turn to look at Maura and Joyce. On the other side is Daniel and his girlfriend and a handful of other friends of Michael's. I smile at them all, wishing the shadows away.

The church is empty but for our small group. They're not here; I keep telling myself this. They're not here and I'm never going back. I never have to see any of them again. I listen to Father Francis and I smile at Michael. I say my vows. The blood catches in my throat as it runs through my veins. I am alive.

CLARE

Mummy makes me put on the full shebang: dress, frilly socks, ribbons in my hair and my good shiny black shoes. I don't want to wear any of it.

'Ye have had plenty of fun now, Clare,' she says. 'Don't be spoilt. We're going to make our visits.'

It's Visitors' Day, which means doing the rounds to see all these old people I don't know and sit on their sofas and watch them all drink tea. It's so boring because Sooty is By No Means Allowed. Sarah, Mary and John can't come, either, because Aunty Joan said we're visiting relatives, and they live here all year round so they're staying put. That means me and Thomas have to sit and behave like a good girl and boy while the adults discuss how are things here and in London, and isn't it sad about your one who died? I don't know who 'your one' is and I don't care. I want to go back to Uncle John and Aunty Joan's and run around until I need to take a puff – breathe in one, two, three, take another puff, breathe in one, two, three, and then breathe in and out nice and slow.

Being in tracksuit bottoms and a top, and normal socks and

trainers, is much more fun, and you can run around and roll on the hay and not worry about getting dirty. When Mummy said I was to wear a dress, I pushed my lips together and folded my arms.

'Wipe that puss off right now, Missy, or I'll put that dog out,' Mummy said.

I unfolded my arms and rubbed Sooty, who was curled up on my lap.

When Mummy was doing my hair and yanked it back hard into a ponytail, I remembered to be good, like Daddy said.

We start with Aunty Anne, who lives down the road. Aunty Anne is Daddy's big sister and Uncle John's big sister, too. She never married, and John told us once it's because she stayed at home to help my granny look after Daddy and Uncle John when they were small, and that the boy she loved went away and she didn't go with him. Then she never met another boy, and now she lives in a small house by the beach and you can even see the sea from her front-room windows, which I think is nice because if I didn't have someone to love, I would at least like to look out the window and be able to see the sea.

She comes out when she hears the car and is there standing in front of the house when we pull up outside. We get out and she hugs us all, one at a time, starting with Mummy and then me and then Thomas and then Daddy, because he's the last out of the car. She squeezes me so tight and I squeeze her back. I feel bad for complaining, because she is the only one that's fun to visit and if she heard what I said she would be upset. She's tall like Daddy and Uncle John, taller than Mummy and bigger, so next to her, Mummy looks teeny-weeny. Aunty Anne has long, light-brown hair and big square glasses and a pretty dress on that's the colour of chocolate. She's the best because she says we're her niece and nephew, so that means that we can have free rein in her house.

We run into the sitting room, through to the kitchen, and see all the food on the table. 'Mummy!' I shout. 'Aunty Anne's made a party.'

Mummy and Daddy come into the kitchen and Mummy says, 'Anne, you shouldn't have.'

'Of course I should have,' Aunty Anne says back. I throw my arms around her.

She tells Mummy and Daddy to sit down in the front room, that she'll be right in and we will help her, which makes me and Thomas smile at each other. We love being helpers. First, I carry in bread and butter and thick slices of cheese on a plate, and then another plate of fat slices of ham and turkey. Thomas brings in napkins, because they're light. Aunty Anne brings in pieces of meat on long, thin sticks.

'Jesus, Anne,' says Daddy.

'Oh, Anne,' says Mummy, when Anne reappears with a bottle of wine and three glasses. Then she comes back with two glasses of Ribena for me and Thomas, which looks the same as wine. She pours wine for the adults and then we all put our glasses in the air and say Cheers and clink them together.

'Dig in,' Aunty Anne says and we all eat and drink, and Aunty Anne puts music on and Daddy says, 'Sure, John and Joan should be here,' and Aunty Anne says, 'Not at all, I see enough of them. I want to see my brother and sister-in-law over from London and my lovely niece and nephew and have ye all to myself.'

Me and Thomas get up and give her a hug then. Visiting isn't bad at all, I think. If only all the rounds could be as fun as this. Me and Thomas cheers again and push our glasses together and Thomas spills Ribena on the carpet, but Aunty Anne says it doesn't matter at all, and smiles at Mummy and they drink more wine.

I'm having so much fun and so is everyone. I just wish Sooty was here and then it would be perfect.

Aunty Anne asks how are things in London and Daddy says, 'Great, great,' and I think, Liar, liar, pants on fire. But then Aunty Anne brings out chocolate cake and they talk about other things, like work and bills, and the costs of things. 'How long are ye here for?' asks Aunty.

'Until next Wednesday,' says Daddy.

'Is that all?' says Anne.

Mummy nods. 'You two, why don't you go outside and see if you can find any snails in the garden?'

'Come on, Thomas!' I say. I know they're going to talk about Mummy's dying mum.

I jump up and get another square of chocolate cake with lots of the chocolate cream on and run outside, where the air smells salty and fresh because we're right next to the sea. I turn and look over my shoulder and there is Thomas, running after me with his chocolate cake, wobbling in his hand.

After we do the rounds, like Daddy says, and visit more people who Daddy went to school with and who he worked with before he got the boat to London, and other old people who were friends of the family, we get to play again. In the hayshed, in the fields, in the forest. And we bring Sooty, Handsome, Fluffy, Blackie and Freckles with us, even though we're not allowed and we've been told to stay away from them. None are allowed in the house any more and we're not allowed into the hayshed under any circumstances. But no one sees us sneak in the back door and, like John says, what they don't know won't hurt them. It's so much fun not being in my good dress that I can't get dirty, rolling around in the hay and letting Sooty crawl over me. I could stay like this for ever.

JOSEPHINE

I notice a swelling in my body and I am sure I'm pregnant. The swelling isn't only in my belly, it is in my breasts, my hips. There is something beautiful about it. About the wonder of the body and what it is capable of. I have never thought of it as something wonderful; as a vehicle for new life. It has been my cage. I am convinced I am pregnant and I am convinced I am not. I run through scenarios of how I will tell Michael. Michael, I have something to tell you. Michael, we're to have a baby. Michael, my period's late. Yet, I expect it to come at any second and snatch it all away from me.

I decide to go to the chemist to get one of the tests I've heard people talking about. I get the bus down the road to the nearest chemist. As I turn to go in I see the man behind the counter. I will myself not to care, to pretend it's for Maura or Joyce. I turn and walk out and go to the next one. This time an elderly gentleman comes in behind me, so before the woman in the white jacket can serve me, I pretend I've forgotten my purse and leave. I go to four chemists but can't muster the courage to go in to buy a test. God only knows what questions they will ask me.

I go home and keep myself busy by putting on a wash and getting the dinner. I don't tell Michael any of the shenanigans, for fear of sounding like a demented fool.

The next morning in the toilet my period comes and I have a good cry for myself. I had been hopeful for new life. I had been hopeful for a transformation.

When my period eventually doesn't come, I wait several weeks before I allow myself to entertain the idea. I make an appointment at the doctor's and they do a test.

On my way home, I buy steak and potatoes and wine and have the table set and myself done up for when Michael gets in. I hear the key in the door and his feet brush against the mat. Then there's the click of the lock and the ring of the keys in the dish. I hide behind the kitchen door and hold my breath and listen to his measured, padded footsteps grow closer as he walks down the carpeted hall and onto the lino floor.

'Where's the most beautiful girl in the whole of England?' he calls.

I hold my breath; keep still. I'm smiling and hot and giddy and my heart is banging loud in my chest.

He peers round the door and I jump, even though I know that's exactly what he'll do. I'm giggling now and step forward towards him and he laughs and says, 'There she is!' He kisses me hello. He smells of tarmac and fumes and still has the faint scent of the aftershave he put on this morning. The concoction is strong and makes my head swim.

'Michael,' I whisper into his chest.

'Yes, my love?' He is smelling my hair and rubbing my back and I am tingling all over.

'We're going to have a baby.' I whisper it because I can

barely believe it. I can't allow myself to get so excited at being blessed like this, but it's too late. I'm already thinking of names and imagining a little baby Michael and seeing the three of us together, a happy family. My family.

He pulls away and looks into my eyes. Then he draws me back to him and squeezes me tight. Then, out of nowhere, he jumps up into the air and lets out a loud Yihaa!

I laugh and he laughs, and I wrap my arms around him.

'How do you feel? Are you okay? Do you need to sit down?' His face is serious with concern.

I laugh. 'I'm fine.'

'Sit down anyway. You're to take it easy.' He leads me over to the table and I sit down. 'Are you happy?' he says after a while.

I nod. I have no words. How to tell him I am the happiest I have ever been, that I am happier than I ever thought possible?

The growth of my body is beautiful, at first, but then on some days it is odious, too. One morning, after my bath, I look at myself in the mirror. Every part of me is swollen. I have been taken over by this creature inside of me, like I have been taken over before. My body is not my own, from the neck down, just like all those years ago.

My tummy is growing and growing, despite me wanting it to stop. Of course there's the baby, but there's the cigarette belly, too. Since I've stopped smoking I can't stop eating. I've tried playing with the cigarette and pretending, just to keep my hands busy, but it's no good.

I wanted to be one of those beautiful, sophisticated pregnant women who are tiny but for their protruding belly. The ones people joke about having swallowed a watermelon.

There's nothing glamorous or sophisticated about me. There's nothing controlled. Once again in my life I find myself looking on at my body, helpless. I stare at my breasts, my tummy, my hips in the mirror; they grow before my eyes. I am sure of it. I'm getting bigger and uglier as this baby grows stronger and more human, as if it's sucking the goodness out of me.

There's a punch or a kick under the skin and it's as if a little monster is alive within me, trying to break out. Maybe it's always been there, and has only just woken up.

I rub this new mound and wonder when we made this living thing. I hope it was one of our nice times together, when I forget myself and allow myself to love and be loved. Other times, I can't help but remember, and it's like I've been taken over again, and again. Then I pull myself away and busy myself somewhere else in the house, or turn over and pretend to sleep. I remind myself it is different, so different. A world away. A sea apart. Get over yourself, Josephine – cop on, for God's sake. Forget about it once and for all. But my body cannot forget. It remembers every time my father has laid a hand on me – whether it was a brush of the arm or a slap – every look, every comment. It remembers every Sunday when Uncle Patrick came for lunch and made jokes and winked and everyone laughed, even me. It remembers my mother on the toilet, and it remembers the stabbing pain, in my head, between my legs, and in my chest. My body is beyond my mind and the words I say inside my head. My body, with its crevices and its muscles that seize up, and its curves that grow.

I put on a dress I bought in the sales and for the rest of the day I feel like a whale. I'm sure everyone is looking at my arse and my legs and my huge chest, and I blush when I have to speak to anyone. I wish the day away, waiting to get in the door so I can change and, when I do, I rip the dress off and put it in the kitchen cupboard to use as rags and put on my dressing gown.

I work until my legs are swollen and my ankles are stiff. The office where I do the books in the mornings barely acknowledges me when I leave, and I wonder where I went wrong. They did get me a bunch of flowers but it was small and mean, and they got me a voucher for a shop that sells baby clothes. Michael says it was lovely of them, and what else were they going to do? I would have liked tea and cake to send me off. Michael says they were busy wrapping up the quarter.

The following Friday, Maura, Joyce and Mister Cohen throw a little leaving party for me. There's chocolate cake and tea and coffee and hot chocolate, and Mister Cohen gives me a card with fifty pounds inside. I hug him and the girls and take the tiny Babygros and bouquet of flowers home. I am full of chocolate cake and gratitude, beaming and not caring about the other office. These are my real friends, bless them. I am also full of nerves and terribly scared of being alone. I imagine Maura and Joyce dolled up to the nines, out on the town tonight, and Michael and myself curled up on the settee, me getting bigger by the minute.

JOSEPHINE

9TH JUNE 1987

When it comes, the pain is like nothing I've felt before. It grips me in sharp, electric waves from the inside out.

I message Michael's pager, like he told me, and wait for him to call. When he doesn't, I ring a cab and take my bag and myself off to the hospital. I try to look calm and don't let on to the cab driver, until a contraction comes and I scream and dig my nails into my thighs and push my knees against his seat.

'Where's your husband, love?' he asks.

'Coming,' I say, 'he's coming.'

'Well, something's definitely coming, that's for sure,' he says with a smile.

I hate Michael for not being here with me.

I have come too early, they tell me. I can either go home, or walk up and down the corridors to help my waters break. I dare not go home to be there by myself, and be humiliated in front of another driver. I shuffle around the hospital. It stinks of disinfectant and hospital food. I tremble as I walk. They will all know what I'm doing. They see me on my own and are wondering where my husband and my family are. I tremble with nerves and anger, and curse Michael for still not being here.

Everyone looks sick. Either on their own sickbeds or sick with worry, and the darkness of it all rubs off on me. I soak it up with each baby step. I look for Michael around every corner, but there are only other men, older, younger, darker hair. His face is nowhere to be seen. I will never forgive him for leaving me with all this sickness and our baby, making its way towards the world.

A trolley comes with a little old lady, her skin loose and empty, and I swear I can smell death.

Further up the corridor, a wave comes. I hold onto the wall, and close my eyes against the stares of strangers. When the liquid splashes over my feet, I pray it's all a dream. They take my hands and put me in a wheelchair and I float along, pretending I'm somewhere else. I'm good at that.

I open my eyes to a nurse helping me onto a bed. She has small, kind eyes and thin lips, like Granny.

'There you go. I'm just going to take your knickers off,' she says, and they're already off by the time she has finished the sentence. 'Move yourself lower down, love.' She speaks in a London accent and it seems wrong; she should sound like Granny.

I shuffle along the length of the bed but she tells me to go further, further, until my bottom is right at the end. She lifts my legs into the stirrups and I want to be sucked up away out of here. I want to die. But I can't die. I'm not here to die, I remind myself. I'm here to have a baby. This is a good experience, a natural experience. I repeat it to myself, and concentrate on my breathing.

All I can do is focus on breathing in, breathing out, as they examine me. A male doctor comes in and joins them, and only after he has looked between my legs does he look at my face and introduce himself. I want to roar at them all, to jump up and run down the corridor and out to the park, where I would sit with my legs together on a blanket and read a magazine.

The tears stream from my eyes without a sound. I count the squares in the ceiling, and listen to them mutter between themselves, the doctor's hands on me all the while. The image of Daddy with the chisel in my mouth, and me unable to breathe a word, fills my mind.

The nurse who looks like Granny comes up to my end of the bed and rubs my arm and says everything is okay. 'Breathe, dear, breathe, try to relax,' she says, and I wish I had a mother who could be here with me now.

I close my eyes and run through the fields behind the house. I skip down the road to Granny's and go in through the back door and kiss her on the cheek. I sit down beside her and eat a biscuit and she rubs my hair. I am in the pub with Bernadette, I'm dancing in the church hall with the girls, twirling around. I'm twirling and twirling. This is what I do. Escape from myself. Run away, down the road, through the fields and the forest and over to the big tree where no one can find me.

All those hours I spent up in that tree, and all I wanted was for my mother to come and look for me.

My body clenches into a tight fist and I let out a roar.

Time moves in waves. In moments of clarity, and clenching and increasing dilation. They tell me my husband has arrived and will they send him in? No, I tell them. He can wait outside. I'm too far gone for him to see me, now. White, sweating, my legs up and open. He can pay for not keeping his word, for doing this to me – for everything.

'Come on, love,' says the nurse. 'One more, now make it a good one.'

I cling to the bed and push and scream but I'm too tired, I can't do it. 'Will you get my husband?' I ask, suddenly sorry for making him stay outside and desperate for him to be here holding my hand.

They tell me to hurry on and push, push, that we need to get the baby out now. Now, I think. Jesus, the baby is in distress. Oh God. I scream that I want my husband, and one of them hurries away and I'm pushing and in he walks with a plastic hat on his head and a face etched with nerves.

He comes to my side and holds my hand and I squeeze it and push.

Then, the sound of a baby crying. My baby crying.

'It's a girl,' a voice says (I don't know whose).

Michael kisses my face while they clean her. 'Well done, my darling,' he says. 'Josephine, I'm so sorry I didn't get here earlier. Forgive me.'

I look at him. 'Where were you?'

'I was at work. I left the pager down and didn't hear the message.' He shakes his head. 'I'll make it up to you, I promise.'

I look away. 'It was the one thing you had to do.'

The nurse brings me my baby, crying, and tells me I can hold her and feed her.

I rub her face and coax her on, gazing at the red wisps on her head and the little fists poking out from beneath the blanket. Her eyes are closed, her eyelids puffy and swollen.

'Hello, beautiful,' I whisper.

The nurse smiles. 'Well done, Mum. Just a few stitches,'

she says. 'You won't feel a thing.'

'Thank you,' I say, reaching out to touch her arm.

'You're welcome, my dear.' She pats my hand.

I can't see yet who my little baby looks like, but I know she will have the best parts of both of us. She will have my eyes, and Michael's pink, full lips. She will have his softness, his way with words and forgivingness, his sense of humour. She'll have my eyelashes and my auburn hair, my warmth and my way with numbers.

She's all mine, I think, mine. My baby. I will watch you grow a centimetre a day, I will feed you when you are hungry, I will shower you with kisses and I will be there for you whenever you need me.

I vow to love her with all my being and give her everything I never had. My daughter will have it all. I tuck my little finger into her tiny cupped hand.

She whines like a puppy and we laugh quietly.

'Look what we made,' I whisper.

'Look what you did,' whispers Michael. 'You carried her and gave birth to her.'

Yes, I think, looking down at her sleeping face. 'I did, didn't I?'

'You did, my darling.' He kisses me on the hand.

At home, the baby cries. I put her to my chest to feed, but she screams with her mouth wide open.

Michael comes in and I ask him to get the bedroom ready. I don't want him to see me and think me helpless and incapable.

'Come on, little baby,' I whisper. 'You did it so well in hospital.'

She cries and I cry with her. I take my breast in my hand and move my nipple back and forth over her lips. I change sides. I get a cushion to prop her up. I squeeze out a drop of milk and wet her lips. I imagine the women stopping me on the street to see my new baby, saying, *Oh, isn't she beautiful?* Cooing over her. *And are you breastfeeding?* they will ask. *Yes, I am,* I will say. Everyone knows breastfeeding is best for the baby. *Aren't you great?* they will say. *Aren't you a fine example to us all, now.*

'Come on,' I whisper. The tears roll down my cheeks. I shake my head. Why would she do it for the nurse and not for me?

I close my eyes and picture myself walking to the shops with the little baby in the pram and all the ladies stopping me to have a look. They'll say how great I look, ask how I managed it at all. And I will shake my head and shrug my shoulders. It just fell off, I'll say. *What a marvellous woman,* they will say back, *and what a beautiful daughter.*

JOSEPHINE

5TH AUGUST 1987

S ome days, when she sleeps I shower with her in the basket on the floor. Other days, nothing will soothe her and I have her in my arms non-stop. Even when she's asleep she senses when I put her down, and I have to scoop her up quickly to stop her from screaming. On those days I end up mooching around the house in my dressing gown, the walls closing in on me as the day draws on. On those days, the weight of this tiny, fragile life depending entirely on me is almost too much. I might have a cry.

It's better when I shower and dress and get out to the shops, even just to buy a pint of milk or the paper. On a good day I take the pram to the park and have a walk around to stretch my legs. She sleeps contentedly and I breathe in deep.

I sometimes remember how Mammy would leave Sean to cry for what seemed like hours. I wonder how long it really was. I imagine myself as a baby screaming in the cot, and her lying in the bed, her head against the headboard, listening. I wonder what she thought about in those moments, and if she loved me. I wonder if she scooped me up in her arms as soon as I made a sound, the way I do with Clare; if she went to the toilet with me on her shoulder.

I can't bear the sound of Clare's cries. I couldn't find it in myself to leave her to cry, like my mother left her children. Michael tells me to. When I jump up and run to her cot, he tells me I should wait longer, that I'll spoil her. I tell him that I'm her mother. Mother knows best, isn't that what they say?

'Sorry,' he says. 'I'm trying to help.'

'Well, I could do without your help.' My tongue is sharp. I am tired from all the waking in the night, from the shushing and rocking, walking around the house, praying for her to sleep. I shouldn't be so mean to him. It's not his fault that he has to sleep, to be up for work in the morning. He has to work. And I have to take care of Clare. That's the way it is. He is only doing his best.

All I know is that I love Clare so much it hurts. With her gurgles and her button-nose, and her lips that swell after she feeds. Her hiccups that shake through her small, chubby, defenceless body. 'My darling girl,' I whisper to her, 'you can tell me anything in the world, whenever you need to.'

I am watching her sleep when the doorbell rings. I wasn't expecting anyone. I look in the basket and Clare is still. I put my hand over her chest and feel the warmth of its rise, followed by the fall. I creep on tiptoes over to the window and look down through the nets. It's Maura and Joyce. They turn and see me and wave. My heart sinks. I have been wondering when they would come, but now they are here, I wish they had let me know they were coming. I wave back, then tie my dressing gown around my waist and tuck my loose hair behind my ears.

I take a look in the mirror and open the door to them.

'Hello!' they say in high sing-song voices.

'Hi, girls! Come in, come in.' My voice sounds flat after hearing theirs.

'Jesus, you look awful,' says Maura. 'You look like you've been hit by a bus.'

'Shut up, you!' says Joyce. She elbows her, thinking I don't see it, but I do. 'You look lovely, Josephine. A little tired is all.'

They are the ones who look lovely, in their skirts and blouses with ties at the neck, all made up.

Joyce leads the way into the kitchen. She takes out a box of chocolates from her bag and Maura hands me a bunch of flowers. I smell them. 'They're lovely,' I tell them. They're from the greengrocer's down the road; I recognize the sticker. I picture them running all the way here, stopping to buy chocolates at the corner shop and the flowers from your man at the greengrocer's. He would have watched them run off, admiring them from behind. He's like that.

Joyce tells me to sit down and asks where I keep the vase. I point to the cupboard. She takes it out and sets about arranging the flowers. I get up to put the kettle on, but Maura shushes me and fills it up and gets out the mugs.

I let out a sigh. It's nice to be waited on. When Michael comes home, I have the shopping done and the dinner on. Clothes have been washed and hung out to dry. The baby's nappies have been washed. She is bathed and dressed and I am sometimes bathed and dressed, too. I make tea and breakfast in the morning. I do it because I want to, because he works hard and I'm at home all day, because this is the deal we made when we became husband and wife, but I am tired.

I watch them, and I miss living in the flat with them, drinking at the kitchen table, getting ready to go dancing.

'Can I smoke in here?' asks Maura.

I nod.

She lights a cigarette and I breathe in deep the grey clouds of smoke, getting woozy. I would love one. Sometimes, when I can't take it any more, I go out the back door and take a few drags of a cigarette while Clare is asleep.

'Jesus, we haven't even seen the baby!' shrieks Joyce.

'Shush!' We all giggle, and it's like we live together again. But it's my baby we're giggling at. I have a baby, I think, and a warm glow ignites within me.

Maura leaves her cigarette balanced on the edge of the ashtray and we creep into the sitting room.

As soon as we go in, I'm aware of the mess. The cot is in the middle of the room. There are dirty mugs on the coffee table with dried teabags inside and the curtains are only half-drawn, casting the room in that half-darkness that is so depressing. A dirty nappy is in a ball on the floor, waiting to be picked up and washed. New nappies sit in clean, folded squares on the table. Michael says we should try plastic throwaway ones, but these are the best.

We gather around the basket and they peer down at her, each reaching for a hand and stroking it.

'Isn't she beautiful?' says Maura.

'She is, isn't she?' says Joyce.

'Oh, look at her little button-nose and her little hands and that fine head of hair!'

'She's as gorgeous as her mother,' smiles Maura.

Clare stirs, so we sneak back to the kitchen to drink our tea. They can't stay long, they say, and apologize for taking so long to stop by. They're both going steady with a fella and, between work and everything, it's hard to find the time. Tonight they're going out to the dance in the church hall.

'Sure, I know. Tell me about it. The days fly by...' I shake my head like I can't believe it. I don't tell them that sometimes the day lies ahead of me like a long, black tunnel.

I close the front door behind them, go into the kitchen and open the chocolates. Just one. I pick out a hazelnut-and-caramel one, then a strawberry cream, then the orange. Then a praline one. I imagine the girls later at the dance, with their boyfriends. I picture them jiving on the dance floor. I pour myself a drop of brandy to take the edge off my jitters.

Clare cries out. I run in to get her and, bobbing her on my shoulder, prepare the milk in a bottle. Back in the sitting room, I sit in the corner of the sofa and prop her up on a cushion. She screams like the Antichrist while I shake the bottle and test a drop on my wrist. My chest tightens and, desperate to soothe her, I shove the bottle in her mouth. I check her ear isn't folded back against my chest.

When she has finished feeding, I burp her on my lap, careful to hold her little face in my hand. A bubble of air escapes her mouth and I congratulate her with a shower of kisses. 'You see, you don't miss breast-milk at all, do you?' I ask her. I am relieved she didn't wake for feeding when the girls were here. I wouldn't want them to know that I have already failed as a mother.

I leave her on my shoulder and wait for her to sleep, soothing her with my shushes all the time.

We have a quiet christening and some food and drink at our house afterwards. That's when it occurs to Michael that we haven't sent photos of Clare home, to his family or to mine. He decides we have to buy a camera and take photos to send to everyone. It has been a long time since I have heard from anyone, and I have no intention of sending them anything, but he wears me down slowly. He says we have to, that our parents will be dying to see their granddaughter.

It's a sunny Saturday afternoon when he sets up the camera and the tripod and insists we sit on the sofa together for a photo of the three of us. I put on a royal-blue dress with a wide collar, hoping it will hide the weight I've put on. I put Clare in a dress that Michael's mammy sent to us. It's yellow with little pink flowers. And I put a bow in her hair and a navy cardigan on top. I spend a good hour putting make-up on myself to take away the bags under my eyes and give myself some colour. Michael puts on one of his shirts and a pair of trousers, but he has no extra weight to hide, his body hasn't just been through a triathlon.

I sit on the sofa with Clare on my lap and he sets up the timer and runs for the sofa, just making it as the flash of the camera goes off. Clare jumps and shuts her eyes and we laugh, and I have to admit it was a lovely idea. He goes back to set the timer again and comes running back, quicker this time, and he kisses me as the flash goes off.

Michael says he'll take some of me and Clare. He goes behind the camera and clicks away, and I tell him not to be daft, that he'll waste the whole film.

'And how would I waste the film on my two favourite girls in the world?' he says, and I think, This is what life's all about. It's these moments of happiness right now, these snippets of us being together.

We go out to do the shopping and buy things for a nice

dinner, seeing as we're all dolled up. Everything is easier on the weekends. Michael is beside me and Clare's cries don't hurt so much, and I don't feel as drained.

The photographs are lovely when they come back. I write a letter to Michael's mother and thank her for the dress, and tell her we are doing well and plan to come out and visit next summer or the one after, when Clare is bigger. To my own mother and father, I send a photograph of the three of us and I choose the one where Michael's eyes are closed. I want the nice one for myself. I write Clare's full name and date of birth on the back. I don't ask how they are or for them to tell me the latest news, so that I don't expect any reply. I enclose cash, as I always do.

It crosses my mind to write separate letters to Sean, Siobhan and Brendan, but it has been so long now that I wouldn't know what to say. Besides, none of them have picked up the pen and paper for me. A flush of anger comes over me, and then I think of Siobhan. I wonder how life has been for her. Maybe I would do things differently if I were to do them over. I asked Bernadette to look after her, and that was about as much as I could do. Any more and I would have exposed myself. Anyway, she is not my daughter, and I can only think of Clare now.

The next time I hear from them is more than a year later, and it's to tell me that Uncle Patrick died in his sleep. No note, just the cutting of the obituary from the local paper. I don't even know who sent it. For days I am subdued. It's the not knowing. Not knowing if finally I am free, and my prison guard is dead, or if poor Uncle Patrick did nothing at all and I have spent all

162

these years hating him for nothing. Michael mistakes it for mourning. He says the next time we go home we should go to my part of the country as well, that it would do me good. I shake my head. I won't go back, I tell him. He sighs with frustration, not understanding, and I wonder if I never should have lied to him at all.

Michael works on the house and I work on Clare, and like that life edges by, sometimes fast, sometimes slow. She shrieks, she giggles, she says Mama and Dada, she walks and then she runs. She helps me with the washing, taking it out of the basket onto the floor, then back into the basket. She runs out into the garden, come rain or snow. Patting at the French windows with her little paws, putting streaks down them until I wrap her up in a coat and boots and scarf on top of her pyjamas. And off she goes, to explore the flowers and the earth and the worms and the snails.

One morning she takes a bite out of a worm and I nearly die with the shock. I scream at her and put my fingers in her mouth and fish out the end of the worm – I don't know if it's the head or the tail, who does? And I throw the rest of the body away and tell her never to do that again, do you hear? She cries and cries for the rest of the morning. I feel terrible. I explain that Mummy got a shock and that worms aren't for eating, and I say I'm sorry for giving her a fright.

Her eyes are wide and watery and she is unsure of me. For the first time I see how like me she is, with that look of hers, those big eyes and auburn curls on her small, intelligent head.

Soon she is at nursery in the mornings and I am missing her terribly, waiting till twelve o'clock when I can go and pick her up. Sometimes I watch her through the window, playing with other little girls and boys, and I wonder where the years have disappeared to.

Then, when Clare is three, we try for another and soon we are blessed again. I am delighted. I think of names for a girl and for a boy. I get out all of Clare's baby things and wash, iron and fold them and put them in the chest of drawers in the baby room. I grow bigger – bigger than last time. I fight the voice and the bad thoughts. Look at you, look at the size of you. A hippopotamus! How does he love you at all?

'Am I like a hippopotamus, Michael?' I ask him one evening, when Clare is in bed and we're watching television.

He wraps his arm round my shoulders, like I knew he would, and tells me that I'm the daftest, most beautiful hippopotamus he's ever seen.

I shrug off his arm.

'What? What did I say wrong?' His voice is desperate, and worry lines are creasing the skin around his eyes.

'This is no time for jokes.' I get up and go to bed.

When he has turned off all the lights and locked and chained the front door, he comes after me. He gets into bed and envelops me from behind, intertwines his feet with mine. They are cold and I move mine away.

'I'm sorry,' he whispers in my ear. He can't see the tear streaks over the bridge of my nose, down my cheek and into the pillow, but he knows me well enough by now.

I release a shaky sigh.

When my breathing has relaxed and the tears are dry, I reach back with my feet and find his, warmer now. I hide myself there, in the crescents of his insteps.

*

I send another photograph when Thomas is born. Thomas, the image of his daddy, with the same blue eyes and blondie hair. With his baby gurgles I had forgotten the sound of, and his cries, more ferocious than Clare's. Unlike Clare, he takes to the breast. Every time I feed him, I am vindicated. With the gentle tug of his suckle, all is right in the world.

Michael gets out the tripod and this time there are four of us on the sofa, and Clare squeals with the surprise of the flash and kisses Thomas on the forehead and holds onto his fists. Michael takes some of the three of us – myself, Clare and the baby – and then of Clare holding Thomas in her arms. I even get behind the camera and there they are, Thomas in Clare's arms on Michael's lap. Clare is a daddy's girl, that's for sure. She adores her daddy. That's what I say to people, laughing as if it didn't hurt me deeply, the fact that she prefers her father to me, with all that I do and give and love.

CLARE

23RD JULY 1997

Me and Thomas and Sarah and Mary get in with Mummy and Daddy. Uncle John and Aunty Joan take John and stop for Aunty Anne on the way. We're meeting at the beach, down by the chip shop. We have a picture of us there on the wall in the sitting room, and I make sure Daddy has his camera, so we can get another photo of us all this year and put it next to it.

I love it here. It's not like the beaches on the TV, it's not sandy and gold and soft. It has stones and pebbles that you have to walk on, and when you walk on them you say Ow-ow-ow! because you can't help it, it hurts so much. It smells of seaweed, which is so salty and horrible, but Daddy loves it and always takes bags of it home to London to eat long after we're back. Me and Mummy scrunch our noses up and she says it stinks the house out to the high heavens, so she makes him keep it out in the utility room, but Daddy and Thomas love it and eat it like it's chocolate. Sometimes Daddy brings some into the sitting room on a nice evening when we're all watching the TV together, and he and Thomas eat it like it's popcorn until Mummy has had enough.

The sun's out, but there's a nice soft wind and the smell of salt and water is refreshing. We have so much fun because everyone says Ow! over and over and we all laugh, which makes it hurt more. Mummy is laughing at the top of her voice and that makes me laugh so much that I wee myself a little bit, but it doesn't matter because we're going into the sea anyway.

When we are down in our spot where we come every year, over past the chip shop, we lay our towels out, one by one, next to each other's. Then it's time to change into our swimming costumes.

My tummy goes tight because I don't want everyone seeing my fanny. I should have changed in the house before we came, but Mummy said not to be silly, that it doesn't matter, but that's not what she told me before.

'Mummy!' I call. 'You hold the towel while I get changed.'

'Come on then, hurry up,' she says. She takes the towel and holds it round my shoulders.

'Promise you'll hold it?'

Mummy tuts. 'Stop dilly-dallying.'

I take off my top, doing my best to keep my shoulders in, so I don't poke open the towel.

Mummy passes me my bikini top and then turns round when Thomas calls her, and the towel falls down to my waist.

I squeal and grab it and hold it close to my chest. 'Mummy!' My face burns and my throat swells up. I look round. Sarah has taken all her clothes off and doesn't even care that I can see her, but she's skinny, so she doesn't have boobies that stick out a little bit like I do. Mary is too small to have boobies yet, so she doesn't care about anything, either, and she takes her knickers off right there and then before she puts on her swimming costume.

'Cop on now, Clare,' Mummy says. 'You don't have any-thing for anyone to see.'

I grip my lips tight together and look at her hard because I remember what she said to me, even if she doesn't. To not let men near me or see me, and that I was growing into a woman and had to protect myself and not reveal myself to anyone. That my parts were precious, and I had to make sure no one ever saw them. It was when I was getting out of the bath one afternoon and she stared at me and I felt weird, even though I never feel weird having a bath in front of Mummy, because we're all girls and we have the same thing, so what does it matter? Thomas has a winkie, but it doesn't matter because he's my brother, and Daddy has a winkie too, and that never mattered before. Until I heard Mummy tell him that he shouldn't be bathing me, that it wasn't appropriate, and he said, Don't be daft, and she said, I'll give you daft. I heard that from the top of the stairs and I wanted to shout down to Mummy that she was being a big stupid idiot, but I didn't. That made me mad because bath time is so much fun with Daddy, more fun than with Mummy, and what does it matter if he sees my bits, because he is my daddy. So when I was drying myself by the bath and Mummy was looking at me in a funny way, I said, What? and she said, Nothing. And afterwards she was all funny with me and spoke in her serious voice and told me I was a girl now, but I would be a woman before I knew it. She said it like it was a bad thing, and it made me scared and I decided then I didn't want to be a woman with precious parts that I couldn't let anyone see.

And now she lets the towel fall down, so everyone can see my boobies, and she says I have nothing and that I'm being stupid. For a second I feel like screaming at her, That isn't what you said before!, but I don't. I know that I don't have nothing to hide and that I have my boobies, and I don't want anyone to see them because she said I shouldn't.

I hate her a little bit when she lets my towel fall down, and decide that I won't trust her when I'm changing, after being in the sea.

The others arrive and we wait for John to change and then we race into the sea, even though the stones hurt. The water is so cold that my teeth chatter like a machine. Daddy says we have to swim to get warm and he picks me up and I scream, and he throws me down and I go under and the sea goes in my ears and up my nose and I gasp for air, but only get water. I wave my arms about like I'm a bird flying, until I'm up again and can get air. My eyes sting and snot comes out of my nose and, when I open my eyes, everyone laughs. I start splashing Daddy to get him back, but he's way too tall and he splashes me and I have to turn round and wade my way through the water to get away. We all try at the same time, but he picks us up one by one and throws us in the water and we all scream and yell and giggle. Daddy says we're water babies because we swim and jump and go under the water and don't care. Sarah teaches us how to do three somersaults in a row and we play a game where you have to swim under two people's hands under the water. Uncle John comes in with a ball and we play 'Piggy in the Middle'. Thomas and Mary are Piggy most of the time because they're smallest and always miss the ball.

Then Mummy and my aunties come in, but Mummy warns us all to stay away from her because she doesn't like the water very much. She slides in like a dolphin, without making a single splash, and lies on her back, floating in the sea. She never swims because she's scared of deep water.

I watch her lying on the silky surface and think I see her smile. The water around her sparkles in the sun, like it's winking a thousand times, and her hair spreads out like the bare branches of a tree. I wonder if she's remembering that time when I got out of the bath.

Thomas comes over. He wraps his arms round my neck and we float in the water, kicking our legs out like we're frogs.

'Hi, Thomas,' I say. We move around in circles.

'Hi, Clare,' he says. 'Can I jump off your knee?'

We hold hands and he steps up onto my legs and I'm kind of sitting down in the water. 'Ready, steady, go!' I bounce my legs each time and hold his hands, and then I kick my legs and fire him off like I'm a diving board, and he jumps through the air with his knees together into the water and makes a pretty good bomb-splash.

When the sun is behind the clouds and it's so cold that we're shivering again, we all get out. We can't run because the stones hurt so much, so we tiptoe over to our towels. Mummy pulls my hair back until it hurts, and squeezes it to get the water out, and then goes over to Thomas to help him dry himself. I go over to Daddy and he takes my towel off me and starts wiping me dry all over my back and my legs, and I stand hugging myself with my teeth chattering. Then I get my knickers and skirt and top and he puts the towel around my shoulders.

'No one will see anything, don't worry.' He winks.

I smile at him because I know I can trust him. I put my top and skirt down on the stones and get my knickers, and put them the right way round and put one foot in the hole and then the other and pull them up. They stick to my legs on the way up because my hair is dripping and making my skin wet again. Then I put on my top and pull up my skirt.

'Ready?' says Daddy.

'Ready,' I announce.

He lifts the towel up and scrunches my hair in it. He never hurts as much as Mummy. Sometimes it feels like she's going to rip my head off, she moves it about so much.

'Are ye ready?' shouts Uncle John.

'Ready for what?' Daddy asks.

'For sausage and chips!' Uncle John shouts.

'Yaaaay!' we all shout. I'm hungry and I love eating sausage and chips on the stony beach. I see a shell just by my flip-flop and I reach down and pick it up. I rub the sandy stuff off it and feel its ripples under my fingers. I put it in my pocket for the windowsill in my and Thomas's room.

All good things come to an end. That's what Mummy says. Why? Why do they have to come to an end? I ask her. Because they just do, she says. But I don't think that's fair. 'We could just live here,' I say to her.

'No, Clare,' she says. 'We've been through this before. We live in London.'

'But this is home!' I say. Because it's true. This is home.

'No,' she says, the way she does to say, You're getting on my nerves and be careful, because you'll get a clap around the back of the legs. 'London is our home.'

'But you always call here home. Always,' I say. 'Home home home. Here is home.' I know I'm being loud and everyone can hear downstairs but I don't care. 'I want to stay here with

Sooty and John and Sarah and Mary,' I tell her. I cross my arms and stick one leg out, bent at the knee, to show her I mean business.

'Enough of that, right now,' she says.

I hold my arms across my chest and stare up at her. Her lips are closed tight together, so tight they have gone white and she looks mad, but I don't care. She nearly died and my granny is dying, even though she thinks I don't know, and her family are a shower of cunts and I don't even want to go and stay with them at all, but now we have to. I just want to sit with Sooty and put my fingers through his warm, soft fluff, because I love him and I know he loves me and that makes me feel warm inside.

'Enough of that,' I say, putting on her accent. I know I'm pushing it.

She pinches me under the arm and twists my skin between her fingers until it hurts so much I cry out. I know it's going to go purple, and it's all her fault.

'When you have learned to behave, you can come downstairs,' she says in the voice that doesn't belong to her. It's the voice of the ugly monster that is horrible and nasty and hits you for no reason. She closes the door behind her.

I sneak downstairs. Everyone is in the back room. I tiptoe through the kitchen, out the door and round to the hayshed. I go in and there is Pretty Lady and all the fluff-balls. That's what we call them. Pretty Lady wags her tail when she sees me and it goes thump, thump, thump against the floor, and Sooty wags his tail in the air, too. It moves so quick it looks like the windscreen wipers on Daddy's car when it's pouring rain and they go wish-wash, wish-wash, so he can see.

I sit down and all the pups climb onto my lap and Pretty Lady licks my face. I hold Sooty against my chest and I cry into his fur. It's not fair.

The metal door opens and the hayshed lights up and I jump. There's nowhere to hide. I can't climb up the hay and there's nothing to hide behind.

Uncle John walks in. 'Well, well, well,' he says.

I sniffle and wipe my eyes with my free hand.

'Look what we have here.'

I cry more, because now I'm going to get in big trouble because I shouldn't even be in here, and Mummy is going to pull my knickers down and slap me on the bum over and over again.

He walks over to me and kneels down.

'Sorry, Uncle John,' I say, through the shakes in my chest.

'Oh, don't you worry, munchkin,' he says, reaching out and drying the tear on my cheek.

That makes me smile, and then I cry even more.

'Easy, easy,' he says, and he puts his arm round me and I lean into his chest, careful not to squish Sooty or his brothers and sisters.

'I don't want to go!' I cry. 'I want to stay here with you.'

'Well, unfortunately in this world we can't always get what we want,' he says.

'But why?' I ask him out loud. Why can't we stay here, where Mummy is happy and Daddy and me and Thomas can play all day and be with everyone we love. And with Sooty.

I sob into his shirt, which smells of hay and cows and a bit of poo. 'I can't leave Sooty.'

Sooty is as upset as me, and whines to show us. I lift him up and look into his big brown eyes; he licks my face.

'What will poor Sooty do without me?'

Uncle John rubs my shoulder and makes tutting noises, which are supposed to make me stop crying, but I can't. 'He'll survive.'

'And what about me?'

'You'll survive, too.'

'But I love him, Uncle John.'

'You love him, do you?'

I nod.

'Oh, Jesus,' he says, shaking his head.

'What's wrong?' I ask him.

'What am I going to say to your mother?'

'Please don't tell her you saw me.'

'Shush.' He rubs my cheeks and smooths my hair down. 'What am I going to tell your mother when I say I couldn't help myself – that Sooty would be lost without you, and he just has to go with you. Besides, I have more pups than I know what to do with.'

I gasp in all the air I can and turn and look at him. 'Really?'

He smiles down at me and nods.

'You'll convince her?'

'I'll do my best, darlin',' he says in an American accent.

I wrap my arms around his neck. 'Thank you, Uncle John, thank you, thank you, thank you,' I shriek.

'Oh, Jesus,' he says, smiling.

JOSEPHINE

Clare is doing her homework at the kitchen table and Thomas is drawing, pretending he has his own. He loves to copy his older sister. I'm making dinner. It's Friday night and the house is quiet, but for the steam screaming quietly out of the pressure cooker and the scribble of their pencils. I pour myself a glass of wine. There's no sign of Michael. He's usually home by now. I go into the back room and put on a record. The kids come in and we have a dance in front of the fireplace.

When the song ends, the two rascals throw themselves on the sofa, hot and breathless. I put on another record and get my wine and tell them they are allowed a glass of lemonade and a biscuit while we wait. I wonder where he is and what's keeping him. Hot anger begins to bubble.

Clare and Thomas run out to the kitchen and I hear the fizz of the lemonade hiss when the lid is turned and the crackle of it when it hits the glass, and the top of the biscuit pot being taken off and put on again. In they come, bounding with excitement and flushed in the cheeks. We get up and dance to the rest of the song, and with my free hand I twirl Thomas around, then Clare. I finish my wine and put the glass down, and twirl them both at the same time.

The dinner in the pot will be ruined. The vegetables over-done, the lamb hard as rubber. By God, he'll get it when he comes in.

The phone goes and Clare gets up and runs to get it, even though she's been told not to answer the phone.

I go out to the kitchen and push the button on the pressure cooker, then carry it to the sink and put it under cold water.

I can't hear what she's saying, but I can hear her chat away. She must be talking to a friend from school. I go to the door of the sitting room and listen. She's telling whoever it is how old she is, and how old Thomas is. My heart goes. It's someone from beyond. She turns to look at me and panic takes over and I wave my hands wildly for her to say I'm not home, I'm upstairs, she can't find me. 'No,' she says, 'she's doing her nails right now.'

I could kill the little madam. I get the bottle and my glass and run to snatch the phone off her. I tell Clare to take herself and her brother upstairs to play, and I take a deep breath and say in my telephone voice, 'Hello, who's that?'

There's a pause on the other end. I watch the children walk out, and gesture for Clare to close the door behind them.

'Hello, Josephine.' The voice is distant, Irish. 'It's your sister Siobhan here.'

If I was standing in front of a mirror I know my face would be white, gaunt, aged in an instant. 'Hello, Siobhan, how are you?' How simple it is to ask that, even though a lifetime has passed between us. The years weigh on me, now that I have her on the phone. Why didn't we do it before? Why haven't I picked up the phone once over the years? I wonder what kind of a woman she is. Then I wonder what kind of a woman I am.

'Grand, now. And yourself?'

I take a sip of wine. My hands are shaking. 'Great,' I say.

'I just spoke to your eldest one, Clare. She sounds like a lovely little girl.'

'She is, now, she is,' I say. 'Do you have any yourself?'

'I do, a little boy called Dermot. He's five.'

'Lovely. They're terrors, aren't they?' I laugh. I am filling in. Filling in for years gone by.

And how are you, Siobhan – I mean really? I'm sorry for leaving you, Siobhan, but things were so difficult for me. You see, what happened... something terrible happened... and I tried to tell Mammy but she forbade me from speaking of it again, and I never knew who it was... but I think it might have been Daddy. He didn't do anything to you, did he?

I've missed you, I have thought of you so many times over the years.

I asked Bernadette to watch out for you. Did she? I've stayed away because I was scared.

Of what?

Of being called a whore, of humiliation, of being ridiculed. It's easier to forget when there is distance.

I run through it all in my head, the words hopping off my lips. 'So... how's Bernadette?' I ask. The rest is locked in my throat.

I was raped, Siobhan.

I've never said those words before. I don't think I've even thought them.

'Oh, sure she went to Dublin and married. She has her mother heartbroken. Anyway,' Siobhan says, as if to say, Enough of this small talk. 'The reason I'm calling is because

Mammy is sick.' She takes a deep breath. I take a gulp of wine. 'She's dying, Josephine, and she wants to see you.'

The news winds me, the way Thomas is winded when Clare is running after him and he falls on his chest and can't breathe and the tears stream from his stunned eyes. I clear my throat. Take a sip of wine. 'I see.' I am sitting on the chair, but I would like to get down on the carpeted floor and lean back against the hard, cold wall. The life I have worked so hard to build is drained out of me in seconds, as if through a drip that's taking instead of giving. I picture my mother on her deathbed; me, a little girl, giving her tea from the cup. Sean, a baby, in the basket. 'Good girl,' she says, her voice thin and raspy. 'What's wrong with her?' I ask.

'Her kidneys are failing, she has pneumonia. She has been unwell for some time.'

'I didn't know.'

'No, you wouldn't, would you?' A rhetorical question. I can't work out if she's being sarcastic, or simply honest.

'I'll see what I can do,' I say. 'The holidays are coming up...'

'All right, so. Do you want my number?'

I tell her I'll get a pen and paper. My mind is blank and I can't think where they'll be. I get a piece of paper from the kitchen table and one of the colouring pencils that Thomas was drawing with. I note it down.

'Take care, now, bye.' She puts the phone down first and I sit for a couple of minutes, listening to the dead tone. I won't go. I shake my head. I said I'd never go back.

The doorknob turns and the children start to come in, but I shout at them that I'm still on the phone. I just need a minute, that's all. I turn the stem of the wine glass between shaky fingers. My head is reeling. I put on a record and whack up the volume to drown out my thoughts. I sing along to the tune, swaying my arms in the air. Then I open the door and the two of them are sitting at the kitchen table, drawing. Such good children, both of them. I kiss each of them on the head, and that's when I hear the tap running on the pressure cooker. 'Clare, didn't it occur to you to turn the tap off?' I shout. I can't help it. I go and turn it off and put the pot back on the hob. It'll be like vomit. And still no sign of Michael.

The music booms out and I tell the children to pack up their things, that we're going to treat ourselves to a takeaway.

They jump up and down and run to me in the middle of the kitchen and wrap their arms around my waist.

I bend down and look into their beautiful, big, innocent eyes. 'Sorry for shouting,' I tell them. 'Mummy was stressed.'

Just then there's the sound of the key in the door and it slamming shut.

Off they run, full-speed. Daddy, Daddy, Daddy! They shout and squeal and jump up and down, clapping their hands.

I watch, still bending down in the middle of the kitchen floor, as Michael scoops them up into his arms and kisses them until they giggle.

My cheeks tingle with humiliation. Ungrateful little bastards.

Everything is undone. I am undone.

I won't go, I won't go. I say it to myself over and over again, making myself believe it. I am at war with myself. I am bloodied, broken, my limbs are twisted. But something in me knows I will go.

I make the arrangements, go shopping for clothes and presents. But it's as if I am looking on from the outside, watching myself do it all. My head hurts. Clare and Thomas scream and squeal and thump about upstairs. They have my nerves hanging out of my sleeves. Worn bare. They have no idea how lucky they are. Running wild in the house, with all the toys they could wish for.

Silence! I shout. It's all I can do not to tear myself up into shreds.

I wake them up in the morning; get them washed and dressed. Take them to school. Go shopping. Do the washing. Hang the clothes out. Pick them up. Sit them down, for Clare to do her homework. Make the dinner. A zombie; a zombie servant. Slaving all day after them, my life spent on them, only for them to go running to their father. Is this what I have become? A zombie servant at war with herself, counting down the days before she meets her maker?

Brandy helps. Michael, with his incessant questions, doesn't. *Talk to me, Josephine. What's wrong, Josephine? What's wrong with you? For God's sake, woman.* He doesn't understand. How could he? On top of everything, I've lied to him. He wouldn't believe another word I said, if I were to tell him the truth. Anyway, he's growing tired of me, I can tell. Losing energy, and patience. He told me. Working, working. Working for the family, the breadwinner. How nice to have a title calling you the winner. Wouldn't I like to be the winner? All I won was a bloated body with a wardrobe full of dresses it can't fit into, and two screaming demons that suck the life out of me – just like everyone has always sucked the life out of me.

I sit at the kitchen table and sip my brandy. I sneak upstairs into the children's room and wake Clare. She is sleepy and warm and when I ask if she'd like a hot chocolate, she says yes. I knew she would. I carry her downstairs and sit her down and make her hot chocolate with milk and stir it until it's high with froth, the way she likes it.

'You're so lucky, Clare,' I tell her.

'I know, Mummy,' she says, sipping her chocolate, with her feet tucked up under her bottom.

I tell her stories – stories to show her how lucky she is. How I would have loved to have everything she has, everything I have given her.

On one of the last Saturdays before we're due to go, we shop for clothes and go out for dinner, the four of us. I go along with it for appearance's sake. Appearances for Michael, appearances for the children. Hunky-dory. Tickety-boo. When we get home I put on music. That way, we keep the party going and we keep drinking and I can hide from myself. I'm drunk and Michael's spinning me round and we're spinning, spinning. I'm spinning through the years and through the prayers and through the sins and through the pain.

Clare has been scratching her head all night and I can't stand to look at her for one more second. She's like a mangy dog. 'They're back again,' I tell Michael.

'What do you mean?' he says; not a clue, as usual.

'You know what I mean,' I tell him, sick of telling him everything. 'Riddled – riddled, she is. Her head's crawling with them. How are we going to take her to meet my mother and father like this?'

'Calm down,' he says.

'I will not calm down,' I scream at him. I can't help it. I can't help myself. I've been holding it all in for so long. Can't anybody see anything? I scream. I don't know whether I'm screaming it out loud or in my head, but I'm screaming.

CLARE

26TH JULY 1997

I snuggle up under the duvet and watch the green fields fly by. I look over at Thomas. He's fast asleep, his head on his teddy as a pillow. Sooty is on my lap, on top of the duvet. He's still a baby, so he sleeps all the time and my lap is the perfect place for him, all comfy and warm.

The colours of the fields change and I watch them and wonder what Mummy's family will be like. I hope I like them, and that they like me and Thomas and Sooty.

I watch Mummy and Daddy's heads and feel my eyes closing. Mummy says sleep is the best thing because it stops me feeling sick. She turns to check up on Thomas and then me and looks down at Sooty and tuts, but it's one of those tuts that isn't very serious.

I smile, and hug Sooty close to me. I still can't believe he's mine.

I start to drift off, all warm and snuggly with Sooty in my arms, and think about what I know about my kind-of-new granny and granddad. Mummy has told me stories about them when we were on our own, and Daddy was working late and Thomas was in bed. She tells me things she shouldn't tell me. The next morning, when her eyelids are black from make-up and she is in her dressing gown and says she has a head on her like a bull, she tells me not to mention any of it to anyone and to forget all about it, so I know that she has trusted me with secrets she hasn't told anyone else, not Thomas, not even Daddy. That's why I am extra-special and need to look after Mummy like she's famous and I'm her bodyguard. Because even though she looks like a film star, sometimes all she wants is for me to hug her and rub her hair while she cries into my chest.

Once, when Thomas was in bed with a temperature, we sat at the kitchen table and Mummy drank her brandy and I ate chocolate biscuits.

She told me that when she was my age she thought babies came from behind cabbages. The room was filled with smoke, because it was one of those moments when she needs a cigarette, so she gets one from the box in the cupboard that she keeps for emergencies. Whenever she gets one, Mummy always tells me that she gave up smoking for me, and that's why she has all these size-ten dresses in the wardrobe that she can't get into.

She said she would look behind all the cabbages in the field in case there were babies there. I started imagining the fields, because I've never seen them, and I imagined lines and lines of cabbages going on for ever and ever, and Mummy pulling back the green leaves to find babies.

Then she told me about the day she found out that babies didn't come from behind cabbages.

She walked into her parents' bedroom and my granny was lying in her nightie on her bed, and her nightie was wet, red with blood. I asked how much blood and she said the whole thing was soaking wet and covered, as if it had been dipped in bright-red paint. I shivered then. Why was there so much blood? I asked, but Mummy carried on. She never answers questions she's not ready to answer. You always have to wait until she has said what she wanted to say and gets there eventually.

Mummy and her sister took my granny to the bathroom. So that's her sister, I think, with my eyes closed and my hands cupped around Sooty. Her name is Siobhan. She's younger, I remember that from the story. And I remember her eyes were like two piss-holes in the snow, which means they were small and dark, like when someone has weed in the snow. I don't really know what that looks like.

Why didn't Granddad help? I asked. Because that's women's business, Mummy said, explaining that her dad and brothers, Brendan and Sean, were all in bed and it was up to her and her sister to help their mum.

In the bathroom, Siobhan lifted my granny's nightie over her head and Mummy got a terrible shock because Granny's boobies were big and black and blue with bruises. She started squeezing her boobies. Why did she do that? I asked. Mummy took a gulp of her brandy and I heard when she swallowed, because there was so much. I thought, That's naughty, because we're not allowed to make noise when we swallow. She smoked her cigarette and the grey smoke shot out of her nose and into my face. She was squeezing the milk out, she said, watching me, waiting for me to say something even though I didn't know what I should say.

She told me her mum had lost a baby. I still didn't understand. But where do babies come from? I asked.

She smoked her cigarette and pushed the yellow bit into

the bottom of the ashtray on the table, wiggling it around, and then she pointed downwards at me. I looked down. She was pointing in between my legs. I looked down and then up at her. From your special part, she said.

While I wondered exactly how that worked, I ate the last of the chocolate biscuits.

Mummy carried on talking. She said that babies who died were buried next to the graveyard, on the other side of the wall. Her eyes got all watery and her nose got snotty.

'The little dead babies in limbo,' she said.

I wondered what limbo was, and if it was nice.

Then she started sounding like she was giving a speech in Mass, like Feathers does. The tiny little babies, she said, denied into heaven, denied the vision of God and the purifying of their soul and left in no-man's-land. Left in the abandoned patch across the road from the graveyard. She wondered if they were any better off for being near the church, or if wild dogs would have found them. She ran her hands through her hair, so it went big and messy, and her eye make-up smudged over her cheeks, and she cried into her hands.

'My baby,' she said. 'One day soon your body will be ready to have a baby.' She smoked her cigarette; took a drink of brandy. 'If you feel uncomfortable with a boy or a man at any time, scream and run. And kick them in the balls.' She was angry, now. 'You have to protect yourself.'

'Which men?' I sniffed.

'Any men,' she spat. 'They're all as bad as each other, all capable.'

'Not Daddy.'

She threw her head back and laughed then, and I didn't understand what was funny.

*

I put the duvet between my head and the window and lean against it, so I can't feel the bumps on the road. I put my hands through Sooty's fluffy warmth and close my eyes, but all I can see are Sooty's brothers and sisters. They're dead and floating on a river of tar, the black liquid Daddy uses to repair roads. That might be what limbo is like.

'There it is,' says Mummy.

The house is huge. I can see it over the hedges far away. It stands tall like a palace, with a triangular roof like the big Toblerones we get on the way home in the shop on the boat. Daddy always gets one to cheer us up when we have the post-holiday bluesy-twos. Mummy tells Daddy to pull in on the side of the road. There's a bump when we go up on the grass. Mummy lowers the thing that keeps the sun out of your eyes and looks in the small square mirror on the inside. She gets her bag from her feet and takes out her make-up bag. Me and Thomas stand up and hold onto the heads of the seats to watch. A car swishes past and Mummy turns to the side and hides her face behind her bag.

'Why did you do that?' Daddy asks.

'I don't want them to see us sitting outside the house!' Mummy laughs, but I can tell she's pretending. 'We should have stopped somewhere on the way to get ready.'

I hold onto Daddy's neck.

'Let's go!' shouts Thomas.

'Shut up, Thomas,' I tell him. I don't want to go in. I don't think any of us should go.

'Clare,' Mummy says. 'Don't speak to your brother like that.' She turns to Thomas. 'Two minutes, darling.' Her voice is high and happy, but thin like the ice that can break and little children slip through and never come out of again.

There's a pond in our park – it's not our park but the one near our house – and when it freezes over Daddy always says it's so dangerous we can never go anywhere near it, do you understand? Yes, Daddy, we say together, to keep him happy. I'm sure I could pull Thomas out if he fell in, but he wouldn't be able to pull me out and I wouldn't like to slide under the ice and never come up again.

Mummy pushes ruby-red lipstick onto her lips.

'Can I put some on?' I ask. I'm scared, too, and I want to paint my face.

'No, you cannot,' she says, looking at me in the little mirror, snapping the lipstick closed and rubbing her lips together.

'Oooooooh,' I moan, and I pick Sooty up, who has been sleeping quietly on the seat beside me. I put him to my face. 'She won't let me put lipstick on,' I whisper into his ear.

'Don't be silly,' she says, and puts shadow on her eyes. 'You don't need any.'

When she has finished, she closes the make-up bag and places it in her handbag and puts that on the floor and turns round. 'Now. The two of you are to be good, do you hear? No fighting, no screaming, no noise. Neither of you are to get in the way of your grandmother and grandfather.'

'Yes, Mummy,' we say, stroking Sooty.

Daddy laughs the way he did when Uncle John told him he'd asked me to take Sooty off his hands as he had too many puppies and Mummy jumped up and said, No way! And Daddy said, Come on, Josephine; and Mummy said, Why do I always have to be the bad guy?

He reaches over to put his hand on Mummy's leg, just like he put his arm round her shoulders before. 'Come on,' he says, 'we'll have a great time.'

Mummy smiles at him and nods, then looks back at us and smiles. But there's something in her eyes that makes me scared, the way she looks at me as if she's going to say something, but doesn't.

Uh-oh, I think. Something smells fishy. Not because I can smell fish, because there's no fish in the car, and Daddy always washes the car so it is lovely and sparkling clean, but because that's what Daddy says when something is weird. Then when something bad happens he says, I knew there was something fishy going on. Or if it's really bad, I can smell a rat.

'Ready?' Daddy asks, slapping Mummy's leg gently.

'Ready!' Thomas shouts.

'Ready! Let's go,' Mummy says.

Daddy turns and looks at me.

'Ready!' I say. My voice comes out high and thin. I rub Sooty under his ears.

Daddy starts the engine, pulls out onto the road and drives until we get to a gate and he turns in there.

The stones swish like the sea when Daddy rolls on them, and I remember the beach and Sarah and Mary and John. I have my shell in my pocket and I put my hand inside to check it's still there. It is.

We stop outside the front door and I get out and then get Sooty. Thomas climbs out and I close the door.

'The dog stays here, Clare,' Mummy says.

'Mummy!' I cry. 'I can't leave Sooty, how will he sleep without me? He'll be all on his own.'

'Clare,' she says, in her I'm-not-messing voice.

'Come on, honey.' Daddy opens the door and puts Sooty inside.

I cross my arms across my chest and close my mouth as tight as I can, to show them both how extremely unhappy I am. I decide not to talk to them for one hour.

Mummy goes to the door and rings the doorbell. We stand behind her. Thomas stays close to me, but I push him away because I am not in the mood.

The door opens and a big, tall, old man appears and smiles a big smile. 'Well, hello there – look who it is,' he says, looking at all of us.

When he looks at me I smile a bit, even though I am not one bit happy.

Mummy steps forward and they hug and then he shakes hands with Daddy and says, 'Micky, so good to see you, how are you?' And then he stands and puts his hands on his knees and leans over and I think he might fall, he is so wobbly. 'And who have we got here?' he says.

I know this means I am now supposed to introduce myself. 'Clare,' I say, looking down at the ground.

'Who?' he says.

'Clare,' I say again.

'I can't hear you!' he shouts, which makes me and Thomas giggle. Thomas hides behind Daddy's legs.

'Clare!' I shout back.

'Hello, Clare,' he says.

'Hello,' I say, because Mummy has always said that when someone says hello, you should say hello back.

He turns to Thomas. 'And who else do we have?'

But Thomas just hides behind Daddy's legs because he has gone shy and doesn't know he should play the game. 'That's

Thomas,' I say, pointing over at him.

'Who?' he shouts, holding his hand up to his ear.

'Thomas!' I shout louder.

He laughs, and his eyes light up and his shoulders shake and then he coughs. Mummy and Daddy laugh, too.

I can't believe how old my granddad is. And he's really fat.

'Would you like to meet my dog, Sooty?' I ask.

'Well, of course I would.' He steps down from the big step outside the house and comes over to the car, and I point through the window at Sooty, who has his paws up against the window and his tail wagging really quickly.

'Oh, isn't he lovely,' he says. 'Sure, why don't you bring him in?'

'Can I?' I ask.

'Of course you can,' he says.

I shriek and open the car and pick Sooty up, and Granddad pushes the door closed again.

We all walk into the house and I just can't believe I have never met my lovely granddad before today.

JOSEPHINE

26TH JULY 1997

I go through the motions, but in my mind I am playing out sequences of how it will be, how it will go. Finally, our days with Michael's family come to an end. It is time to get in the car and drive across Ireland. The ground, the trees, the sky are soaked after the rain. Shells of houses lie broken in the middle of fields, left to crumble. A single corner attempts to stand, a reminder of what was once there. I am like those jagged brick stumps. A part of me is trying to stay alive when the rest of me is dead.

Villages, towns, those corners of houses grow familiar. Finally I am near to being put out of my misery.

The dog whimpers. I had forgotten all about it. A mongrel Clare picked up on the way. What lunacy! We all know who is going to be cleaning up its mess, letting it out in the morning and walking it twice a day. But what could I do, there in front of everyone, with them all in cahoots for us to take the damned dog? I was forced into a corner. They say you should never force a rat into a corner, because it will bite.

Shut that thing up, I want to shout. But I bite it back. I wind down the window and the wet wind hits my face in bursts that force my eyes shut. After all these years, I smell home. My clothes are soaked with the strong sweat of fear.

It's all smiles and how-do-you-dos. It's like a dream. I tremble my way through it. My father is smaller than I remember. Michael is taller than him. Who would have known?

'Josephine.' He opens his arms wide.

I turn to Michael, the children, wondering what to do, wishing someone would tell me, help me. They smile back at me.

There's nothing else for it. I go to him. 'Hello,' I say, as he plants kisses on my cheeks and hugs me. His kisses are like glass paper across my skin. His arms, like tentacles pulling me underwater. I fight the urge to be sick.

'Daddy, this is my husband Michael, my daughter Clare and my son Thomas.' I watch him shake Michael's hand, clap him on the back, bend down to the children. *Get away from them! Don't touch them, you monster!* But I don't say a word. I watch, mute, as he manipulates my family – my family who I have kept safe and far from here, until now.

He is full of loud, low-belly laughter. There are no signs of the tyrant I grew up with.

When I demand the dog stays in the car so as not to make him angry, he sweeps out, all arms and chest and belly, and says he wouldn't hear of it. Out comes the dog. Clare flocks to him. The dog flocks to him. The sun breaks out from behind the charcoal clouds, the dog yaps playfully. I am in a nightmare that will never end. Sweet Jesus, will it never end?

In her room, as I had pictured, is my mother. Lying up against the headboard, with machines going in or coming out of her, I'm not sure which.

195

I go to her, sit on the edge of the bed, hold her hand. Seeing her like this makes me forget. 'Hello, Mammy.' It's my voice but it's not.

'Hello, Josephine.' There is no smile. Just an older version of the woman I remember as my mother. A thinner, meaner-looking version of Granny. The cheekbones are there, the hair. But the eyes are not kind and sparkling, and the lips are a gripped line of bitterness.

I bring the children in and she looks at them. I tell them to go and give her a kiss; they do. She touches their small hands.

'Off you go now,' I tell them. 'Be quiet and keep out of your grandfather's way. Play outside with the dog.'

'Sooty!' Clare corrects me.

'Play outside with Sooty.'

They run outside. The door stands gaping open after them.

Had I expected tears? Love? Everything to be different, after all these years? I don't know. I don't have any of the answers.

Siobhan comes to visit. She doesn't bring her son and she doesn't look me in the eye. She talks to Michael and the children, but with me she is shy, she makes sure to stay away, and when I try to talk to her alone in the kitchen she finds an excuse to leave. She is a stranger. I wouldn't know her on the street, neither in London, nor here. Sean comes, too, another stranger. A grown man with a beard, no longer the little boy I knew so well and cared for as if he were my own. He is pleasant, making jokes and getting everyone laughing. It's as if we're all playing roles in a film, playing it out until the end. Brendan is spared the charade; he is making it big in America. America. Now that's far away.

*

I ask where Granny's grave is and they tell me it's on the far side of the graveyard, up the hill. We walk through the moss and the stones, careful not to step on the dipping graves that could collapse at any minute.

I tell the children to say sorry to the dead for stepping by their graves, so all the way through the graveyard all I hear is, 'Sorry, sorry.' Michael is at it, too, and I wish we were somewhere else, somewhere far away from here. Maybe then I would say sorry with every step I took and laugh at us all, acting the eejit.

Clare and Thomas lay flowers at Granny's grave, and I pull out the weeds that have grown around the headstone.

'What was she like?' asks Thomas, his eyes scrunched up, the way they do when he's being inquisitive and thoughtful.

'She was a lovely lady,' I say. 'She was like a mother to me.'

'But you already have a mum,' says Clare. Such an observant child.

'She was more of a mum than my own,' I say, gazing at the headstone, tears filling my eyes. 'But don't tell her that.'

'Shall we head off?' says Michael. Always on hand to calm the storm, even before the storm has hit.

I clean my mother, I clean the house, change the sheets, dust, mop. I count the minutes until we are free of this place and curse myself for ever coming back. It's beyond me why she asked to see me. Maybe Siobhan was lying, just to get me to look after her for a few days. It looks like no one has been here to do any housework in a while. I do not talk to my father. I tell the children to stay outside.

My father has Michael wrapped around his little finger. 'What's your poison?' Drinking partners. He's an entertainer, all right. Great craic, altogether.

Everyone comes round for a night of drinking and it's all wonderful. The games, the games. With their smiles and their hugs and their laughing and their jokes, and it's lovely to see you, and it's lovely to meet you. And, Josephine, why didn't you bring him over to us before? What a lovely man. Didn't you do well? When they don't call or write, and take my money without a word of thanks, year in, year out.

I smile and nod, the tick-tock, tick-tock going in my head.

CLARE

26TH JULY 1997

Mummy goes in after Granddad. I tiptoe behind Daddy, and Thomas follows me. There's a mirror on the wall beside the door and I try to look in it when I go past, but it's too high so I can't see myself, only the wall on the other side. We pass a door that's a little bit open and I can see the nice fluffy chair and I know that's the good room where guests go, but we don't go in there. Me and Thomas will have to sneak in later. We have plenty of time anyway, because we're staying here for three whole days.

We go into the kitchen and sit down. Mummy tuts at me when I sit at the table with Sooty and I don't know what to do. I put him on my lap, so no one can see him, and hope Mummy forgets about him and doesn't make me put him outside.

'Tea?' asks Granddad.

'That would be great,' says Daddy in a happy voice, rubbing his hands together. He puts his arm across the back of my chair and stretches.

'It's a long drive, isn't it?' says Granddad. His voice is so big it fills the room, it's much louder than Daddy's. He is funny even to look at. He has loads of black and white hair that sticks up, and his cheeks are big and round. I bet when he was a baby all the women pinched them. He doesn't look anything like Mummy. She has lovely big eyes, but his are small and funny-looking. She doesn't have fat cheeks, either. And he's fat and she's slim. And he's tall and she's short.

'It is indeed,' says Daddy.

'Tea would be lovely,' says Mummy. 'Do you need any help?' She goes to stand up and stops halfway, like she doesn't know what to do.

'Not at all. Sit down and make yerselves comfortable. And what will the two little ones be having?'

'Squash!' shouts Thomas.

'Shhh,' Mummy says. 'Quieten down, like a good boy.'

'Not a bother on you,' says Granddad. He turns to Thomas. 'There's no squash, now. A nice glass of cold milk?'

Thomas scrunches up his face and his nose goes all wrinkly, like he's an old man. I laugh, but Mummy shoots me an evil look and I stop.

'That would be lovely, thank you,' I say in my good-girl voice.

Granddad nods and says, 'Two glasses of cold milk coming up.'

We never have milk at home and I don't want any, either, but I'd better be a good girl or Mummy will give me a slap across the legs when we're alone. I can tell by her face. It's so straight and her lips are so thin when she smiles that she looks fuming, which is even angrier than angry.

I turn to Granddad. 'Are you Mummy's daddy?'

'Clare!' Mummy says in her warning voice.

I huff and rub Sooty, who is being a good little boy on my lap. I can't say anything.

Granddad laughs and his belly moves up and down, up and down, and then he coughs into a white square hankie that he pulls out of his pocket. He wipes his mouth and nose and I scrunch my nose up, but then un-scrunch it when I remember that I have to be a good girl or else there will be consequences.

'I am indeed.' He smiles when he has put the white square into his pocket again. 'I'm her daddy, which makes me your granddaddy!' He comes over with two glasses of milk and puts them on the table, one in front of me and one in front of Thomas. He ruffles my hair and it falls all over my face and that makes me laugh. 'You're the spitting image of your mother, so you are,' he says to me.

I smile up at him and Mummy laughs, ha-ha-ha, out loud. 'Really?' she says. 'Would you say? Everyone says she looks like Michael.'

I shake my head. 'No, they all say I look just like you.' Everyone always says I look like Mummy. Even she says it. I take a sip of milk. It's cold and it tastes good. I gulp it down because I'm thirsty.

Thomas copies me, like he always does, and gulps it down, too. Then he puts the glass down on the table and I burst out laughing because he's got a milk moustache all over his top lip, almost up to his nose. He laughs, too, and starts pointing at me and I point at him and we laugh out loud.

'That's enough out of you two,' Mummy says. 'Clean yerselves up, please.'

I wipe my mouth with the back of my hand and so does Thomas. We look across the table at each other and keep laughing, but silent laughing. I can see his chest going up and down and that makes me laugh even more and I think, Oh no,

I've got the giggles, and I try to hold them in and then a big snort comes out like a pig is in the room, but it's me and that just makes me and Thomas laugh even more.

'Clare and Thomas, that is enough, right now,' Mummy says in her I-mean-it voice.

'Come on, now,' Daddy says.

'Ah sure, leave them,' Granddad says, chuckling. 'They're fine.' He brings over two cups of tea for Mummy and Daddy, and another one for him, and sits at the end of the table, which is between me and Thomas. 'Ah, I forgot the sugar,' he says and starts to heave himself up, with his hands holding on to the table.

'I'll get it,' Mummy says, and she goes over to cupboards and starts opening them up. She opens one after the other and giggles and then turns round. She is a bit pink and bites her lip, like I do when I'm embarrassed. 'Sure, I don't know where it is,' she says.

'It's in that one, there.' Granddad points at the one she hasn't opened.

'Typical,' she says, smiling. But it's one of those tight smiles that make her lips go white. It reminds me of when she was on the phone to Aunty Maura, saying, We'd have to see the lot of them. I wonder now who 'they' are. They can't be Granddad, because he's a ball of laughing and coughing with his sticky-up hair that waves from side to side when he coughs.

'When was the last time you were home?' asks Granddad.

Mummy takes out the sugar and brings it over to the table.

Granddad takes some and she stands waiting until he's finished: one spoon, two spoons, three spoons.

'Three spoons of sugar!' I say. 'That's sooooo much.

Mummy never lets Daddy have three. He's only allowed one and a half.'

'I'm sure she's right, too,' nods Granddad, then he leans towards me and says in a quiet, hush-hush voice, 'Your granny doesn't let me have any, either, but what she doesn't know won't hurt her.' He winks and when he does, he moves his whole face to the side. I will have to learn that, I think to myself. That reminds me. Where is Granny? I want to ask but I don't dare.

'It's been a few years now, sure it has,' Daddy says. 'Time flies when you're having fun, isn't that what they say?'

'It certainly does, and they certainly do,' Granddad says.

The way he talks is funny. I like it.

Mummy drinks her tea.

'So ye liked the milk in the end, did ye?' Granddad says, looking from me to Thomas.

We both nod. Sooty squeals and is turning round in circles on my lap. I go red. Mummy won't forget about him if he makes noise like this. He already weed a bit in the car, but Mummy doesn't know yet and I hope she doesn't notice. He wants to get off my lap, but I can't let him because he'll run around and Mummy will go fuming.

'What's the little man's name?' asks Granddad.

'Sooty,' says Thomas.

'Ah, Sooty. Will we give him some milk, will we?'

I nod.

Granddad puts his hands on the table and heaves himself up like he's moving a mountain. He goes over to the cupboards and gets a bowl out, and then gets milk from the fridge and pours milk into the bowl. He carries the bowl of milk past the table and over to the back door, which is closed and isn't the door we came through, and leans down to put it on the floor but he gets halfway and can't go any lower.

'Here, let me,' says Daddy, getting up and taking the bowl off him to put it on the floor. Then he beckons me over with a nod of his head.

I get up and carry Sooty over and put him down. I can feel Mummy's eyes on me. Thomas comes over, too. We all stand and watch Sooty. He turns round and starts sniffing Granddad's slippers and then Daddy's shoes, and then wanders over to the table where Mummy is sitting.

'Sooty!' I call him, but he doesn't hear me because he carries on under the table. 'Naughty boy. Sooty!' I go over and crawl under the table and carry him out and take him over to the bowl and dip his nose into the milk. He licks his lips. I push his face towards the bowl. 'Come on, Sooty.' But he turns round. Thomas crouches down and watches, and Mummy and Granddad are still watching. I push his nose into the milk again and he licks his lips, so I push his nose in again. I decide that's what I'll do because it's the only way to make him drink, and all babies need their milk.

'Would ye look at that,' Granddad says and Mummy laughs a little laugh. 'I'd go back to that age in a second, so I would.'

'No worries, no hassle, no nothing,' Daddy says.

Granddad goes back over to the table and Mummy sits still, her arms folded, looking down at us and watching me and Thomas take turns in dipping Sooty's nose into the milk.

After a while she tells us to go outside and play.

Granddad opens the back door and we take Sooty out and they close the door again, which means they want to talk in private. Closed doors always mean talk in private, and mind your own beeswax. I know what they're talking about anyway, so I don't mind. And it's better to be outside because it's boring inside. The only thing is I want to go for a snoop around the house, but we can't do that because we have to go through the kitchen and then they'll see us. We'll have to wait until we need the toilet. That won't be long anyway, because Thomas always needs to wee right after having a drink. Mummy says it goes straight through him.

We play with Sooty in the big garden around the back of the house. It's a huge garden, much bigger than ours, and there are no flowers so we can run anywhere we want. A hedge borders it along the end, and the first thing Sooty does is run to the hedge and try to eat the twigs. Then he does a wee and a poo, and I'm so happy he waited until we got outside. I don't know what to do about the poo, but don't want to disturb their private conversations, so I move it to the corner with a twig and forget about it.

We run around and Sooty follows us and then, when we get tired of that, we play Hide-and-seek. We go through the gate and walk around the house until we choose a spot for Thomas to count. He faces the wall and covers his eyes with his hands and counts to ten. I pick Sooty up, so he won't give me away, run through the gate to hide behind the corner and watch Thomas. He takes his hands off his eyes and turns round and looks my way and then the other way, but he doesn't see me, and Sooty is being super-quiet. He's tired after running around. He's still a baby, so he gets tired really easily.

Just when I think Thomas is going to come towards me, he turns and walks the other way. When he turns the corner, I run as quiet as I can, holding Sooty close to my chest like I'm his mummy and he's my baby, and I go back through the gate, past the back door and over to the next corner and peep round the edge and see Thomas walking along. When he goes round the next corner, I peep around the corner I'm at. It's the front of the house where Daddy's car is parked, and there Thomas is, walking round the car and looking underneath and I have to put my hand over my mouth or I'll laugh out loud.

He walks around the front garden all the way over to the big gate we drove through when we first arrived, and I think he's going to see me, so I have to run back a bit. I hide in the shade of the house as close as I can to the wall, and stand still like we're playing Freeze. I hold Sooty in my arms nice and tight. I think he's asleep.

That's when I hear voices and I think the grown-ups are coming from around the back of the house and they're going to ruin our whole game and Thomas will discover me, but I turn and no one comes. I look up and I can see a window, but even on my tiptoes I can't see into it. I listen and I can hear Mummy's voice speaking softly. Then there's silence and then there's another voice. It's soft like a murmur. I'm sure they are saying words, but I can't tell what they are. I stay still and listen. That's Mummy. Then there's the other voice. It's a woman, and it sounds like she's whispering. I listen as hard as I can. She sounds a bit like Mummy but smaller. And then I understand. It's Granny. So that's where she is. I smile. I'm glad Mummy is seeing her. I imagine they're hugging really tight.

I remember the time I heard Mummy talking to Aunty Maura, and I hope Granny isn't too ill because I won't know what to do – not like Mummy knew what to do when she was little. I wonder when we'll meet her. I wonder what she looks like. I wonder if she'll be as nice as Granddad. I wonder, I wonder, I wonder.

I remember I'm supposed to be hiding from Thomas. I tiptoe over to the corner, where I saw him go over to the front gate. I can't see him. I run along the front of the house, past the pebble drive and the front door and the flowerpots on either side of it, and I look round the next corner. He's not there.

'Found you!' shouts Thomas from behind me.

I jump and Sooty squeals.

'Ha-ha-ha-ha,' he laughs. 'Scaredy-cat, scaredy-cat.' He comes over and rubs Sooty. 'Can I have him now?' he asks. 'And will you look for me now?'

I give Sooty to him, because Mummy says we're brother and sister and we have to share. 'Be careful to hold him tight,' I say. He is big in Thomas's small arms and I'm scared he'll wriggle and fall.

Thomas wraps his arms tight around Sooty and starts walking away from me.

I turn to face the wall and fold my arms and put them round my face. I start counting. 'One, two, three, four, five, six, seven, eight, nine...' I pause and then shout, 'Ten!' I take my arms down and turn around and look left and right. No Thomas or Sooty. I set out to find them.

CLARE

'Clare and Thomas, can you come here, please?' I hear Mummy call in her I'm-not-messing-you're-in-big-trouble voice. I don't know why she's using that tone, we've done nothing wrong.

'Come on, Thomas,' I call, and he appears from around the corner and we start walking towards the house.

Mummy is at the back door. She closes it and steps down onto the grass. 'Right, I'm going to bring you in to meet my mother now. She's not feeling too well, so be nice and quiet, okay?' Her voice is soft and her face is white and sweaty. She's not having as much fun as we are. It must be true, then. Her mum really is dying. I hold Sooty close and rub him under the ear; he leans his nose in close to my chest.

'Are you okay, Mummy?' I ask. I don't think she is. I don't think she's been okay for a while.

'Of course I am, munchkin,' she smiles, and taps my chin playfully. She hasn't called me munchkin for ages. I smile.

'I need to go to the toilet,' Thomas says in his whiny voice.

'You go on ahead, love, it's the first on the left after the kitchen,' Mummy says.

'Can't you and Clare come?' Thomas tugs at her hand.

'We'll be right behind you, darling. Go on, you're a big boy.'

After Thomas looks from Mummy to me and Sooty, and back to Mummy, he decides that he'll have to go on his own. He goes up the steps and pulls the handle downwards and manoeuvres himself around the door.

Mummy pushes it closed after him. 'Do you like it here, Clare?' she asks. She sits on the step and taps it beside her, so I sit down, too.

I put Sooty down to have a little run around. 'Where's Daddy?' I ask.

'You know you don't answer a question with a question.'

'Yes, I like it,' I say. We're not allowed to answer a question with a question, but Mummy is allowed to do it, and she does it all the time. 'I like the house and the garden. And Granddad – he is really funny!'

'He is, isn't he?' Mummy smiles. 'But he's old now, Clare, and I don't want you disturbing him, do you understand?'

I nod, but I don't think I do understand, so I shake my head instead.

'I mean, I want you to leave him alone. I don't want you bothering him or going near him. He gets tired. He needs to rest. And under no circumstances are you to be alone with him. I want you to stay where Daddy and I are. And don't get separated from Thomas, under any circumstances.' All the time Mummy keeps looking straight ahead, over the hedge at the bottom of the garden to the fields.

I am scared.

She turns to me. 'Do you hear me?' Her eyes are shining and her lips are tight and I don't know why she is so angry. I haven't done anything, only played out here with Thomas, like I was told to do. And I wasn't bothering Granddad, I was only talking to him when he talked to me.

I nod. I let out a big sigh and my shoulders slouch, the way Mummy doesn't like, so I straighten my back again.

'Good girl,' she says. She puts her arm round me, pulls me towards her and squeezes me so tight it hurts. She holds me with both arms and her chin is digging into my head, but I dare not complain. My face is squashed against her chest and I can smell her perfume. It's so strong I can't breathe.

'Let's go and get Thomas,' she says, standing up and opening the door.

The room is dark. The curtains are drawn and the bedside lamp is on at the side of the bed, making strange black shapes on the walls. Daddy is looking after Sooty and I don't know what to do with my hands. I put them at my sides and play with the folds in my dress. All of a sudden it is tight on me, and I want to take it off right now and put on tracksuit bottoms and a T-shirt, like Mary and Sarah and John. I'd love to be back at their house right now playing in the hayshed, rolling around or beating Sarah at an arm-wrestle.

Mummy is in front of me and Thomas is holding onto the back of my dress and I pull at it, so it's free of him. As soon as I do it I feel bad, so I stretch my hand backwards and find his. It's hot and clammy and grips me tight.

'Children, this is your granny,' Mummy says when she has reached the bed and sat on the chair beside it, so we can finally see the woman lying in the middle of it.

She is old and wrinkly and doesn't look anything like Mummy. Her face is so thin and dry that it looks like paper. All it needs is lines on, and it could be straight out of my exercise book. She is covered by the blankets, but her hands are out and she lifts one up and it is full of blue lines that look like they're going to burst any second and splash us all with blood, just like that story Mummy told me about when Granny lost her baby and she was covered with blood and it looked like paint. I imagine the black shapes on the wall as splashes of blood. I hold Thomas's hand tighter. I wonder if I'm hurting him, like Mummy hurt me before, when she was hugging me so tight I couldn't breathe.

'Say hello.'

'Hello,' I say.

'Hello,' Thomas says.

Our granny smiles. 'Aren't you very pretty?' She looks at me.

Me and Thomas stand next to each other, holding hands.

'Like your mother,' she says.

I smile. Yes, I am pretty like my mummy, I think. 'Nice to meet you,' I say.

Thomas copies me. 'Nice to meet you.'

Mummy and Granny laugh then, which makes me and Thomas giggle.

'Nice to meet you too, Thomas,' she says.

I wipe my nose with the back of my hand because snot is starting to drip down, even though I'm not allowed to. Then I breathe in through my nose to make it go back up, and swallow.

For the first time I notice a huge machine by the wall. It looks like a robot. I want to ask what it is, but I don't. There's a jug of water and boxes on the bedside table and a photo in a frame, but I'm too far away to see who is in it.

I'm hungry. I wonder how much longer we'll have to stand

here. Me and Thomas start playing secretly with our hands, tickling each other's palms.

'Give your grandmother a kiss,' says Mummy.

I walk over to the bed and lean in, but I can't reach her, so she leans her head towards me. I give her a peck on the cheek and she takes my hand and rubs it between her fingers. I smile at her and wait for her to let go, but she doesn't, so I pull it back. Then I stand to the side to let Thomas in. When we've both given her a kiss we go back to where we were and hold hands.

Finally Mummy says, 'Okay, you two, off ye go now and leave your grandmother to rest.'

In my head I say, Yipeeeee, but what I really say is, 'Okay, see you soon.' We go outside and I close the door behind us.

'I'm hungry,' says Thomas.

'Me, too,' I say. 'Let's find Daddy.'

We walk along the hallway to the kitchen, and Granddad is sitting at the table.

'Look who we have here,' he says, smiling.

Thomas giggles and runs over to the table and sits down, but I don't know what to do. 'Do you know where our daddy is?' I ask.

'Yes, I do indeed. He's gone down the road to the shops for a few things. Now I bet ye two are as hungry as can be, aren't ye?' he says.

My tummy growls. Thomas squeals and I laugh, too. I nod.

'Sit down there now and I'll make you a nice fry-up.' He heaves himself off the table and I sit down.

I feel dizzy. It's been hours since we've eaten.

'Are you okay, little one?' he asks.

I nod. 'I feel dizzy.'

'Here, up you get – come into the front room and lie down on the sofa.' He pushes me up with his hands on my shoulders and guides me out of the kitchen. If it wasn't for him holding me, I would sway all the way to the floor.

I shake my head. I cannot be alone at any time with my granddad.

'Shush, now, don't worry,' he says. He pushes open the door to the posh room with the nice chair and leads me to the sofa. I sit down and he pushes my head down and lifts my feet up. He rubs my face. 'Now, you rest there for a minute and I'll make you something to eat and a nice, warm milk.'

I'm just thinking that Mummy's going to kill me and cut me up into little pieces, like I'm a piece of steak on her plate, and she's so hungry she could eat a horse, when I nuzzle my face into the soft cushion on the sofa and fall asleep.

Thomas wakes me up. 'Clare, Clare.' He pushes my shoulder and rocks me backwards and forwards. 'Come on, Clare, Granddad has made us a big fry-up.'

I get up and take his hand and follow him through to the kitchen, where Granddad is sitting at the end of the table. There are three plates on the table, one in front of him and one on either side of him. I sit down where I sat before, and Thomas sits opposite.

'Are you feeling better, Clare?'

I nod. I have been very naughty, leaving Thomas on his own, and if Mummy finds out she is going to have my guts for garters. I think about crying, but that would be no use. I'm hungry. I look down at the plate. There is a sausage and two slices of bacon and beans and half a tomato and a slice of something fat and black. I ask Granddad what it is and he says it's black pudding. I don't know what that is. I decide not to ask, because Mummy said not to bother Granddad, so I pick up my fork and stick it into the sausage and put the end of it into my mouth. It's delicious. I chew and swallow and then take another bite, and then again and again until it's gone.

I look up, because I'm waiting to be told off as I'm eating like a little pig with no manners at all, but Granddad isn't even looking at me, he's focusing on his plate, which is piled high with his own sausages and bacon and beans and tomatoes. There is another plate in the middle, with slices of bread on it. Granddad puts butter on one and folds it in two and gives it to me, then gives another one to Thomas and keeps one for himself. I bite into it. It's yummy. We're not allowed to eat white bread at home because Mummy says brown is better, so I gobble it up really quick in case she comes in and catches me and takes it away. It has loads of butter on it and reminds me of my cousins.

This visit is turning out to be much better than I thought. Coming to Mummy's side is a lot of fun and I wonder why we didn't do it sooner. If Granny was better, it would be even more fun, but as Mummy says, you can't ask for everything. And I'm sure she's not really dying, she probably just has asthma like me and it's really bad at the moment. Maybe I should lend her my pump.

I kick my legs under the chair because Granddad doesn't mind anything. With Mummy, we can't kick our legs or laugh or sing or anything. We have to sit and eat like a good girl and boy. I kick Thomas under the table and he laughs and kicks me back. We eat until our plates are clean. By the time I finish I am so full that my dress is tight. I undo the ribbon around my waist and do it up again, but that doesn't make a difference. I imagine my dress popping at the sides like I'm a cartoon character with super-powers.

Granddad is mopping up the sauce from the beans with some bread when Mummy comes in. She smiles at the three of us and looks at me. 'Where's your father?' she says. I wish she would call him Daddy, like she used to, and let him cheer her up with a kiss.

'He's gone to the shops to get some bits,' says Granddad.

'I see,' says Mummy.

I jump off my chair.

'What is it?' Mummy says in a fright, coming over to me.

'Sooty. Where's Sooty?' I look from her to Granddad.

'He's gone with your dad,' says Granddad.

I sigh a deep sigh, like people who have a shock, and then everything is okay. How could I forget Sooty? What kind of mother am I to my little puppy doggie?

'I made some food,' Granddad says to Mummy. 'Help yourself, it's on the side there.'

'Thanks,' says Mummy. She goes over to the frying pan and finds a plate and dishes the food out.

'Did you manage to bath her?' Granddad asks when she is sitting down.

She nods.

'Thanks a lot. Siobhan will come over tomorrow and take care of it, so you needn't worry.'

'Is Siobhan not coming tonight?' Mummy asks. Her voice sounds different. She sounds more like Aunty Joan and Uncle John and Granddad, not like me and Thomas. I have to remember to speak like them, I think to myself, my hands under my bum and my feet swinging.

'Clare, be a good girl and stop swinging your legs, will you?'

I sit still. I just hope Thomas and Granddad don't say anything about me lying down in the front room.

'She's stopping by, she said. Sean said he'll come down as well.'

'When are they coming?' I ask.

'After your bedtime, little lady,' Mummy says. She smiles, but it's not one of her lovely film-star smiles from the cover of a magazine, it's a tight-lipped one. Her make-up has rubbed off her eyelids and her lips, and now she just has the black lines around her eyes that make them look like they're really deep in her face, even though they're not.

'Can't we stay up to meet them?'

'No, ye cannot. It's been a long day for everyone.'

I don't say anything else. We sit and wait until Daddy comes home with some shopping, and then I tell him we have to get ready for bed and we're not allowed to see our aunt and uncle who are coming to visit.

'Surely they can stay up late one night?' he says.

I knew he was my one last hope.

She looks at him like she's talking to him without using words. He replies with a shrug, and she lets out a sigh and says, 'Okay, okay.'

'Yay!' Me and Thomas jump up and down. I take his hands and we start skipping around in a circle.

We get ready for bed and Daddy sets Sooty up with a bed outside, which I'm a bit worried about because he'll be outside on his own and tied up, so he doesn't go wandering off during the night.

After we've brushed our teeth and put our pyjamas on, we play on the big bed in the room where we're going to sleep.

The doorbell goes. Mummy told us to stay here and that she'd come to get us, but I'm too excited to wait, so I get off the bed and lift Thomas off and open the door and peep outside. There's no one there, so I creep along, holding Thomas's hand and pulling him after me. We go towards the voices and, when we get to the end, I peep round the corner and there are all the grown-ups standing in a circle.

A man with a beard sees me and beckons me with his finger. 'Who's this little lady?' he says, and then he sees Thomas after me and says, 'And this handsome little chap!' Everyone laughs.

Mum steps forward, takes our hands and leads us to him. 'This is my daughter, Clare, and my son, Thomas. This is your Uncle Sean.'

He crouches down and opens his arms, so I walk to him with Thomas behind me and he wraps his arms around us and gives us a hug. Then he gives us a kiss each. The hair on his cheeks tickles and his eyes are sparkling and smiling. I like him. He has Granddad's spiky hair and Mummy's brown eyes, which I guess are like mine.

There's a lady too, Mummy's sister Siobhan, who I spoke to on the phone. She looks serious, but when she sees us her face breaks into a smile. 'Oh, Josephine, they are gorgeous,' she says, touching Mummy's hand. Mummy puts her hand on top, and for a second they look at each other, smiling.

Then she pulls her hand away and comes to gives us a kiss and ruffle our hair with her hands. She puts her hand in her pocket and takes out a green hairband with green flowers on and a green scarf with the same flowers, and says the hairband is for me and the bandanna is for Thomas.

'Thank you!' we chime together.

She explains that the green flowers are shamrocks – four-leafed clovers – and will bring us good luck.

I decide to wear mine tomorrow.

It's way past our bedtime, so we say goodnight and Mummy brings us to our room. She pulls the curtains and sits on the bed. Thomas is next to the wall and I am on the outside, and she reaches over me to kiss Thomas and then kisses me. She strokes my hair and Thomas's and tells us to cuddle each other. I put my arms around Thomas and he puts his around me. 'Now,' she says, 'hug each other like that all night. It gets cold here, so you hold onto each other to stay warm now, won't you?'

'Yes, Mummy,' we say together.

'Promise me you'll hug each other all night.'

'Promise.'

'Promise.'

'Clare, don't let go of your brother,' Mummy says one last time, and then she turns the light off and closes the door. I squeeze Thomas tight.

'Ouch,' he says, squirming in my arms, but I don't loosen my grip one little bit.

CLARE

29TH JULY 1997

Someone getting into bed wakes me up. I open my eyes, but it's black-black-black and I can't see anything. I freeze and think of screaming, but then I would scare Thomas. I think of calling out but everyone would hear, including Granny, and she isn't feeling well so I can't wake her up. I squeeze my eyes tight shut. Tears fall down the side of my face, and even though I hate when tears tickle on their way down and always wipe them away, I don't move because I don't want to wake Thomas and I don't want whoever it is to know I'm awake. I lie as still as I can and hope that whoever it is will go away. I squeeze my eyes and legs together, and wish I was still cuddling Thomas like I promised I would.

Something lifts up and then there's an arm over me, and I squeeze my eyes even tighter because that will make it all go away. This is why Mummy told me to cuddle Thomas all night long. I knew she was saying something that she wasn't really saying. I think of Father Feathers and Mass, and I say the 'Holy Mary' in my head as fast as I can. The arm around me pulls me close, and then there are kisses on my face and I can smell the strong scent of Mummy's perfume and the sweetness of her hair, mixed with cigarette smoke.

'Mummy,' I whisper, 'is that you?'

'Shush, go back to sleep, my darling,' she says.

'Mummy! You scared me!' I wipe my face and hug her tight and nuzzle my face into her neck, where I fit perfectly.

'It's okay now, honey. Off to sleep you go.' Her words are soft around the edges because she has been drinking. Her skin is warm. I close my eyes and let out a deep breath.

When I wake up I am as snug as a bug in a rug. Mummy is on one side and Thomas is on the other and it's so hot I'm sticky and sweaty, but in a good way. I love being snuggly under the thick blankets they have in Ireland that mean you can't really move. At home we just have one duvet, and it's light and fluffy and boring. Thomas kicks me.

'Ow!' I say, even though it didn't hurt, but I still don't want him kicking me or he'll just do it all the time. 'Cheeky monkey,' I say.

'Sorry, Clare!' he sings. Then he comes and hugs me round my neck really tight. I tickle him until he lets go.

'Shhh,' Mummy says.

Thomas lifts his head up to look over me. Then he cups his two hands round my ear and whispers, 'What's Mummy doing here?'

I cup my hands round his ear. 'She came to sleep with us last night,' I whisper back.

He does the same again. 'Why?'

I do it again, too. 'To keep us safe.'

'From what?' He leans back and scrunches up his nose so that he looks like a tiger when it gets angry and wants to fight another tiger.

I don't really know, and what I do know is too hard to explain, but if I say that he'll make me tell him every detail. I shrug my shoulders.

'What?' he whines. He hates it when he doesn't know something, even though I say I'm older and that's the way it is. I've even explained that adults don't know everything, they just know more than us. It's God that knows and sees everything.

'Shhh!' I say, pointing at Mummy who still has her eyes closed. That works a treat. He lifts the blankets up and puts his head underneath and then pokes his head out and his hair is electric and wiry.

Mummy moans.

'How's the head?' I ask, the way Uncle John asked when he came down to the kitchen when we were at his house.

She bursts out laughing. 'Where did you hear that?' she asks.

'At Uncle John and Aunty Joan's,' I say.

'You cheeky monkey.' She puts her arm round me and kisses me on the cheek. Thomas whines, so Mummy reaches her hand out and Thomas comes in and we have a three-way hug, which is when all three of us hug at the same time. Mummy squeezes us tight. 'I love you both so much,' she says.

'I love you, too, Mummy,' I say.

'And I love you, Mummy,' Thomas says.

She squeezes us tight and flattens our hair and then kisses us on the head. I smile a big smile because I'm so happy.

'Come on, it's time to get up,' she says, and she pushes back the blankets. Me and Thomas get up and go into the bathroom to shower and get dressed. Then Mummy showers while we brush our teeth, and we go into the other room where Daddy is still in bed. We jump on top of him and he lifts us in the air like we're aeroplanes, one at a time. His face is all puffy and his breath stinks, so we moan and fan the air in front of our noses and he laughs and calls us monsters.

'Come on, let's go and have breakfast and leave your father to get dressed,' Mummy says. That's another time she has called him father. I hope it's not Sooty's fault.

She makes us scrambled eggs on toast, and Granddad comes in just as she's sitting down at the table to eat.

'Morning, kids,' he says, smiling a big smile.

'Morning, Granddad!' we say together.

Mummy doesn't say anything. There's just the sound of my fork and Thomas's against our plates. I look from her to him, waiting for her to say, Good morning, but she doesn't.

Granddad goes over to the kitchen and sees the scrambled eggs in the frying pan. He dishes them onto a plate, but Mummy says, 'Er, they're for Michael.'

Granddad laughs. 'Are they, now?'

I feel bad. 'You can have my scrambled eggs, Granddad,' I say.

'And how am I going to take your scrambled eggs off you, young lady? Sure you're a growing girl.' He laughs. 'I like them nice and hot anyway. I'll make some fresh in no time.'

We have one day left. Mummy and Daddy have to see someone about something and they say we have to stay at home. I'm glad. It means we can play with Sooty and run around and make as much noise as we want and talk to Granddad, and he can make us more bacon and sausages. Granddad is lovely. I feel bad because Mummy seems angry at him, but I don't know why. I don't think she should be angry at him. He's made us lots of food and is always laughing and happy, even though Granny is ill.

Mummy tells us they will be as quick as they can, and to be good and stay out of trouble and Granny and Granddad's way. She says Sooty is By No Means Allowed inside the house, so we should put our coats on and stay outside and play with him. We put our coats on and I hold Sooty while we wave them away and watch the car disappear out of the drive. We go out the front to the pavestones. I find a stone and draw squares for Hopscotch and we play that for a while, but Sooty keeps trying to eat the stone. Then we go around the back and find some rope, so I do some skipping. Thomas doesn't know how to skip, so he sits on the ground and holds Sooty, otherwise he'll come and try and eat the rope.

There's a sound of knocking on a window. Me and Thomas look around, but don't see anything. Then there's the knocking again. I look up at all the windows and see that the one over by the corner has the curtain pulled up a bit. I walk over. Granny is holding the edge of the curtain. She's waving her hand.

'I think Granny wants us to go in,' says Thomas, who has snuck up beside me with Sooty in his arms. Sooty is scrambling to get down.

'Put him down, Thomas,' I say, in my adult I'm-telling-you-off voice. He is always holding him, and sometimes I want to hold him, too, but Sooty needs to get to run around like a normal puppy.

Granny waves.

'Do you want us to come in, Granny?' I say loud, calling up to the window. It's high up, and we're still little.

She nods.

'Can we bring Sooty?'

She nods.

'Come on, Thomas,' I say, turning and taking Sooty. He is mine, after all. Thomas is always taking him off me. I'm grumpy. Mummy said to stay clear of Granny and Granddad, and now Granny is calling us in to her dark and smelly room with tubes and machines and things from scary films.

We wipe our shoes on the mat at the back door like we do at home, apart from when we're running and just can't stop. We go into the kitchen. Granddad isn't there. We walk through the door to the hallway; it's quiet and spooky and I'm glad we have Sooty to protect us. We walk along the hallway, me first and then Thomas. I always have to go first because I'm the Big Sister and it's my job to look after him because he's still small.

'I need to go to the toilet,' Thomas says.

'Can't you wait?' I say, because that's what Mummy always says when we say we need to go to the toilet.

'No!' he says.

I turn left at the bathroom door and lock it after Thomas is inside. I put Sooty in the bath and he's so funny because he tries to climb up the side, but it's too slippery for him, so he keeps sliding up and down, up and down. Me and Thomas giggle while we watch him. Thomas does his wee and I decide I might as well do a wee, too, now that we're here, so I do one and then flush the toilet. After I flush it I jump away quickly because I hate getting wee-spray on my legs. Thomas always forgets and then complains when he gets splashed, and I laugh while he wipes it away with toilet roll.

We wash our hands with soap and water and then dry them with the towel on the back of the door. I pick Sooty up from the bath and he licks me all over my face because he's so happy to be out. He doesn't like baths, like me and Thomas do.

I carry on along the hallway and, when I get to Granny's room, I knock on the door.

'Yes, yes, yes, come in,' she says, and when I push open the door she is coughing into her hands. I want to put my hand over my face, but I know that would be rude. I turn and look at Thomas and he is scrunching up his nose, so I give him an elbow in his side to tell him to stop-that-right-now.

Granny puts a clear plastic mask over her face, which makes me take a big breath of air. She pats the bed next to her, which means we have to go and sit down. I sit first and Thomas sits next to me. I keep a tight grip on Sooty because if Mummy knew he was in here she would kill me, so I better not let his lovely hairs go all over the place.

We sit and wait while she gets her breath through the mask and then takes a sip of water from the glass on the bedside table. She sits up and wipes her mouth with a hankie. I hate hankies. Mummy makes us keep one up our sleeve when we have a cold, so when you blow your nose, you have to put it back up your sleeve right after and you get all wet. Granny does exactly that. I suddenly think how funny it is that Mummy makes us do that and Granny does the same. I decide to ask her what Mummy was like when she was little, like me and Thomas.

She shakes her head from side to side like she's thinking. 'Ah, sure, you know, a little girl like any other.'

'But what was she like?' I ask again, the way I do when Mummy doesn't answer a question properly and I have to ask it over and over again.

'She looked like you,' she says, pointing to me.

I smile, happy with myself. That means I'm going to be beautiful when I grow up.

'What about me?' Thomas says in a high-pitched voice.

'You look like your father,' Granny says.

He pouts and folds his arms. He always wants to be the same as me.

'Don't be stupid,' Granny says to him, and the seriousness in her voice makes Thomas look down, his chin on his chest. 'There are a lot more important things in life than looking like your mother.'

I wonder what she means but I don't dare ask.

'Her looks are what started it all.'

I stroke Sooty on his chin and he holds my hand with one paw and licks my fingers to say he loves me. I give him to Thomas, because I think he needs a cuddle. I need a cuddle, too. 'Do you need anything, Granny?' I ask.

She closes her eyes to small slits and looks at me through them. 'Make me a ham-and-cheese toasted sandwich,' she says. 'I'm famished all of a sudden.'

'Okay,' I say, climbing off the bed. 'Come on, Thomas.' I have never made a ham-and-cheese toasted sandwich, but I've seen Mummy make them a trillion times, so I'm sure I'll be fine.

We go into the kitchen and get the ham and cheese out and find the bread. I put the bread into the toaster and get out a plate, a knife and the butter. When the bread pops, I try to take it out but it's too hot. We wait. Thomas pulls over a chair and climbs up onto the worktop so he can watch.

'Where's Granddad?' he asks. He's still sulking after Granny telling him off.

'I don't know,' I say.

'Maybe he wants a sandwich.'

'Okay,' I say, 'I'll make him one, too.' I get more bread out and wait for the toasted slices to cool. Then I take them out and put the other ones in. I butter the bread and then put a slice of ham on one piece of toast. The cheese is a big block, so I have to cut it. I cut bits off the corners, because I can't cut a whole slice like Mummy does. I put the other piece of toast on top and cut it in half. When the other pieces are cold, I take them out, put some butter on them and do the same with the ham and cheese. I cut it in half, but one side comes out much bigger.

'Ready!' I say, happy with the sandwiches.

Thomas climbs down and I give him one sandwich to carry.

Sooty follows us along the hallway, each of us carrying a plate. We go right to the end to Granny's room and knock on the door. I open the door and Thomas goes in and gives her the sandwich, then turns to leave.

'Where are ye off to?' she says.

'To give Granddad his,' I say, pointing at the plate I'm holding.

Granny taps the bed and points at Thomas. 'You stay here and keep me company while your sister gives it to him.'

Thomas sits down and Sooty runs over and licks his shoes.

'I'll be really quick,' I tell him.

I go to find Granddad, even though I'm breaking all of Mummy's rules. I go back along the hallway to the kitchen to see if he's there. Nope. I go into the fancy room – nothing. I look out the window. Not outside. That means I have to go upstairs. I go up and call out but there's no answer, so I go along the hall to the end where I've never been. I knock on the door.

There's a cough and then, 'Come in.' It's Granddad.

My heart is beating like a drum. If Mummy caught me, she

would kill me. I'm scared. I open the door and go in and there is Granddad, lying on the bed with his shirt open so I can see the vest underneath, and his trousers on.

'I was just having a rest,' he says, sitting up.

'I brought you a sandwich,' I say, feeling stupid, because this was a stupid idea.

'Isn't that lovely?' He laughs, and when I don't move he says, 'Well, come in and give it to me then.'

I go over to him and give him the plate.

'So, sit down and talk to me for a minute.'

I sit on the edge of the bed and watch him eat his sandwich. My tummy is tight and I'm hot and my heart is still going full drum. I keep turning to the door to see if Sooty or Thomas come in.

'What do you like to do?' Granddad asks, taking the last bite of the first half.

'Erm.' I try to think but can't come up with anything. 'We like to... play in the garden, and the park,' I say. I turn back to the door, but there's no sign of Thomas or Sooty. I want to go but I can't leave.

'What else?'

'Hopscotch, and drawing.'

When he has finished, he asks me to put the plate on the table.

I get up and go to get the plate from him, and when I reach to take it, he jumps forward and shouts, Boo! really loud. I jump and drop the plate and crumbs go all over the bed. He laughs and I smile, but really I want to cry.

I'm picking up the plate when Sooty comes running in. He squeals and tries to eat my laces. Then Thomas comes in.

'Thomas!' I run and hug him.

'Hello, Thomas,' says Granddad. 'Let's have a cuddle with this puppy, then,' he says, so I pick Sooty up and put him on the bed. After they've been playing for a minute, I think we really should go. 'Mummy said Sooty has to be outside, so we better go.'

'Well, do as your mummy says.' He smiles.

I take the plate and close the door after us. There is something scary about Granny and Granddad.

When Mummy and Daddy get back, we have to pack and get ready because we're leaving tomorrow. Mummy is in our room with us, folding our tops and my skirts into halves and putting them into the suitcase.

'How was it when we were away?' she asks.

'Fine,' I say. 'We made Granny a ham-and-cheese sandwich.'

'Really? How did you manage that?'

'It was easy,' I say. I don't tell her we made one for Granddad as well.

'Granny said I don't look like you, and Clare does,' says Thomas.

'Did she now?' Mummy laughs.

'Yeah, she was mean to me. She said it's better not to look like you anyway, because that's what started everything.'

'Shut up, Thomas,' I say and I throw a teddy at his face.

Mummy stands still. Her face turns white and she grabs my arms, her fingernails digging into my skin. 'What?' she says.

I cry out. 'Mummy, it hurts!' I yell. I wriggle and try to get out of her grasp, but she holds me so tight I can't get away.

'Tell me what she said, right now.'

I keep wriggling.

'Right now!' she screams.

Tears roll down my cheeks. 'She said there are bigger things in life than looking like you. And then she said your looks started everything.' The tears run down my cheeks.

'What did she mean?' She squeezes my arms tighter and I know I'm going to have big bruises when she lets go.

'I don't know! Mummy, I don't know!' I cry.

'Mummy, let go of her!' shouts Thomas.

Mummy waves her other arm, and the back of her hand lands slap against Thomas's face. Thomas yelps and falls back on the bed. Sooty whines.

'That FUCKING CUNT!' Mummy screams. 'I knew it, I knew it.' She says it over and over again, shaking her head. Her face has gone yellow, like the ends of the cigarettes she leaves in the ashtray on the nights she smokes, and her eyes are wide open with the white bits glistening. She lets go of me and runs her hands through her hair. Then she runs out of the room. I climb onto the bed next to Thomas and put my arms around him. I know now what that word means. It means someone is so horrible that you really, really hate them.

Mummy screams so fast I can't understand. She's screaming and sobbing at the same time, and I hear her say all the bad words I have ever heard and she says, 'I knew it, I knew it.' Then a door slams and there's a huge crash that shakes the bed, and the sound of glass shattering into a thousand tiny pieces. I remember the wooden unit in Granny's room with mirrors in the doors. Me and Thomas stay still, hugging each other. We get under the covers and let Sooty under, too. There's more screaming and shouting and then there's Daddy's voice. Then, after lots of hushing and muttering, everything goes dead.

Just when I'm falling off to sleep there's another loud bang, this time from the other side of the house; maybe the front room. Everything is shattering to smithereens. Daddy comes running into the room. His cheeks are wet and his hair is mad and messy, the way Mummy hates.

'Daddy, what's happening?' I whisper.

'Don't ask questions,' he shouts. He goes over to the suitcase and heaps the last things on the bed inside, in one big pile, and zips it closed. 'Get your rucksacks together as quick as you can,' he says. 'Now!'

I start crying. Daddy never shouts. I get out of bed and get my rucksack and Thomas's and put our teddies and books and crayons in. I zip them up. I wipe my face. Stupid Thomas. If only he hadn't said anything. He's such a stupid big-mouth that now he has caused the whole house to shatter, and driven Mummy mad.

'Come on,' Daddy says. He picks up the suitcase and wraps Thomas in his arms and tells me to stay there. He carries Thomas out and closes the door behind him, so I'm left on my own with Sooty. I wait. There is no sound. I need my pump. I go into my pink rucksack and get it out and take a puff and hold – one, two, three – and then I do the same again. I put on my pink rucksack and hold Thomas's in my arms.

Daddy comes back. He picks Sooty up by the back of the neck and Sooty squeals.

I cry harder.

He hands Sooty to me, takes Thomas's rucksack and picks me up. He opens the door and carries me into the hallway and out the front door. On the way past the lovely front room I can see that none of the framed photographs are on the wall. Now they are all over the carpet, shining like the sea under the sun, winking a thousand times. The nice red sofa that we played Noughts and Crosses on with our fingers is sliced into bits, and I can see the yellow stuffing poking up, like when I have a scab and it gets infected and yellow pus explodes out of it.

Daddy puts me and Sooty in the car and closes the door and goes back inside. Thomas is crying. I try to quieten him, but give up and cry, too.

Daddy comes out with his arm round Mummy. She is screaming. Her hair is wild and her make-up is all over her face. Spots of blood are all over her arms and her hands. Daddy brings her to the car and opens the door and helps her in. She puts her face in her hands and rocks back and forth, making these horrible whining noises that make me and Thomas cry even more.

JOSEPHINE

I have to see Siobhan.

'No,' says Michael, 'let's get far away from here and never come back.'

But I mean it. I have to see her. I can't leave it like this. He says it's a mistake. A big mistake. You're not in the right state. Why don't you wait until we're home and you can ring her.

No. No. No. Take me to her, Michael. Please.

I direct him to her house and get out of the car before he has the handbrake on. I walk straight in the front door and call out Siobhan's name.

She's in the kitchen with her son. She takes one look at me and tells him, 'Go to your room and play for a while, I'll be in in a minute.'

We stand still, watching each other, while he walks slowly to the door, eyeing me suspiciously. He turns the corner.

Siobhan walks over to the door and closes it. Then she goes to the cupboard and gets two glasses out and a bottle of whiskey. She pours us a glass each and hands me one. 'Here,' she says.

'I don't want it,' I tell her.

'You're shaking – look at the state of you. It will calm you down.'

I look down at my hands; she is right: my hands, my arms, my whole body is in tremor. I take the drink and down it, wincing at the taste and the heat in my chest. 'I was raped, Siobhan.' The words are out. All these years unsaid, and there they are, floating in the air between us as if they didn't weigh anything at all. 'The night Sean was born. Someone came into my room. Daddy, he came into my room.'

It sounds so simple, put like that. I gaze out the back window at her view of the garden. Her son's clothes are drying on the line.

'It wasn't Daddy.'

I look back at her. I shake my head. I don't understand.

'Shall we sit down?'

I shake my head. 'What do you mean?' My voice is a whisper. 'What are you saying?' I wipe my eyes with the back of my hand.

'When Patrick was dying, he confessed to Mammy. I wanted you to come and see her because I thought she should tell you.'

I lose the feeling in my legs.

Siobhan lunges forward and catches me in her arms, then leads me to a chair to sit down.

'You mean... you mean Mammy has known since he died?'
She nods.

'And you?'

She nods again, tears falling from her eyes.

I hold my face in my hands. I don't want her to see me. I don't want anyone to see me. I want to crawl into bed and never get out. I stay like that, I don't know how long for. Finally I take my hands away and look at her. She is sitting opposite me, looking down at the floor, her hair hanging around her face. 'Why?' I ask. 'Why have you never told me?'

'She said she would never forgive me if I told you. She said it was long in the past and there was no point in digging up old dirt.' Siobhan starts crying. 'I told her she had to tell you. Last night I said she should tell you before you went.' She goes and gets tissues, gives some to me and keeps some for herself.

'I went to Mammy, all those years ago. I tried to tell her. She shut me up.'

'She didn't know then.'

I hear a loud cackle. It is me. 'She didn't know then! Oh, well, that's fine then, isn't it?' The realization hits me. All these years – all the time spent going over every memory with a fine-tooth comb. Thinking it was my own father. But it wasn't. It wasn't him. It was Patrick.

'So he confessed on his deathbed, did he? How good of him!'

'Josephine, I'm so sorry.' Siobhan takes my hand in hers. I look down at our hands, but I can't feel hers on mine. I can't feel my hand at all.

There's the sound of the front door opening and closing; footsteps coming. Of course. Michael, the children. They're all out in the car.

The door opens and there is Michael. He stands still, looking at us. You can see from the red colour of his face that he has been crying. He rubs his nose. He doesn't speak.

'I should go,' I say.

'Whenever you want,' Michael says. 'I just wanted to make sure you were okay. I'll be in the car.' He turns and walks out.

I blow my nose and wipe my eyes. I should go. 'I should go,' I say out loud, to her, to myself. I walk out to the front door. She follows me. When I get there I turn round. 'Did he ever do anything to you?'

'No.' She shakes her head.

No. Of course not. Instead of relief, I feel bubbles of anger under my skin, in my throat, in my eyes. Tears of anger drip down my cheeks. 'Goodbye, Siobhan,' I say, and I step down onto the mat and walk along the path to the car.

'Goodbye, Josephine.'

I hear her, but I don't turn to look back. I get into the car and do up my seatbelt and wait for Michael to start the engine and drive away.

CLARE

15TH SEPTEMBER 1997

I sit backwards on the sofa facing the window, with my elbows resting on the back and my hands on my chin. 'One, two, three, four...' I count out loud.

Thomas has ten seconds to hide. I count slowly to give me more time. I don't want to play. There's nowhere to hide here anyway. I know Thomas will be behind one of the chairs. There's nothing else in here. Four chairs. A fireplace, a bit like ours, but bigger, with tiles on it. This one isn't real like ours, though, it has plastic logs in that you can turn on with a switch. They go red when they're hot.

We're in the room with toys in the big building in the nice wide road with lots of huge trees on it, where Mummy takes us after school. We can draw on a big white board with felt-tip pens and play anything we want, while she talks to a lady called Jane in the room next door. I play with Thomas, so he thinks everything is normal and we're really here to play, but it's cold and dark outside and I want to go home. I know we're in a room for children while the adults go and talk about what's happened, just like when we went to hospital before the summer.

'Six, seven...' At least I'm out of school, I think. I don't want to see anyone, not even Mandy and Hannah. They want to compare our holidays and hear every detail about mine. And I can't tell them about mine, because then I would have to tell them about my new granny and granddad, and Mummy shattering the house into smithereens and us leaving without saying goodbye. So I am staying away from them.

'Ten!' I say, spinning round. I get off the sofa and walk slowly, over to the fireplace, because that way the chairs are facing me. I can see Thomas's elbow sticking out from behind one of them. I sit down. 'Where is he?' I say out loud. 'Hmmm.'

Thomas giggles.

I stand up and go around the back of the chair. 'There you are!' I say.

He jumps up into a star shape.

'Do you want some water?' I walk over to the corner where there is one of those water-thingies. You have to press the lever and nice cold water comes out, and the water does a big burp and bubbles go to the top. You have to take a plastic cup first from the tube at the side and put it underneath, or you'll splash water everywhere. Thomas wants to pour his own, but he spills it, so I hold the plastic cup while he pushes on the lever.

The door opens and Mummy comes in, followed by the lady called Jane.

'Ready?' she says. She smiles and her voice is light and fluffy, but I know she is just pretending. We play Let's Pretend all the time. Thomas might fall for it, but I don't.

We nod and gulp down our water and put the cups in the bin beside the water-thingy.

'How are you both today?' Jane says.

'Fine, thank you,' I say.

'Fine thank you, too,' says Thomas.

She smiles and turns to Mummy. 'See you next week.'

'Great, see you next week,' Mummy says. 'Come on, you two,' she calls to us.

I get my cardigan and Thomas's jumper from the sofa and go over to the door. I give Thomas his, and tie mine around my waist.

Mummy doesn't say anything until we're outside in the dark walking down the steps. 'Clare, take your cardigan from around your waist. You know that stretches the sleeves.' Her smile has gone.

I kick the pavement as I walk, to make scratching sounds with the pebbles.

'Clare, stop that,' Mummy says.

It's cold in the supermarket, so I put my cardigan back on. We follow Mummy around while she looks at things and puts some of them into the trolley. When we get to the best aisle, she won't let us go down it. 'We've talked about this,' she says, which means, We're not talking about it again.

Since we've got back she won't let us have one single teeny-weeny piece of chocolate or crisps or biscuits, or anything that tastes nice. She says the holidays were the holidays and we all over-indulged, and now we have to eat healthily. I don't think it's fair that she has been on a diet for as long as I can remember, and now she's making us go on one, too. I walk down the sweets aisle by myself and pick up a packet of sweets. I keep them in my hands and walk all the way down the aisle until I get to the bottom and turn round the corner into the next one. When I turn the corner I push the packet of sweets up my sleeve. My face is hot, like it's on fire. I look down, but can't see anything under my cardigan. I breathe out slowly and try to walk like normal, holding onto the sleeve of my cardigan, so the sweets won't fall out.

'Wipe that puss off your face,' says Mummy.

I have to turn away because that makes me smile. She doesn't know that I'm going to have sweets all to myself for dessert. The big decision is if I risk giving one to Thomas or not.

I stay three steps behind and make sure Thomas is always on my left, so there is no reason for either of them to touch my right arm, with the sweets up my sleeve. We go up the last aisle and Mummy picks up some bottles and then we go to the tills. My face is on fire when I walk through the tills bit, because I think maybe something might go off. Mummy packs up all the bags and pays the lady and then pushes the trolley towards the door. Thomas takes my hand and I squeeze it; he pulls his hand away and says I'm sweating. We go through the doors and there is no beep-beep-beep. I'm free, and I have my sweets! I skip ahead to the car and wait at my door, which is the back passenger seat one on the left. Thomas can go in the front.

I do my homework in my room with Sooty in my lap and then we go downstairs to watch TV. Mummy is at the table writing a letter. I'm so excited about the sweets that I just cannot contain myself. That's what Mummy and Daddy say, when me and Thomas are so excited we could burst. I have hidden the sweets between my pillow and the pillowcase. No one will ever find them there until the weekend when Mummy washes our sheets, if she washes our sheets. I sit down next to Thomas on the sofa and watch TV, but all I can think about are the sweets upstairs. I say I'm going to the toilet and leave Sooty with Thomas, and go up to my room and open the sweets and take the first one out and pop it in my mouth. It's yellow and tastes of lemon, and I chew it as fast as I can. I take out one more. Purple. I eat it. When I have chewed every last bit and have none in my teeth, I go downstairs and sit next to Thomas. I want another sweet.

I say to Thomas, 'Thomas, do you want to see my homework?'

He nods. I knew he would. He always wants to see my homework. He loves it. Sometimes he even wants to do it, so I tell him what the homework is and he does his beside me.

We go upstairs and Sooty pitter-patters up behind us, the way he does. I close the door and whisper, 'Thomas, I have a big secret to tell you.'

His eyes go big, like the round bits of Mummy's bras. 'What?'

'I've got sweets!'

He gasps, just as I'd hoped. 'How did you get them?'

I put my hands over his ear and whisper into my cupped hands, 'I took them from the supermarket!' He lets out a shriek and I have to put my hand over his mouth. 'Ssssh! Mummy will hear you!'

I climb up to my bunk – one, two, one, two, one, two – and Thomas climbs up after me. We leave Sooty on the floor and he keeps trying to get up the ladder, but can't reach higher than the first step. I get the sweets out of my pillowcase and give him an orange one and take a pink one for me. When they're finished, I take out another two – purple for Thomas and another pink one for me – and we gulp them down. When

244

they're gone, I take out another two and we gulp them down, too – yellow and orange. Then I give Thomas a pink one and I have the last purple one, and the packet's gone.

We climb down the ladder and I hide all the wrappers in the side pocket of my schoolbag and we go downstairs to watch TV.

'DON'T lick your lips,' I warn Thomas before we go into the sitting room.

We sit down. I get the remote and flick through the channels to see what's on, and stop at whales sliding through the sea. Thomas snuggles next to me and I put my arm round him. Sooty can't jump up yet, so I lift him up and he curls up on my lap.

Mummy is over at the table, writing her letter and smoking a cigarette. Since we got back from holiday she is smoking all the time. She gets up and puts the paper and pad and pen into the drawer of the cabinet and says she's going to get dinner ready. The whale spits out of the sea with a big sneezy noise, and me and Thomas laugh. I tickle him under the arms because it's good to hear him giggle, and hearing him makes me laugh harder. We lie back and I snuggle my feet under his bum so they are nice and warm. I twiddle my toes and he says, 'Ow!' but I tell him to be quiet or else Mummy will come in.

After we have played in the big playroom and Mummy has talked to the nice lady, she always comes back and writes a letter. She seems okay, but you just never know. It's like tying my shoelaces. I can never guess how the bow is going to look. One time one of the loops is huge, another time I don't have enough lace to wrap around to make a loop; sometimes they last all day, and sometimes they come undone ten times and

I fall over my foot and everyone laughs. I can never guess how they are going to be. Or Sooty's poo. It's all different colours and different shapes and sizes, and sometimes he does it in the kitchen, sometimes the garden, sometimes on the patio or the grass, sometimes in the sitting room. It's different every day. And that's just like Mummy. I never know how things are going to end up.

When I think she is good and try to give her a hug, she shouts at me to get away from her and give her some space. Then when we stay in our room, she comes in crying and gets into Thomas's bed with him and makes me get in, too, and she holds us tight and cries all over our hair.

I haven't asked her what happened with Granny and Granddad, or at Aunty Siobhan's. I don't ask her anything any more. Because if I ask something she doesn't like, she might slap me across the face or pinch me really hard.

The half-moons I had on my arm are fading now, and so are the pink blood-spot stars. When the stars and moons are gone, I won't have anything to remember – it'll be like it never happened. Maybe it didn't ever happen. Maybe it was a dream. No one has said anything about it, so maybe I fell asleep and it really is all a dream.

'Thomas,' I whisper. 'Do you remember what happened at Granny and Granddad's?'

'When the lightning hit the house and the glass broke?' he says.

'Yes,' I say. 'That was scary, wasn't it?'

'Yes,' he sniffles. 'I don't want to go back there. Lightning is scary.'

I rub his soft blond hair and he leans his head on my chest.

My throat hurts and my eyes sting because I want to cry,

but I hold it back. I have to be strong for Thomas. I pick Sooty up and hug him close. He makes everything better. He understands like no one else does. Thomas is a baby, and Daddy is working all the time. He has lots of work and they're against the clock, he says. But I think he's upset with Mummy, because I heard them talking after we got back and he was telling her to go to the police, and she screamed at him that he was crazy and stupid and what was she going to go to the police for? The bastard is dead, she screamed. He said then that he was only trying to help and that whatever he did or said was wrong. And since then he's been looking nearly as sad as Mummy. They don't speak like they used to, they don't dance, and he doesn't kiss her when he comes home, or at surprise moments to cheer her up.

Mummy carries my plate and Thomas's first. She puts them down on the table so fast that the food slides to one side.

I pick up my fork to move it back to the middle.

'You don't start eating until we're all sitting down, Clare,' Mummy says, giving me evils from the oven.

'I wasn't,' I say.

'You got too used to all that food in Ireland. You're too hungry for your own good,' she says. She's angry.

'But I wasn't—' I try to say.

'No interrupting.' She shakes her head. 'I will have to start cutting your portions down. And you will have to ask my permission before eating anything.'

I tuck my hands under my legs, but instead of kicking the chair legs with the backs of my shoes, I pinch one of my thighs. I'm so fat that loads of skin goes in between my fingers. I am a little fatty. Mummy's right. She wants me to be nice and pretty and slim, like her and women on the ads in the magazines she buys and on the inside pages of the newspaper. But instead she's got me. A round ball of fat. If I fell off the chair now, I would roll across the kitchen floor and fall off the step and into the utility room. Sooty would think I was a ball and would push me along with his nose and paw at me, scratching my arms and legs, the way he does that drives Mummy mad and makes her say I look like a tinker. My face burns.

Mummy comes and sits down. She blesses herself, and Thomas and me do the same. 'In the name of the Father, and of the Son, and of the Holy Spirit,' she says.

'Amen.' We say it so perfectly in time that it sounds like there is one of us here, not two. Sometimes I stay so still, so Mummy can pretend I'm not here at all, so I'm not driving her crazy and getting under her skin. We say together:

> Bless us, O God, as we sit together,
> Bless the food we eat today,
> Bless the hands that made the food,
> Bless us, O God. Amen.

We bless ourselves, and Mummy and Thomas pick up their knives and forks. We can eat now. But I'm not hungry. I keep my hands under my legs. Mummy cuts into the chicken Kiev and the oil oozes onto her plate. She gets a big piece on her fork and puts mash on top of it and opens her mouth wide so it fits in. That means she's hungry. But she's not starving, because when she's starving we don't even have to say our prayer and she puts the plates down and picks up her knife and fork straight away. On those days she says she could eat a horse. On those days she piles her fork so high she can't close her mouth. When we eat with our mouths open, she slaps us across the legs.

Today she isn't starving, but she's too hungry to eat like a lady. That's how she likes me to eat. Cutting up little pieces on my fork and putting it into my mouth, closing my lips around it and pulling the fork out, and then chewing lots of times with my mouth tight shut.

I pick up my knife and fork and cut a little piece of chicken Kiev off the end. The garlicky oil seeps out into the mashed potato. I cut that bit into two and put it in my mouth, making sure I close my lips around the fork, and pull it out slowly. It tastes good. I chew it lots of times. I go back for the second piece. Now that I have the taste in my mouth, I am a teeny-weeny bit hungry. But I remind myself that if I fell off the chair, I would roll out the door and Sooty would maybe even chew me up, the way he's chewed the corners of the tables and some of Mummy's shoes with heels. I cut an even teenier piece and decide to count how many times I chew it. I get to twenty-eight and it's goo in my mouth, so I swallow it. I decide I will eat one section of the Kiev and draw a line across the mash to mark where I can eat up to. I cut another little piece of Kiev and get a teeny bit of mash and put it on top, and chew it thirty times until it doesn't taste of chicken Kiev and mash any more. I swallow it. The next forkful I chew fifteen times, and the one after that is so good I chew it ten times, and then I forget to chew and keep eating.

By the time I remember the line on the mash and the section of Kiev I was supposed to eat, I've gone way past it. It's too late now, I decide. I will do it tomorrow. I keep eating until I have finished.

CLARE

I want to go to Uncle John's and run round the back of the house and in and out of the trees, careful not to run into them and bang my forehead so my head bounces around inside itself.

We only have our garden. We're not allowed on the flowerbeds because they're Mummy's and we'll destroy them, and we're not allowed to make a noise.

The car's not working, so we have to walk to school through the park. Mummy doesn't like it. She says it's too cold and miserable and dark to be walking through the park. But I like it because it reminds me of Uncle John's.

I was looking forward to the summer holidays for so long and, now we're back, it's only worse. It was what Mummy needed, Daddy said. But I don't think it was a good idea at all.

Me and Thomas run ahead. Sooty runs after us, his tail wagging one way and the other, the way it does when he's happy. We're not allowed on the grass, but she's looking down so I run on and off the grass, slithering like a snake. A snake has no legs, so it needs to move in swirly swirls. That's what they do in my dreams. Slither in swirls through the sea and jump up in the sky and into my hair. I run onto the grass, onto the path, onto the grass, onto the path.

'Clare, wait for me,' Thomas calls.

I look back. I don't want to stop. 'Catch me up,' I call back, the wind blowing my words away as they come out. It's cold. Fingers touch mine and I cling to them, and then his hand is in mine. I turn and he smiles, and I smile back and we run, holding our hands with our school bags out, onto the grass, onto the path. Onto the grass, onto the path.

Sooty barks. Woof, woof! Shush, Sooty. Woof, woof! He will take Mummy out of her dreams and make her look up.

I feel a hand on my shoulder and first I think it's Thomas's, but then I remember that Thomas's hand is in my hand. Just when I turn to see whose it is, my shoulder is yanked and I'm thrown backwards onto the grass. I feel the tired tears of the morning grass soak through the bum of my dress.

'What do you think you're doing?' Mummy screams. 'How many times do I have to tell you?' Sooty comes and licks my face and puts his paws on me. They're all wet and, when he moves them, there are muddy prints on my coat. When he's happy he puts his paws all over you, playing. Stop it, Sooty, I think. Down, Sooty.

Mummy pulls him by his collar and he yelps as he's yanked into the air away from me.

I don't want to be a cry-baby but I can't help it. My bum is cold and wet and my school bag is muddy and Mummy is mad. I start crying. Thomas cries too. His shoulders shake before anything else. He is quiet like a mouse, but his shoulders shudder and then the sound comes and the tears roll.

'It's okay, Thomas,' I tell him.

'God help me – both of you, be quiet!' Mummy screams.

Other mummies and their children go past and they are all staring at us, but Mummy doesn't care.

'You both have me driven mad! And this fucking dog!' She yanks Sooty's lead and pulls him into the air until he yelps again.

Please be quiet, Mummy, I think. Everyone is looking. But she doesn't care. She's in one of her monster moods when she doesn't see and there's nothing you can say or do. She just keeps screaming until you're red in the face and everyone is looking with their mouths open, like they are at the cinema.

Then she whispers, which she sometimes does. I don't know what's worse. 'Get your arse up off that ground.' She says it with her lips tight and white, and I am scared.

I get up and make to run away, but she catches me and squeezes me under the arm and it hurts so much my eyes sting and the tears come out by themselves.

'Be-have,' she says.

I walk beside her the rest of the way. I don't touch Thomas and I stay away from Sooty, because I know that's what she wants. I don't cry, because that will just make her worse. I don't rub my arm, because that will make her angry.

'Goodbye, Mummy,' I say when we get to the gate, because that's what I have to say. 'Bye, Thomas,' I say. I want to give him a hug, but that will just make Mummy mad, so I look at him quickly and then look away. Thomas goes to the school next door because he's littler than me. I will look for him later in the playground and see if I can find him through the fence.

*

Miss asks me what happened and I say I fell over playing with my new dog. She laughs and shakes her head and I smile as much as I can, even though my chest is still popping in and out and I feel like I should take my pump.

When I sit down at my desk, Mandy and the other girls ask me what's wrong and I say I was running on the grass and my Mummy got mad and they tell me not to worry. That's nothing, they say. I nod. I say, 'Here' when my name is called and then I gaze out the window. Miss asks me a question, but I wasn't listening, so I don't know what she said. 'Sorry, Miss?'

'Pay attention, Clare,' she says.

'Yes, Miss; sorry, Miss.' I hope she doesn't pinch me under my arm, too.

At breaktime I go to the toilet and pull up my jumper and look under my arm. It's all purple. I poke it and it hurts. I poke it again.

At lunchtime I go to look for Thomas but I don't see him. I sit on the end of the table in the canteen, so I don't have to talk. Mandy fancies Dominic and she thinks he likes her, too. I'm not hungry, so I give my sandwich to Rebecca. Rebecca is always hungry and when someone doesn't finish their lunch, she always wants it. I give her my sandwich and the cereal bar I have for dessert and I eat my yogurt.

'Are you okay, Clare?' they ask.

I nod and say I just don't feel very well.

Last class is history and we have a quiz and I know the answers, so I forget I'm sad and shoot my hand up in the air and go, 'Miss, Miss,' and she picks me and I tell her that the Children's Crusade was in 1212. I'm the best in my class at history. It's so much fun. Dates and things that happened before even

Mummy and Daddy were born. Just when I'm smiling and happy, it's home time. I wish I could stay longer and that I was in the after-school club, which is for children whose mummies work and come to pick them up late. I go out and meet Thomas and we walk to the gate together. He's forgotten all about this morning and starts telling me about everything that's happened today. I smile and listen. Then Mummy comes with Sooty and we both say, 'Hi, Mummy!', which we have to do before we go and say hello to Sooty, or Mummy will get mad.

Mummy smiles. I run to Sooty and wrap my arms around him. He licks my face and squeals with delight. He's such a baby and I love him so much. His tail goes wild wagging-wagging-wagging. When you stand next to him, his tail beats against your leg. Sometimes I stand next to him when Thomas is hugging him, just to feel it thumping like a heartbeat.

I don't run on the way home. But I do ask Mummy for the lead, so I can take Sooty. He pulls me along because he's so strong, and me and Thomas take it in turns to hold the lead.

At home we get changed and play in the utility room with Sooty until we're called for dinner.

We wash our hands and sit down at our places at the table. Daddy isn't home. I don't ask where he is. I say thank you for dinner and bless myself and wait for Mummy to say the prayer, but she picks up her knife and fork and starts eating. I'm not hungry, so I eat little bits here and there until Mummy tells me not to play with my food. When she's not looking I give some to Sooty and he gulps it down, with his tail wagging-wagging-wagging like mad.

When we are putting the things away I hear the click of the front door. I drop the tea towel and run to the door. Thomas runs after me. 'Daddy Daddy Daddy!' I shout. I'm so happy to see him. He kneels down and is there to catch me when I get to the door. He wraps an arm round me and then catches Thomas in the other arm and lifts us up into the air. He still has his coat on. I kiss his cheek. It's cold. I wrap my arms around his neck and snuggle my face into his shoulder. It's so warm and safe there. I don't even mind his hairy chin that pricks me. I don't care about the pricks today. I like them. They remind me of him; that he is here. Now that he's here, we can play and run around and Mummy can go upstairs.

He carries us into the kitchen and sets us down on the floor. He goes over to Mummy, who is making a cup of coffee, and says, 'Hello, love,' but she doesn't look at him or smile or anything. She looks as angry as she looks all the time.

I feel bad for running to the door. I think that might have made her angry. The three of us should have gone to the door together.

When I have a lovely man, I think, I will run to him and let him pick me up as soon as he gets in the door.

Mummy wrinkles up her nose and sniffs. 'I can smell shit,' she says to Daddy, looking at him for the first time.

Daddy sighs a big sigh that means he's tired. 'Here we go.'

'I bet you brought it in on the bottom of your fucking shoes.'

Me and Thomas stand still and watch them, hoping everything will be okay and they will make up, and Daddy will sit down to have his dinner and we can tell him about our day.

'Lift up your shoes,' Mummy says to Daddy.

'Come on now, Josephine.' He turns to us, not smiling any more. 'You two, go upstairs to your room.'

I take Thomas's hand and walk out of the kitchen. We walk upstairs until we get three-quarters of the way up and sit down. I make the shush-sign at Thomas and he nods. They start up again.

'Come on, Josephine,' says Mummy, putting on Daddy's voice. 'I can smell shit in my kitchen, which I spent the whole morning cleaning, and you're telling me to come on? Ha!' she laughs. The horrible cackle she does when she's not really laughing. 'I'm not the one who, when they cook, it smells of shit.'

'What do you mean?'

'I mean you can't even cook, is what I mean. Now lift up your shoes,' she shouts.

I feel bad for Daddy. I wish Mummy wouldn't shout at him.

'Come on. I'm not a child.'

'Oh, really. Unless you told me, I really wouldn't know.'

'Josephine, what are we going to do?'

'Well, you're going to show me the soles of your shoes, and if you brought dog's shit through those carpets that I spent hours cleaning today, so help me God.'

I run up the rest of the stairs into our room. I pick up my shoes and turn them over. They're clean. I pick up Thomas's. There is brown sludge on the bottom. I look at the floor in our room and see brown sludge on the carpet, too. I keep my head down all the way to the stairs and follow the poo-sludges. I go downstairs and see the sludges all the way into the kitchen. They're shouting now. Mummy's voice is high and swirly, like the night the snakes were in my hair.

'Mummy,' I say, keeping my head down. 'It was me.'

As soon as I've said it, a thump comes down on the side of my head and my ear rings. She's screaming at the top of her voice. Daddy has her wrist in his hand and he's shouting, too, telling me to get upstairs to our bedroom.

I turn and run, and all I hear is Mummy screaming, 'Trodden through the whole fucking house! That dog! That fucking mongrel!'

On Saturday, Daddy says we've been good all week, so we're going to the big park with cows and sheep and peacocks. I ask if we can go for a Family Night Out after, but he says no – no Family Nights Out for a while. Me and Thomas huff and fold our arms and he says there'll be none of that, so I unfold my arms and Thomas copies me. Daddy's eyes are small and watery and he has lines around them that he didn't used to have.

'Is Mum coming?' I ask.

'No, she's got things to do.'

'Can Sooty come?'

'Yes,' he says.

That makes me and Thomas jump up and down and clap our hands. Sooty comes running in from the garden and barks. Woof-woof. I rub his head and under his chin and he jumps up on me. He puts his paws on my tummy and I take them in my hands and make him dance. Thomas laughs and so does Daddy, and that makes me laugh. I get a fit of giggles and the tears sneak out of the corners of my eyes and my face goes red, I'm that hot.

'Right. Eat up your breakfast and we'll be off,' Daddy says. He gulps down his tea.

I let Sooty go, and I sit down, but he jumps back up and rests his paws on my lap. Daddy doesn't say anything. If Mummy was here, she would scream that it's disgusting and to get that dirty mongrel outside this minute. I'm glad she's not coming. Everything is so much brighter when she's not here. The sun peeps out from behind the clouds and we can play and run around, and Thomas can squeal like a mouse when I tickle him.

I gulp down my cereal and barely even chew, but the Krispies are so small I can swallow them right down. Daddy goes out and it's just me, Thomas and Sooty. I look at the kitchen door to make sure it's all clear and then put the bowl on my lap. Sooty licks up the milk like he's a mop and splashes me. When he's finished, his whiskers are all white like he's an old man, even though he's only a baby like Thomas. I wonder if Uncle John got my letter.

When we get presents, Mummy always makes us write a Thank You Letter. So I got the writing paper and pen out of the cabinet in the sitting room and wrote a letter. It said:

Dear Uncle John,

Thank you so so so so so much for my puppy. I love him more than anything in the world (apart from Mummy and Daddy and Thomas). I promise I will look after Sooty for ever and ever. Amen.

Love you, Clare

P.S. Thomas says thank you too.

P.P.S. Tell Sarah and Mary and John we miss them.

I made Mummy send it, even though she said there was no need. She hates Sooty. I don't know why. He's done nothing to her.

Sooty licks his lips until the milk has gone. I get my bowl and Thomas's, put them in the sink and turn on the tap. I want to be quick, so instead of using the sponge like Mummy has shown me, I wipe the bowls with my hand under the cold water. I don't use the hot tap because I might burn myself, and that hurts. If Mummy knew I was washing the bowls in cold water, she would give me a slap across the back of my legs.

Me and Thomas run upstairs to the bathroom to brush our teeth. I make a worm of toothpaste on my toothbrush and hold it under the tap. Thomas makes a worm on his toothbrush, but it's long and skinny and looks funny. 'Yours is skinny,' I say, laughing and pointing at his toothbrush.

'Well, yours is fat, like you!' he shouts.

I stand on his foot and elbow him in the tummy. Saying you're fat is the worst thing you could say to anyone. No one wants to be fat. Everyone wants to be slim and beautiful. I hate Thomas right now, so I make my eyes really small like black holes and stare at him with pursed lips.

He squeals and hits me with his toothbrush. I look down at my top; it has blue toothpaste on it.

I clip him round the ear with the backs of my fingers.

He starts crying.

'Shut up, you idiot,' I tell him with tight lips, like Mummy's when she's angry.

'*You're* an idiot,' he shouts.

I finish brushing my teeth without looking at him again in the mirror. I rinse three times and storm out of the bathroom and into our bedroom. I shut the door and lock it, even though we're not allowed to. I pull my top up over my head and throw it on the floor and stamp on it. I look up. My eyes are burning. I can see myself in the mirror. I look like a big blurry blob. I sit on the carpet and cry into my top, so no one will hear me.

I wipe my eyes and look at myself. My boobies look big. Mummy is right. I'm fat.

I hear Daddy call up from downstairs, asking if we're ready. I wipe my eyes again and get a new T-shirt from the wardrobe, put it on and go downstairs.

In the car Daddy puts on a funny face and says, 'Seatbelts, everyone,' like he's the captain of a big ship. Normally I would laugh, but I just smile this time. When he turns on the engine he makes voom-voom noises that only he can make, and he pulls out and we whizz down the road.

We make a stop at the petrol station because Daddy needs to fill up. We wait until he puts the pipe in the back of the car and feeds it, and then we go into the shop with him. We can each choose some treats for our day out. I choose a packet of salt-and-vinegar crisps and a chocolate-and-caramel bar, and Thomas gets a bar of chocolate and a packet of sweets. Daddy goes over to the ice-cream fridge and gets one out for himself. When I see the ice-cream in his hand I say, 'Oh!' because I want one, too. Thomas copies me the way he does, and Daddy says, 'Do you want an ice-cream, too?'

We nod, so he lets us choose an ice-cream. I choose my favourite with caramel and chocolate, and Thomas gets the strawberry cone he always gets. We skip out the door to the car. I sing when I put my seatbelt on because I'm so happy.

At the park we walk by a little stream of water and see baby pigs and sheep and cows eating in the fields. There are peacocks in a garden and they open their tails and show all the green eyes with make-up on their feathers. 'They're beautiful,' I say to Daddy and Thomas, pointing at the ones with their tails like rainbows. 'They look like Mummy.'

Daddy laughs and Thomas takes a bite of his chocolate. 'How's that?' he says.

'All they have to do is open their arms and they look beautiful, showing all the colours on their feathers, just like Mummy.'

Daddy gazes at them and nods.

'I want to look like that,' I say.

Thomas holds his chocolate in his hand and runs around in circles, flapping his arms.

CLARE

All the other children's mummies have come to get them already.

Me and Thomas sit on the wall outside the gate and swing our legs, knocking the backs of our shoes against the wall, the way Mummy hates. She says it's unladylike, just like sitting without putting your legs together or scratching when you have an itch. We play a game, looking out for Mummy's car to see who sees it first. We don't walk through the park, now the car is back from the car doctor, which means Sooty can't come because Mummy says he's not allowed in the car.

Thomas sees her car first and holds his arm out, pointing. 'I spy with my little eye,' he shouts.

I start laughing because he got confused. With this game he's supposed to say, as quick as he can, 'I spotted, I saw, I won.'

He laughs, too, and I help him off the wall.

'Silly billy,' I say, taking his hand. The car is coming closer. It's grey and has a big front and a big bum, and a scratch on one side from when Mummy went too close to a lamp post when she was parking.

We wait at the edge of the pavement, which is as far as we are allowed to go, and watch Mummy come towards us, closer closer closer. She's going fast and not going slower like she normally does, so I grab Thomas's arm and jump backwards. She stops in front of us with a bump and a screech and waves for us to get in.

I open the back door and crawl in, and Thomas climbs in after me and pulls the door shut with both hands.

I hold on to the head of Mummy's seat to stand up and give her a kiss on the cheek. Her skin is wet and leaves a taste in my mouth of salt-and-vinegar crisps. Her face looks all shiny.

'Hi, Mummy,' I say, and sit back so Thomas can give her a kiss.

'Hello, my darlings,' she says. 'Did you have a nice day?'

'Yes,' I say.

Thomas nods.

'Good,' she says, smiling. 'I'm taking ye for ice-cream.'

Thomas jumps up and down and claps his hands.

'Really?' I ask.

'Yes. Because you've both been so good.'

I stand up and put my arms around the seat until I feel her hair. I tickle her neck and she puts her hand over mine and I smile and my cheeks get hot.

She turns the key and the engine croaks and then chugs to life. She looks in the mirror and pulls into the road. I turn and look behind us, just in case a car is coming, because sometimes Mummy doesn't see them and then, when they beep at her, she winds her window down and shouts at them.

We drive to the High Road and Mummy parks. In the ice-cream café she says we can pick whatever we want. I get a banana split with chocolate and caramel, because that's my favourite. Thomas gets strawberry and chocolate ice-cream with strawberry sauce and nuts. Mummy gets a coffee. She smokes while we eat our ice-cream and, because I'm sitting in front of her, the smoke comes into my face and makes me cough, but I don't mind because my ice-cream is so good. We haven't been allowed to eat any sweet things since we got back from holiday, apart from when we're with Daddy.

'Is that nice?' Mummy asks.

I nod and she laughs. 'You have ice-cream on your nose,' she says.

I giggle and wipe my nose and look at Thomas. He has ice-cream all round his mouth and chin, but because Thomas is next to Mummy, she hasn't seen him. I point at Thomas and start laughing and we all giggle. Mummy laughs and smokes her cigarette. She gets a tissue and wipes Thomas's face and then tries some of his ice-cream. I ask if she'd like to try mine and she says yes, so I give her a spoon, but try not to give her much caramel because I want it.

'Mmmm,' she says, 'that's delicious.'

When we have finished, we drive home and wait at the front door while Mummy finds the key for the top lock. Her hand is shaking. She's pale and her skin is shiny, like when she picked us up. She opens the door and we wait for her to take the key out of the lock and go in. Sooty always pokes his nose out, so we have to close the gate so he can't run away, but he's not there today.

We go in and take our coats off and hang them up on the hooks by the door. Mummy puts her bag on the table and walks inside. There is still no sign of Sooty. He always comes to kiss us hello. 'Sooty!' I call. 'Sooty Sooty Sooty!'

Me and Thomas run inside. We go through the kitchen into the utility room. The door is locked, so he is probably outside. We run to the front door to put our shoes on, and run back. I unlock the door and open it. Sooty is always jumping at the door when it's locked. He must be at the glass doors to the sitting room. Sometimes he sits there and watches us inside, or jumps up and paws at the glass. Then he leaves muddy pawprints, which makes Mummy angry.

I run along the alleyway by the side of the house and Thomas follows me. I jump over Sooty's poo and warn Thomas not to step on it. At the end of the alley, I turn right into the garden. The patio is empty. Sooty isn't anywhere by the doors. I run onto the grass. We have an apple tree in the middle that falls sideways. He must be the other side of it. 'Sooty,' I call.

'Sooty,' shouts Thomas.

We run all round the garden, careful not to stand on Sooty's poos. He's not there.

My heart bangs in my chest. Maybe he got through a hole in the fence, maybe he jumped over the fence. I didn't think he could jump that high. He's still only little. I go over to the flowerbeds, where we're not allowed and Sooty's not allowed, but he doesn't know that, so he's eaten lots of the tops of the flowers. I check he's not hiding in the bushes.

'Where is he, Clare?' asks Thomas.

'I don't know,' I whisper.

We go back into the utility room and I open the cupboards to see if he got inside one by mistake. I open the toilet door and look inside. We go into the kitchen. The kettle is boiling. I can hear the water bubbling inside and humming, like it's going to take off and fly over the worktops. I turn on the light to the sitting room. 'Sooty,' I call.

Me and Thomas look under the table and the sofa and the chairs. I check in the fireplace. I think he might be playing Hide-and-seek, only he doesn't know how to play. We go upstairs and check the bathroom: the shower and the bath, and the unit under the sink; and then the back rooms. Thomas starts crying. We go into our room. We check under our bunk beds, in the wardrobe and in Thomas's bed under the duvet. I even climb up to my bed and lift the quilt to see if he's sleeping.

I knock on Mummy's door.

'Come in,' she calls.

I open the door and Mummy is sitting at her make-up table in front of the mirror, smoking a cigarette.

'Sooty has escaped,' I declare. 'We have to find him – let's get our coats.' I run to Mummy and tug at her sleeve.

'Mummy, Sooty's gone,' Thomas sobs. 'Poor Sooty.'

She shakes her arm free to smoke her cigarette. She blows the smoke into the mirror and stares as she disappears in the glass. She stays still, her back straight, one arm holding the cigarette. I watch as she rubs her thumbnail and fingernail against each other, the way she does when she has chipped one.

'Sooty's gone,' she says into the mirror.

'Gone?' I say, my bottom lip wobbling.

'Gone?' Thomas says in a sob.

'Yes, he's gone.'

'But where's he gone?' I ask. 'He must be lost. He'll be looking for us.' The thought of small, fluffy Sooty wandering the streets, looking for me and Thomas, is too much. 'Mummy, we have to go NOW!' I scream. 'NOW!' I pull at her jumper.

'NOW!' Thomas shouts. 'NOW, MUMMY, NOW!'

'He's gone!' she shouts, still looking straight ahead.

I watch her face from the side, the smoke shooting out of her nose like a dragon breathing fire. 'But where?' I whisper. The tears roll down my cheeks.

The front door clicks and then closes. Daddy's home. He'll help us find Sooty, I think. He'll show Mummy. I turn and run out of the room, along the hallway and down the stairs. 'Daddy, Daddy!' I scream. 'Sooty's gone and we have to go and find him,' I say as fast as I can, holding on to the rail and running down the stairs. I run into him and wrap my arms around his waist.

He kneels down on one knee and looks at me.

'Daddy, we need to go,' I squeal, pulling at the neck of his jumper. I sniff and wipe my nose with the back of my hand.

'Clare, Sooty has left us,' Daddy says. He looks up at Thomas, who has come down, and waves him to come over.

'Where has he gone?' I whisper.

He looks at me, then shakes his head like he is saying no, but there is nothing to say no to.

'WHERE?' I shout.

'We couldn't look after him,' he says. 'He needed too much care and time, and Mummy couldn't manage it. He had to go.'

I try to get away, but Daddy holds on to me. 'Clare,' he says, 'Clare!'

'No!' I scream. 'Leave me alone.' I lash out at his face with my hands and hit him away. 'I want Sooty!' I scream. 'I hate you, I hate you both. I hate her!'

He lets me go and I fall down. I get up and run up the stairs on my hands and feet. I run into my room and up the ladder and get under the duvet and push the pillow against my face and I scream and scream and scream.

*

When I wake up I still have the picture from my dream in my mind. It's Sooty lying in the middle of the kitchen floor. He has been caught in a trap, and the pin is going through his head and he's squealing like a mouse.

CLARE

I climb down the ladder as quick as I can – one, two, one, two – and get my pink rucksack. I unzip it and turn it upside down and everything falls out onto the floor. I go over to the wardrobe and take out two tops, a dress and a skirt, and then take out five pairs of knickers and two vests and stuff them in my rucksack. I get my pencil case with my colouring pencils and a notebook and put them in. I run to the bathroom and get my toothbrush. Then I zip it closed.

I put my rucksack on my shoulder and place my other arm through the loop, so it's on my back, and run down the stairs, right, left, right, left, holding onto the banister in case I slip. No one is in the kitchen. I go into the sitting room. Thomas is sitting on the sofa on his own, watching cartoons. He doesn't see me, so I back out slowly and run through the kitchen to the utility room. Daddy isn't there but the back door is open, so I know he's pottering around, which is when he's doing bits and pieces. I go out the door along the alleyway. The long hose snakes all the way along, moving every now and again, so I am careful not to stand on it or I'll trip. Daddy is watering the flowers. I get to the end of the alley and see him at the bottom of the garden with the hose in his hand, pouring water over the flowers that are left on the flowerbed, where me and Thomas aren't allowed to go.

He turns and sees me and smiles a sad kind of a smile. I walk over to him. 'Daddy,' I say. My tone is serious. I am serious. I mean business.

'Yes, honey?' he says in a soft voice because he is upset and he knows I'm upset, too.

'Daddy,' I say again, because even though I'm serious I'm scared and nervous and don't know where to start. My bottom lip is shaking, but I WILL NOT CRY.

He carries on sprinkling the water over the leaves, even though there are no flowers there.

'We need to get Sooty back,' I say, like I'm an actress playing a part in a film and I mean business.

'Now, Clare—' he starts, but I don't let him go on.

'No, I mean it, Daddy,' I say. When Daddy is serious about something he says, 'I mean it', and me and Thomas know there is no messing. So I think if anything will make him listen, that will. 'I love Sooty so much, and I just had a dream he got caught in a mouse-trap, like that mouse we caught and it was still alive and squealing...' I run out of breath. I huff and puff and continue, 'And I've decided that if Sooty goes, I go, because he is the only thing that makes me and Thomas laugh sometimes, and without him we will be miserable.'

He stares at the end of the hose where the water pours out onto the ground. His trainers and the bottom of his trousers are all wet and muddy. If he brings that mud into the house, Mummy will kill him.

'And it's not fair what you did, taking Sooty away from us like that, when we were at school. So I want you to take me to get him back.'

'Clare, darling,' Daddy says.

'I'm serious, Daddy,' I say, holding my head up and staring at him hard. My eyes sting but I hold back the tears. 'Or else I'm leaving.'

He looks at me and laughs, but then sees I'm not laughing and my face is stony-straight, like the poker by the fire, and his face goes serious.

I stand firm, looping my thumbs around the straps of my rucksack and staring at him. 'Please, Daddy, please, please, please,' I say, over and over again, with my eyes.

He looks back at me, then across the garden to the French doors. I turn round. Thomas is standing inside the glass, watching us.

'Come on,' says Daddy and he starts walking across the garden, taking the hose-snake with him. I follow him all the way along the alley to the tap, where he turns it off. Then he gets down on his knees and gives me a hug, but I don't even want a hug – I want to go and get Sooty.

'Please, let's go,' I almost squeal. My cheeks are all red, and I'm hot and my heart is going bum-bum, bum-bum.

We go inside and Daddy stamps his feet on the mat, and from the kitchen he calls to Thomas to turn off the TV and come on.

At the front door I throw my rucksack on the floor and put my coat on. We go out and Daddy closes the door behind us.

He unlocks his car door and lifts up the little button, reaches round to the back and lifts up that button. I open the door and get in. Thomas climbs in after me.

'Where are we going?' asks Thomas.

I don't say anything, because I'm not really sure where we're going and I don't want to make any promises. Daddy always says you shouldn't make promises to anyone that you can't keep.

'We're going for a drive,' says Daddy.

'Yeah,' I say. 'We're going for a drive.'

We put on our seatbelts.

Daddy says, 'All strapped in?'

'Yes,' I call impatiently, wanting to shout, Go, Daddy, go!

'Yes,' says Thomas.

Daddy drives and I look out my window and Thomas looks out the other one. I sit back and watch the trees go by, and then I close my eyes and imagine seeing Sooty again. I try to imagine the softness of his fur in my hands and the cold, wet stickiness of his nose against mine.

'We're here,' Daddy says, turning off the engine.

Me and Thomas undo our seatbelts and I look round to see where we are. All I can see are houses, on both sides of the street.

'Hang on,' Daddy says, turning round in his seat. 'I'm just going to go and talk to a workmate of mine for ten minutes. You two stay here, okay?'

'Okay,' I say.

'Keep your doors locked, and don't open to anyone.'

'Okay.'

He gets out and locks his door with the key, and then checks our doors are locked.

When he's at my side, I wind down my window and call him closer by wiggling my big finger.

He leans down. 'What, love?'

'What about Mummy?' I whisper.

He straightens up and squeezes my hand hard.

I know then that everything will be okay, and he will make Mummy see that we need Sooty. I squeeze his hand back.

We watch him walk across the road and go into one of the houses with a big hedge in the front, so you can't see any of its windows. My heart goes bum-bum, bum-bum.

'What are we doing here?' says Thomas.

I wonder if I should tell him or not. I decide not to. 'Daddy is talking to his workmate,' I say. I turn and face the back, so I can watch the house, but all I can see is the hedge and the wooden gate.

Is that where Sooty is? I wonder. I put my head out the window to see if I can hear him. Nothing. Just the chirp of a bird in one of the trees.

I cross my legs and my toes and two fingers on both hands, and close my eyes tight, and say in my head, Please, please, please let Sooty be here. I will be good for ever, and I will look after Thomas and Mummy and Sooty, and I'll walk him and pick up his poo and tell him he's being naughty when he jumps up with mud on his paws.

My cheeks burn and my bottom lip shakes. I try to keep it still but it won't stop trembling.

Thomas gets bored and draws on the window with his fingertip. I watch him push his finger round in circles that get bigger and bigger. It's the body of a snail. Then he adds the head and the long, thin ears.

A loud yelp breaks the silence and I spin round to look out the back window at the house. I can't see anything, but the yelping continues. Sooty!

'Thomas, it's Sooty!' I squeal. I can't help it. It's Sooty, I'm sure it is.

'Where?' he shouts, looking out the windows.

'He's in that house, there.' I point at the house Daddy went into.

Daddy appears at the gate, looking behind him and waving goodbye, and I can see a strap in his hands. Sooty trots through the gate after him.

They cross the road and I unlock my door and jump out, and so does Thomas, and we run to meet them and Thomas screams, 'Sooty, Sooty, Sooty!'

Sooty sees us and gallops towards us like a horse. He jumps on me and licks my face and then jumps on Thomas and he falls over, and he giggles, and I giggle, and I hug Sooty round the neck. His fur is soft and warm and I hug and kiss him and he barks and squeals. 'Sooty, I love you so much,' I whisper in his ear, and he hears me and he licks my face over and over and over again.

CLARE

10TH OCTOBER 1997

Daddy opens the door, and me and Thomas run in. We've even got chicken and chips to celebrate. I feel as happy as when I'm on the swing in the playground in the park, when it gets to the highest bit and I could almost jump, but I don't. That's one of my favourite moments of my favourite things, ever. That, and when we were all happy a long time ago.

Me and Thomas run through the hallway and then the kitchen, into the utility room.

Daddy has Sooty by the lead, and Sooty is running after us, pulling Daddy along, and I can hear him puffing and panting. Sooty sounds like he's choking, but he's not really. He just does that to make Daddy let him go.

Me and Thomas giggle. I get the key from behind the plant pot and open the back door.

Daddy has the bag with the food in one hand, and the lead in another, and is red-faced and laughing when he bounces through the kitchen door.

'Yippeeeeee!' I shout, and then Thomas shouts just after me.

'Ten minutes to play and then we'll have dinner,' Daddy says, unhooking Sooty's lead from his collar.

'Yaay!' we shout together and run out the door.

We run around the garden and Sooty runs after us, jumping up on us and licking our faces and making us scream with delight.

It feels like we're out there for just a minute when Daddy calls us and says it's time to have dinner because it's going cold. I wave to Thomas and we run in. Sooty trots in with us, running in between my legs and nearly tripping me up, then in between Thomas's legs. I can tell he's his happiest ever, to be at home with us again.

We take our shoes off inside the back door and I point to the rag on the floor and make Sooty go and stand on it, but he thinks I'm playing and keeps coming to me to lick my finger. 'Cheeky monkey,' I tell him, and put my face down to his, so he can kiss me.

He licks my ear and Thomas gets into a fit of laughter because he'll have all my ear's wax on his tongue.

We go into the kitchen, where Daddy has taken the plastic boxes out of the carrier bag and put them on the table. There are only three sets.

I look round and see a plastic bag on the counter. 'Isn't Mummy having dinner?' I ask.

'She's not hungry,' Daddy says. He's smiling like everything's okay, but I can tell it's not the same smile as before, because his eyes aren't smiling. When he is truly happy, they sparkle.

I had forgotten about Mummy. It all comes crashing back and my smile freezes and my tummy feels empty.

'Come on,' says Daddy. 'Wash up your hands and let's gulp down this feast.'

I help Thomas wash his hands and then I wash mine, and we sit down to eat.

I open the yellow plastic box with the chicken burger inside and take a bite. It tastes good. I hold the burger in one hand and with the other I reach down and pinch my thigh to remind myself. I squeeze and roll the fat, so it doesn't hurt too much, but just enough so that when I let go it will tingle. Instead of taking another bite straight away, I sit still and feel the tingle in my thigh fade. When it's gone, I take another bite. Then I pinch my thigh again. I put the burger down and wait. Then I get a chip and dip it in ketchup and eat it, but it's already cold and gone soggy, so I decide not to have any more. That way, I can have some more of my burger in a minute. I watch Daddy and Thomas eat theirs.

'Not hungry?' asks Daddy.

I shake my head.

'Don't worry about Mummy,' he says. 'She'll come round.'

Later, when I'm in bed, I'm woken up by shouting. There are Mummy's shrieks, and then there are roars. I don't know who they belong to at first. I'm not sure if they are Mummy's or Daddy's. Daddy never roars. But after a moment of squeezing my eyes shut and concentrating really hard, I can tell they belong to Daddy.

I sit up and listen.

'I've had enough,' he shouts. Then there are mumbles and then, 'I will not live like this.'

Daddy never shouts at Mummy. It must be serious. He's been at home more lately, which is good because we see less of Mummy. That means I don't have to worry whether she's going to be good, or bad, or really good, or really bad.

'*You* won't live like this?' she says. 'That dog has me driven demented, and you go and get him back? I am the one rearing your children; you barely see them for five minutes and, as soon as you walk in the door, it's as if I didn't exist. A few days off and it's you making the demands! Ha!'

JOSEPHINE

15TH OCTOBER 1997

There goes the click of the front door and the key in the double lock. How strange that he should double-lock the door with me in the house. Has he forgotten altogether I'm here? The diesel engine chugs to life and he drives off down the road. Clare will be complaining of feeling sick by the time they get to the traffic lights. The house is quiet, at last, but for the incessant barking of that filthy mongrel in the garden. My body is heavy as a corpse. My head is foggy. Some peace and quiet is all I ask for. Is it too much?

The cheek of him. Going and getting it back. Bringing that dirty, diseased thing back into my house; and it crawling with fleas. Scratching itself and sniffing itself between the legs. Its stools alive with maggots.

They have him twisted round their little fingers, the two of them. Daddy, this, Daddy, that. Daddy, Daddy, Daddy.

I can't stand it – its barks and squeals and wheezing, pretending it's being choked, just to get my attention. All day it's at it. Clawing for a piece of me, like the rest of them. There will be none of me left. They brought it back to spite me. For it to taunt me. Playing games, like all of them. I thought I was rid of it all, but I'm not. I never was. I'm surrounded by them. Cunts, the lot of them.

I pull the covers around me. I close my eyes and drift off to the school gates. I'm waiting for them. Clare appears swinging her book-bag, then Thomas. I wave. They don't see me. Then they smile their big toothy grins and start running through the groups of other school children, their book-bags swinging, swinging, and they run all the way into their father's arms.

He kneels down and kisses them and they squeal with the tickle of his beard.

I turn and walk down the road, my breasts leaking milk, as if I gave birth to them the other day. My babies. I wake up crying, my chest going with the sobs. I go to the dresser and pour into the glass the brandy that's left in the bottle and drink it.

There it is. The barking. Bow-wow, bow-wow. My father would have put a boot in it long ago. My father. My daddy. He was no angel, but he wasn't what I thought he was. All those years I thought it was the divil and his wife. I didn't realize it was the divil and her husband.

I choke on the brandy, on my tears. *Good girl. You're a good girl, Josephine.* All I wanted was for my mother to love me. *You deserve life, Josephine. Get out there and eat the world up. You show them.* Jealous, she was. Twisted – twisted to the core with jealousy. That her husband didn't love her, that he was as miserable and angry as she was, that she was stuck there in that house, washing and cooking and cleaning and rearing. Jealous, too, that her own mother loved me more than she loved her. Granny knew that she wasn't deserving of love.

I've had enough. I pound the mattress with my clenched fists. I won't stand for it for one more second. Being taken for a fool, used up and spat out. I sit up, breathless, my head spinning. I put on my dressing gown and go downstairs.

The disease-ridden animal knows I'm in the kitchen. It scratches and whines. It clambers furiously at the door as if it were digging a hole in the ground.

I try to think. What will I do? How will I get away from them all, from myself, from this house that's falling in on my chest? My head is throbbing to bursting point. I put on the kettle for a cup of coffee, get a mug out and see an envelope in the middle of the kitchen table. Michael will have left it there.

I don't know the writing. I get a knife from the drawer and cut it open. Inside there is a thin slip of paper. It contains a short note:

Dear Josephine,

I'm writing to let you know that Mammy died peacefully in her sleep on 3rd September, and her funeral took place three days later. I am sorry things didn't go smoother when you were here. For what it's worth, so was she. I wish you all the best.

Love, your sister, Siobhan

My hands shake. I'm left reeling. *Sorry things didn't go smoother. For what it's worth, so was she.* They don't sound sorry. They don't sound like they care. If they did, they would pick up the phone, but no, they stay away. Now she's gone, I want to ring her up and tell her exactly what I think of her. Now she's gone, she's freed from her guilt, if she had any.

Died peacefully. What difference does it make to me? May she rot in the ground.

The kettle boils and the steam wets the wall beside it. I pour the water in on top of the coffee granules, add milk and sugar. I take a sip. It burns my mouth. I fire the mug at the kitchen door and watch the hot brown coffee splash over the door, the walls. It trickles down over the skirting board and onto the linoleum with diamonds in it.

There is the screaming. It's off again.

'Yeah, yeah,' I say. 'I'm coming, I'm coming.'

I go through the kitchen to the utility room and open the door. In it gallops, on top of me. I scream for it to get down, and it sees the coffee and runs in and starts licking it up, its tail wagging madly. Blood mixes with the coffee, from where it has cut its paws on the broken mug. I shoo it away and it goes off to its rag in the corner and licks its bloody paws.

I will ring him, that's what I'll do. I will ring him and ask him if he was in on it all. If he knew, too, like the other two did, or if he even knew on the night itself. Sure, where would he think Patrick had gone? I make a new coffee and light a cigarette and go into the sitting room to dial the number. After two long rings of the international dialling tone, I hang up. My heart is popping in my chest. I ring again and hang up. I'll taunt him and drive him as mad as they have me. He'll think his beloved is back from the dead.

Take it easy, Josephine. Breathe, breathe. Jane would tell me to breathe, to think through the breaths. She would tell me to write it all down. To write it in a letter, even if I didn't intend to send it. I get out the notepad and pen and begin to write. My hand is slow and the writing comes in wobbly scrawls.

The dog has come into the sitting room and is gnawing at

the leg of the coffee table. It has made a trail of coffee and blood all the way through the room. I scream at it but it doesn't stop. It eats away at the expensive mahogany wood. I kick it with my slipper and it snaps at my foot, with its mouth curled around its sharp teeth. The dirty mongrel bastard. It got its teeth into my foot. I check for blood, but it didn't break the skin, though it has left purple marks from its teeth. That's it. On top of everything else, it's dangerous. It could snap at one of the children's faces.

I tap my leg as if I'm going to play with it, and get its lead from behind the kitchen door. It follows me, its tail wagging. I open the front door and walk down the path in my dressing gown, not caring if anyone sees me. I pull open the gate and turn left, and off it bounds down the road.

I turn, close the gate and go inside.

CLARE

After school, Daddy drops us off and says he has to go on some errands for a couple of hours. He will be home shortly. He lets us in the front door, and me and Thomas both kiss him on his stubbly cheeks and watch as he closes the door behind him.

We run straight to the kitchen. I open the door to the utility room. Sooty's not there. I open the back door. Sooty's not there, either. I call him – Sooty, Sooty Sooty! – and walk out to the garden. Thomas is behind me. We walk back inside, holding hands. 'He must be inside,' I tell Thomas, in my adult I-know-everything voice.

Just when I'm going to step into the kitchen, something catches my eye. I tell Thomas to go and look in the back room, and when he has gone into the kitchen, I turn round. Sooty's rag is on the floor in a pile. On the top corner, poking out, is a splash of red, like paint when Daddy's decorating. But we don't have any red walls. I pick up the rag and hold it with both hands. It's covered in dark-red paint and Sooty's black hairs.

Everything goes fuzzy and suddenly I'm burning hot. I remember the story Mummy told me, about Granny having a baby that died, and them burying it beside the graveyard. After that, I had dreams of babies dangling in the limbo-air, dripping with blood. I can see them now: half-babies, half-Sooty, and they are drip, drip, dripping blood all over Sooty's rag.

Hot liquid runs down my legs, warming me. I fall into it, and it is comforting, after my face hits the hard floor of the utility room.

CLARE

'Our Father, who art in heaven, hallowed be thy name. Forgive my mummy, for what she has done, to our dear and beloved Sooty.'

I get on my hands and knees and dig up the earth that's loose around the bushes. Thomas kneels down next to me and does his best to dig up the dirt, even though he's crying so hard.

When we've made a hole big enough, I open my rucksack and take out Sooty's rag with red paint-blood on it. It's already folded nicely. I lay it down in the hole carefully.

I stand up and pull Thomas towards me; put my arm around his shoulder.

I cough to clear my throat, the way Father Feathers does. We could go and get him, his house is nearby, but he would ask where our mother is and make us go and get her.

'Clare, why are we here?' Thomas asks in his smallest voice. His shoulders are shaking and his cheeks are shiny with tears. He has mud all over his arms and legs.

I look round.

A woman is walking nearby, looking at us. I stare at her with my worst eyes until she looks away.

'Because this is Sooty's favourite place,' I say.

'How do you know?' Thomas asks.

'Because whenever we walked to school and then home, we used to have the most fun here, ever,' I tell him.

'But,' Thomas sniffs, 'how do we know Sooty isn't hiding?'

I think of a funeral we once went to, and what Father Feathers said. He talked about wings spreading and birds flying. 'Because Sooty has spread his wings and flown the nest,' I tell him. I don't tell him about the half-babies, half-Sooties floating around in my mind.

I kneel down. Thomas kneels down, too. Together we put the earth on top of the rag until it's covered.

When I stand up, I wipe my knees. Blood begins to drip from where a stone was digging into my knee.

'Clare!' Thomas says in his whiny voice that Mummy tells him off for. 'What are we doing?'

'We're laying Sooty to rest.'

'But he's not even here.'

'It doesn't matter. Things don't always have to be there to make them more real.'

I don't know if he understands or not, but he stands quietly beside me, looking at the grave. I don't know if I understand, either.

A breeze whispers through the trees and raindrops begin to fall. Daddy always says it's good when it rains. The water clears the air and feeds the flowers, and the birds have baths. I tell Thomas I'll race him home, and we run down the hill, the rain pelting against us, mixing with the tears on my face.

JOSEPHINE

18TH OCTOBER 1997

I realize that I am all alone in this world. I always have been, and I always will be. It used to be that Michael and my children linked me to the earth, put my feet on the ground and gave me a sense of place. Now not even they can ground me. They drive me to oblivion, to a dark place in my head that I am screaming to get out of.

I take a photograph off the wall. It's of me when I was a little girl. I'm standing out in the fields by the stream. I have a tummy full of blueberries and a dress on. It was the day I made my communion and I took Granny to my favourite place. I rub the dust off the glass with my sleeve and look closer at my smiling little face. I was happy then. I take another picture off the wall, this time of my two little darlings in the park, holding buttercups up to their chins. Two white squares gape from the wall like holes. I wonder if they'll know which ones are gone. I wonder if they'll notice I am gone. I hope they do and I hope they don't. Hope, hope, hope. I hope there is a better future awaiting them, and awaiting me, even if we can't be together in it.

I pick up the pen and write the date carefully in the top right-hand corner. About three-quarters of the way down the page I begin:

Dear Michael, and my beloved Clare and Thomas,

Michael, do you remember our first dance? I do. It was a good dance. I'm sorry I didn't succeed at being the girl from that dance. God knows I tried.
My darlings, Clare and Thomas, I have not been very well and I have to go away to get better. I hope you can forgive me, and that one day you understand. I hope one day you can remember our dances, too. Please know that I will miss you both and think of you every day, and that leaving you is like leaving a piece of myself. I love you both very, very much.

Mummy xxx

My eyes are dry, my tears spent. I have water running through my veins instead of blood. I am cold. I fold the letter in half and put it in an envelope. I leave it on the kitchen table, propped against the salt. I wonder what they had for dinner yesterday. What they'll have tonight. Michael will have to learn how to cook. He will help them do their homework. No doubt he will be better at it than I was. He'll know the answers.

He will bath them. He will break up their fights. He will pick them up when they fall and graze their knees. I hope they cry for me, and I hope they don't. I hope they know I love them, that I will be thinking of them every waking moment. My throat is blocked with dry tears. My head heavy with brandy.

I carry the photographs upstairs and lay them on top of my clothes in the case. I do my face, and zip the case closed.

I stop at their door, go inside and look round the room. I run my hand over the duvets, smell their pillows. My babies.

I leave my keys in the dish and pull the door to behind me.

It's a cold, grey day. I pull the collar of my coat up over my chin. The wind scratches at my eyes. I turn left towards the station. I will go to Paddington and get a train from there. Jane says it is all arranged, and they will be expecting me. The case is light in my hand. I walk quickly, nervous I'll hear the diesel engine any second.

CLARE

We reach the bottom of the hill and race along the path. I'm way in the lead. The wind is blowing in my face and the tears running into my hair when Thomas starts shouting behind me. I turn around, not wanting to lose speed in case he's trying to trick me.

He's waving his arms, pointing towards the flower gardens.

I stop running. 'What?' I ask, out of breath.

'Can't you see?' he shouts, and he runs off the path and across the grass, even though it's not in the direction of home.

I watch him go into the distance, and as he approaches the ivy wall of the garden my eye is drawn to something moving at the side. It's a dog in the bushes. Thomas approaches and shouts out and the dog looks up and starts running towards him, barking.

I don't believe it. Could it really be Sooty? He's jumping up on Thomas and licking him and barking and Thomas is laughing and rubbing his head.

I squeal and run towards them. 'Sooty!' I shout. 'Sooty!'

He hears my voice and leaps out of Thomas's arms,

bounding towards me. I can't believe it, but it's true, and when I reach him and wrap my arms around him and he licks my face over and over again, I can't believe how lucky I am to have found Sooty again. Wait till I tell Mummy and Daddy.

Acknowledgements

Thank you to each and every friend who has read this book while it was in the making, for their time, encouragement, critiques, insight and wisdom that have helped me along the way. Especially to Margarita, Nicola, Andrew, Jacintha, Laura, Clare and Clive.

Adriann Ranta Zurhellen at Foundry Literary + Media and Sam Brown at Allen & Unwin, thank you both for believing in this book, and letting it see the light of day. Thanks also to the teams at Foundry, Abner Stein and Allen & Unwin.

Thanks to my family for their undwindling love and support, and for always being there when I need you. To my husband, who has been my biggest cheerleader since our first date when I told him about this book, and who has been by my side, telling me I could do it, ever since. I did – thanks to you. And finally, to my baby, who slept soundly on my lap while I worked on the final manuscript. I love you.